Divorced from Number Thirty-Eight

Grizzlies Hockey #2

Elise Faber

DIVORCED FROM NUMBER THIRTY-EIGHT
BY ELISE FABER

Newsletter sign-up

DIVORCED FROM NUMBER THIRTY-EIGHT
Copyright © 2025 Elise Faber
Print ISBN-13: 978-1-63749-245-1
Ebook ISBN-13: 978-1-63749-182-9

GRIZZLIES HOCKEY

Married to Number Twenty-Two
Divorced from Number Thirty-Eight
Knocked Up by Number Ninety
One Night with Number Nineteen
Friends with Number Ten

ONE

GRAY

"THIS IS A BAD IDEA," MY TEAMMATE MUTTERS.

I pause next to Leo on the sidewalk and can't help but agree.

This place is bigger than Costco.

And it's filled solely with baby products.

The Baby Emporium is...terrifying.

And I'm saying that as a man who plays professional hockey for a living.

But as captain of the San Jose Grizzlies, I can't show fear.

I'm expected to lead—even if part of me knows my teammates are wondering when I'll screw up again.

When the shit in my life will overflow and impact the team.

Again.

My temple throbs, but I shake it off, know I've spent far too many nights lying awake, staring up at the ceiling, shame the worst kind of bedmate.

"We got this," I say, mostly to myself, and trudge toward the bank of plate glass doors, grabbing the handle and yanking one open.

Then wanting to promptly slam it shut and get the hell out of here.

The noise.

Good God, the *noise*.

"Fuck," Leo mutters from next to me.

"Buck up, boys!" Smitty, another teammate who, along with Ryan, is accompanying me on this shopping trip.

Or hijacking it, really.

Because Aiden's baby shower is next weekend.

His *co-ed* baby shower.

What kind of fresh hell is that?

One that's going to have me attending a co-ed baby shower on my day off when I'd much rather be rotting in front of my TV or if I'm feeling energetic, getting dressed in adult clothes and driving to the movie theater not far away, buying a huge bucket of buttered popcorn and a soda big enough to quench the thirst of an elephant, then rotting in front of a giant screen while an action hero diffuses bombs with seconds to spare and makes jumps between buildings that are impossible and always gets the bad guy.

Though, as much as I like going to the movies, I don't often feel energetic on my days off because my work days include hockey games, hockey practices, off-ice hockey training to keep honing my hockey skills, and working out for hours in the weight room to strengthen my hockey-playing body.

So, usually if I have a choice, I'm flat out on my couch.

Something that hasn't prepared me for this shopping extravaganza.

"I didn't know I could hear this frequency," Leo mutters.

I want to chuckle because Leo can be fucking funny.

But I'm too busy trying to focus so we can get this shit done.

I turn to Smitty, who has the most experience with kids. He and his wife, Kailey, don't have any of their own, but when he was playing with the Breakers, his teammates popped them out on the regular. "Where do we start?"

A particularly loud scream—do babies seriously have the ability to screech like pterodactyls?—has us all jumping.

But we're hockey players.

We block hundred-mile-per-hour shots. We enact or take center ice hits. We slash and crosscheck and battle along the boards or in front of the net. And we do all that on three-millimeter-wide blades that are sharp enough to wound.

So we get it together.

And when Smitty leads us to the clothes section, we dutifully follow him.

———

I hold up the tiny outfit.

Are kids seriously this small when they're born?

Apparently so.

And since it looks like something that could work—meaning it's sized for babies and I found it in the baby section—I toss it in the cart.

"Dude," Smitty says—or really booms because the man doesn't have the ability to modulate his volume.

He comes in loud.

And louder.

"What?" I mutter, grabbing another item that also looks like it could work and chucking it in the cart.

"You can't just buy newborn-sized stuff."

I blink.

Then blink again.

"Is the kid not going to be newly born?" I ask.

But he's not answering. He's digging through my cart, sighing. "Seriously, man, more than half of this shit won't work."

"Why not?"

"Why not?" He grabs a hanger and holds it up, shaking it so the bag-like thing for sleeping is at risk of sliding off the plastic and falling to the floor.

I snag it from him, toss it back into the cart.

"Why *not?*" he asks again then holds up another. "Quantity isn't quality my man."

"Don't kids throw up?" Leo asks. "Like a lot?"

"They do," Ryan says with some authority (and considering he's in love with a single mom who won't give him the time of day but whose kid loves hanging out with him, he would know).

Smitty gives another aggrieved sigh. "Yeah, they throw up. But they also grow fast, dude. We need variety."

"What's a onesie?" Leo asks.

"What's a—?" Smitty is at a loss for words. Which is a miracle. One that lasts for a few seconds, anyway.

Then he grabs a series of hangers.

And suddenly we're having a chalk talk on onesies versus sleep sacks versus rompers versus footed pajamas.

Do I absorb any of that breakdown?

Nope. Not really.

But do I grab the shit he says I should?

Yup. I sure do.

A full cart of it.

As do Leo and Ryan.

Smitty's not far behind us.

Yeah, Aiden's kid is going to be kitted out.

Considering that Aiden comes from a big family himself, it's not like he needs us to chip in and set him and his wife, Luna, up. They're going to have plenty to fill their nursery.

But he's also part of another family.

The Grizzlies.

So yeah, the kid is going to be kitted out.

That's what being the first guy on the roster to have a kid on the way means.

I always thought that'd be me, that kids were the next logical step in my life.

Then I seriously fucked up.

Now...it's Aiden's next step.

And he gets to deal with the attention, the shit-giving, and the...sleep sacks, rompers, footed pajamas, and onesies that say *I have the Best Uncles Ever.*

In multiple sizes.

My mouth twitches.

Because the most important thing we learned today?

Apparently, kids grow, and they do it fast.

Funny that.

We still bought Aiden's kid the *I Have the Best Uncles Ever* onesie in newborn size, though.

And in three-to-six months and six-to-nine and nine-to-twelve and...all the way up to every size they carry.

Because...priorities.

Two

FAYE

I SIT BACK IN MY DESK CHAIR AND SIGH.

I've just typed The End on the final book in the series and...

I'm unsettled.

It's good.

Maybe the best thing I've ever written.

And I'm terrified.

Because it's the end and I'm not sure it's good enough.

No. It's good enough. I've never worked harder on a book. Not ever.

So, the terror is coming from...not being ready to let it go?

Or maybe a worry because once this series is complete, my readers will forget about me and won't read another one of my books.

Ever.

Maybe they'll even hate this one.

Maybe—

"Jesus, Faye," I whisper, slamming the door on those thoughts and shoving in my keyboard. "Enough."

It's good.

My hero is swoony.

My heroine is confident and sassy—the type of woman I've always wanted to be (and won't *ever* be, but that's the beauty of getting lost in a fictional world, am I right?).

The steam is...off the charts, so hot I'm shocked the words even came from my brain because just typing them on the keyboard made me blush. Speaking them aloud is absolutely never going to happen.

And my favorite part?

The thing that ties all of my books together—from small town to sports to romantasy—is the way the hero sees something special in the heroine, something that may seem normal to the outside world, may even seem boring to everyone. Except that hero. And those small pieces, the simple ones, the quiet parts that are so often overlooked...*those* are the reasons he falls for her, why he thinks she's the most beautiful woman in the world, why his heart is hers and hers alone, and why he would do *anything*—put his body between hers and a bullet, battle a mystical mage, hit an asshole on the other hockey team for besmirching her honor—all just to keep her safe.

Emotionally. Physically.

That's the part I live for.

That's what has tears clinging to my lashes as I write the scenes where he shows the heroine she's not ordinary—not only because she can wield a sword or has magical powers the world has never seen, not because she plays a sport better than any other woman or has the business acumen to take on powerful billionaires.

Because she's *her*.

And that means she's perfect for him. That he'll bend over backward to be the perfect man for her right back.

My book is that.

It's more.

It's one of the special ones, the book babies I've tinkered with, agonizing over each and every comma placement, trying to be intentional about adjective and word choice, making certain the dialogue is tight and snappy.

Some books come easy.

This isn't one of them.

It was a struggle, a slog, a gritting my teeth and forcing myself to sit in my chair, to move my fingers on the keyboard, to push through the tough scenes...

And now I'm through to the other side.

And it's beautiful.

But there's no one to share this moment with.

No lover, no friend I'm close enough with to call and celebrate with.

My neighbors are nice enough to include me in their monthly Book Club, but that's mostly just an excuse to drink wine and shit talk men.

Since I don't have one of those, I usually stick to drinking wine.

My editor—speaking of whom, is waiting on the manuscript so I take the opportunity to email it to her—and I are in different countries and frankly, neither of us are the type to sit on the phone and chitchat.

So...it's just me.

Me to celebrate.

Me to find peace.

Me to do something that isn't sitting in front of my computer for another second.

I exhale and shove my chair back, pushing up to my feet and stretching out my sore back and shoulders.

My hands and wrists ache, my neck is tight.

Though I try my best to use all the ergonomic tools I've acquired in the years since I became a full-time writer, I regularly find myself hunched over my keyboard like a gremlin, jabbing away at the keys, trying to keep up with the rapid-fire way my characters talk to me.

My aching body at least gives me something to do.

I go to my closet, pull out my yoga mat, foam rollers, and massage balls.

Then I spend the next hour stretching and rolling out the sore spots, using my massage gun as necessary.

It's exhausting, just stretching and rolling and massaging...or maybe it's that sitting in my chair for six or eight or *ten* hours a day isn't conducive to a well-conditioned body.

I should take up some sort of exercise that's good for me.

Like walking.

I wrinkle my nose. Yeah, that's not going to happen.

Or I could exercise by lifting my wine glass up to my mouth repeatedly.

Yeah, that sounds a lot more fun.

Grinning, I keep stretching and rolling and massage-gunning until my sore spots are no longer sore and my arms are crying out for a wine-glass-filled workout.

I stow my stuff, head down to the kitchen, sniffing slightly when I make it there. It smells almost like my heater has turned on for the first time during cold season—the faint odor of burning dust or whatever—and even though it's spring, it hasn't been what I would call cold. Not for weeks now.

Definitely not cold enough to warrant the heater kicking on.

In fact, the flowers are blooming and the sky has been clear.

The fog we sometimes get in the South Bay not even clinging to the early mornings like it can in the fall and summer.

It's just...pleasant.

So pleasant, I take my wine into my back yard, staring up at the clear sky, watching the clouds float by, listening to the wind rustling through the trees shading my deck, lining my fence.

Pretty flowers. Old-growth trees. A narrow patch of grass. A tiny pond that used to be filled with koi fish when my grandpa was alive but is now just a water feature.

But a pleasant one.

I sit and listen and drink my wine.

And when it's finally late enough to go inside and make dinner, I push up to my feet and do just that.

Alone.

THREE

GRAY

Say what you will about my teammates, but they're funny—
Most of the time, anyway.

The rest of it, they're annoying as shit.

The only good thing after spending the afternoon in a marathon shopping spree at The Baby Emporium, is that we grabbed beers and burgers.

And fries.

It has to be said that I may or may not have consumed my weight in garlic fries.

I can practically smell it coming out of my pores.

Whatever.

I'm going home to rot anyway.

There's a terrible action movie calling my name.

And an entire bag of microwave popcorn.

Maybe if I get crazy, I'll toss in a handful of M&Ms, get that sweet and salty combination going.

My stomach growls—and seriously, how I can possibly be

hungry after the huge burger and shared pitcher of beer and the body weight's worth of garlic fries is almost unfathomable.

Except that the Pavlovian response of freshly popped popcorn can never be denied.

Mouth twitching, I turn down my street and navigate along the quiet road filled with old-growth trees, but I do it slowly. Carefully. My neighborhood is a well-established one not too far west of where the Grizzlies' home arena is located, and it's mostly families and empty nesters.

With those families, sometimes balls roll out into the middle of the street, followed by kids who aren't paying the closest attention.

Occasionally, the family dog follows them.

Or sometimes it's a rogue squirrel crossing the road or one of the empty nesters going to a neighbor's house for a glass of wine.

An adult playdate, if you will.

And the kids have those too, dashing across the street to play hopscotch or four square—

Both of which they take extremely seriously.

Ask me the difference between skimmies and aces and cherry bombs.

I dare you.

So yeah, my neighborhood is cool.

It's the right mix of close and not—neighbors who know each other's names, who look out for my house when I'm out of town with the team (and I do the same when they're traveling for work or on vacation). We'll bring in mail or Amazon deliveries, I'll put Lizzy—my neighbor across the street's Labrador—back on the rare occasion she escapes her yard, and we'll share adult beverages on a fairly regular basis. But they also know when to mind their own business.

My next-door neighbor especially does that.

Faye Sullivan is about all I know of the woman who occupies the house beside mine.

Along with the fact that she works from home and takes her

turn hosting the neighborhood's Book Club (or Wine Night as the men on the street call it—based on the cackling I've heard through the fence and then later, the sheer volume of glass bottles hitting her recycling bin after everyone goes home).

That's it.

Oh, we exchange waves and neighborly smiles on a fairly regular basis.

Just not words.

In fact, I don't think I've ever heard her say more than a dozen of them.

Something that works for me.

Women...

Well, women and I don't mix.

Not that I don't love women. I do. I love their curves, their hair spread out on my pillow, their sexy little smiles, and their tight, slick pussies. I love all of that and more—the scent of their perfume, their high heels, their lacy bras, their soft skin.

I love it all so much I seem to lose all common sense when it comes to the ones I invite into my bed.

And my heart.

Rolling my eyes because the last thing I need to be doing is worrying about my heart, I hit the button on the opener attached to the sun visor, wait for the garage door to roll up, and then pull inside. I'm just popping the trunk, pulling out far too many bags of clothes when I hear my name.

That voice...

It's a prime example of me having lost all my common sense.

No. It's *the* prime example.

Because that feminine voice strokes down my spine like fingers tracing nonsensical patterns over my naked flesh, moving further and further south, sliding forward, rounding my body and encircling my cock, stroking once, twice, *three* times—

Without looking at the woman who's the embodiment of my mistakes with the opposite sex, I slam the trunk and turn for the interior door, hating myself a little as I walk.

Because I know she's going to follow me.

She always does.

And, sure enough, before my fingers reach the panel to shut the garage door, she's there, a foot behind me, her floral scent in my nose.

It's intoxicating.

It's fucked up.

But that's Courtney and me—fucked up to the nth degree.

I still let her into my house anyway, holding the door wide as she walks inside.

I follow her through the hall, the fucked-up part of me who first invited her into my bed enjoying the view of her shapely ass lovingly cupped by her tight dress as I go. We move into the kitchen and I head for the fridge, pulling out a beer, popping off the top, knowing I'm going to need it in order to survive the next interaction.

I take a long pull, swallow, then face my nightmare. "Why are you here, Court?"

She strolls over to me, hips swaying, heels clicking on the floor, smile full of feminine confidence.

She knows she's beautiful.

The clothes she chooses to wear add to that allure, as does her precisely applied makeup, her hair curled carefully and hanging down her back in gentle waves.

Those blonde locks have spent a lot of time spread out over my pillow...almost as much as her legs have been spread on my mattress.

But even sex was deliberately enacted.

Each and every single move carefully planned and prepped.

Courtney is beautiful, but nothing is natural. Nothing is real. It's all a carefully curated show.

And as much as my dick likes how beautiful and confident she is...my heart is done with it.

I just want something real.

Something like what Aiden has. What Smitty has.

Court—as usual—stymies my plans before I can show her the door.

She plucks the beer out of my hand, lifts it to her lips, and even the sip she takes is designed to tempt and titillate.

And my dick responds.

Christ, I'm a fucking disaster.

"I need to have a reason to be here?" she asks after she's swallowed, fingers stroking—deliberately—along the neck of the bottle.

Yes, she does.

And she damn well knows it.

But I don't say that out loud, don't bother arguing (because it won't make a difference). Instead, I ignore my dick and turn for the fridge, intending to get my own beer.

To numb my idiocy with alcohol.

How could that go wrong?

Fuck. I need to be done with this shit.

I need—

"I want a divorce."

I freeze.

Because those were the words I was thinking.

The words I should be *saying*.

I spin back.

Before I can reply, she launches herself into my arms, and, reflexively, I catch her, beer sloshing over the rim of her bottle, dripping down onto my pants.

"Court—" I growl.

I don't know how I would have finished that statement because...

She kisses me.

And the worst part?

I kiss her back.

FOUR

FAYE

GASPING, I WHIP AROUND, TEARING MY EYES FROM THE window.

From the sight of Gray Roberts—captain of the San Jose Grizzlies hockey team and the most gorgeous member of the opposite sex I've ever had the privilege to lay eyes on—and the beautiful woman who showed up, strolled in, and dared to kiss him with barely any preamble.

And he kissed her back.

His wife. Or soon-to-be-ex-wife. Or is it *wife?*

I can't keep up—just know from the neighborhood hubbub (and maybe my online research, for book purposes *only*)—that his relationship with his wife (or not), Courtney, brings complicated to a whole new level.

I've tried to leave it at that, to not invade his privacy...

But *that*—my eyes go back through the window—doesn't seem very *not.*

Unable to stop myself, I keep watching them as I do the dishes from my dinner for one—daydreaming about a life that isn't me waking up at home by myself. That also isn't making breakfast for myself and working at home...you guessed it, by myself. And eating lunch by myself, taking my after work walk (by myself), eating dinner, also by myself, and then bingeing whatever hot TV show is on social media until I'm too tired to stay awake—and doing it by myself.

And then—worst of all—going to sleep.

By myself.

I have friends, though they're mostly online. I have a job I love, though that's also mostly online. So it's not like I'm a total loner.

I just...spend a lot of time on my own.

Gray picks up the beautiful woman, lifting her like she weighs nothing and setting her on the kitchen counter. Then—

"Oh!" I exclaim, dropping the dish I was washing and ripping my gaze away.

That's...

Well, *that's* a version of oral sex I've never seen before.

I've thought about it.

Written about it.

I've just—

My gaze drifts back.

Never seen it in real life.

Heat floods my cheeks, fills my middle...flickers between my legs.

And right on the wake of that wave of pleasure, shame chases me, nipping at my heels. I close my eyes, count to ten.

"Enough," I whisper, slitting them open, focusing on the task at hand.

I find that at least I didn't break the plate.

Moving slowly and deliberately, I pick it up from the basin and finish washing it. Then move just as slowly and deliberately as I reach over, set it in the rack to dry, then repeat the process with the remaining cutlery and my wine glass and the pan I used to sear my single chicken breast, to cook my single serving of asparagus.

I promise myself I'll give Gray—and his woman, whatever

state they are—privacy, but the pervert in me can't stop my eyes from drifting back out my window, from sliding across our adjoining side yards toward *his* window, from—

Being disappointed when I find his kitchen is empty, though the lights are still ablaze.

I lift on tiptoe, lean over my sink, searching—

"Jesus, Faye," I mutter when I do it for so long I get a crick in my neck.

I shake my head at myself and dry my hands on my towel. Then I get crazy and grab a new wine glass, filling it nearly to the top as I treat myself to a second glass of wine. Sipping, I deliberately stride from the kitchen, only slowing to flick off the lights before I pad into the living room.

No more Peeping Tom-ness for tonight.

I'm going to be normal...and alone.

Sighing, I shove down the loneliness. Alone is normal. Alone is my status quo. Alone is my reality and has been for almost my entire life.

I wouldn't even know what to do if I *had* a partner.

So why do I yearn so intensely for one?

Why do I make my living writing about happy endings and hunky heroes and heroines who demand their men fall hard and fast and desperately?

The only one who's falling in my life is me.

Likely because I'll trip coming down the stairs with an overflowing laundry basket.

Because laundry is my nemesis and I never stay on top of it.

Even if it's just me. Alone.

"Lame, Faye," I whisper as I sit on the couch and flick on my TV, navigating to one of the streaming apps (*one* because I have them all).

Lame is right.

Maybe I need a cat.

No, he or she would probably just eat my face off if I died during a laundry-basket-induced fall down the stairs.

A dog wouldn't eat me, right?

No way. They're man's—or *woman's*—best friend.

So, yup, I definitely need a dog.

That decided, I shove the morbid thoughts from my mind, drink my wine, and spend the next few hours watching my show until my lids grow heavy.

Only when I feel ready to pass out do I shut it off. Pausing to check the thermostat and the stove since I can smell that faint burning smell again (and finding both off), I climb the stairs to my bedroom, making my sleepy way through my nighttime routine of washing my face (and moisturizing), brushing my teeth (and flossing). Then I crawl into bed.

Alone.

Of course.

"Enough," I mutter to myself as I yank the covers over me, as the loneliness ramps back up, threatening to escape.

I deliberately shut it down, deliberately close my eyes and spend the next couple of heartbeats clearing my mind.

Unfortunately, that means I'm not ready to drift off.

I don't get up, though.

And I don't pull out my phone and doom scroll until unconsciousness takes me.

Instead, I lay in the dark as I wait—a long, *long* time—for sleep to come.

But when I jerk awake what feels like minutes later, it's not to sunlight pouring into my bedroom, morning having come to draw me out of my slumber.

It's bright, yes.

And warm—uncomfortably so.

I sit up on a gasp...and then immediately start choking.

On *smoke*.

Because flames are licking up the walls of my bedroom.

For once, I'm glad I'm by myself, that I'm the only one in this danger. But that thought flits through my mind and out of it in a flash. Because that quickly, the heat is overbearing and the smoke is burning my eyes and lungs and...

I realize I'm in danger.

Danger that is far, far more serious than laundry-basket-induced death.

Move, Faye!

I throw the covers back, drop to the floor, start crawling for the hallway, coughing harder and harder with each foot I progress.

There's more smoke—

No. There's *too* much smoke.

But I have to make it downstairs, have to get outside where there will be fresh air.

I pull my tank top up, covering my mouth, getting a bit of relief from the smoke, and keep crawling.

Heat ripples through the air, seeming to scorch my skin, but I don't stop.

I know I *can't* stop.

Then I'm in the hall, turning to the right, squinting in the flickering darkness for the stairs—

"Ow!" I cry out as I tumble headfirst down several steps, having found them in the least helpful way.

Falling.

Yeah, now I understand that would be a bad way to go.

My face hurts and my wrist is screaming, but the smoke is getting thicker.

I can't stop.

Not when it's getting hotter by the second, hotter than anything I've ever felt in my life.

Not when it's getting harder to breathe with each passing moment.

I keep half-crawling and half-falling down the stairs, not stopping until I crash hard onto the landing. Then I roll to my side, searching for the front door and the freedom it will bring.

But I can't see anything, not through the thick blanket of smoke.

Panic rises up, clawing at my insides.

Too hot.

And I can't breathe, no matter how hard my lungs work to draw in breath.

Get up, Faye. Get. Up!

I shove up to my hands and knees, try to crawl forward.

I don't make it far.

Lack of oxygen has weakness seeping into my legs, my arms, and the fabric of my tank top isn't protecting me any longer, not with the heat and smoke closing in.

It's so dark, so disorienting...

I don't know *how* to get out, don't know how to do this...

Alone.

But just as those words slide through my mind, as my arms give way and I crumple to the floor—

There's a loud *crash.*

I finally spot the front door, giving way in a splintering of wood, a shattering of glass.

And the last thing I see before black sucks me under...

Is the gorgeous man from next door.

FIVE

GRAY

"YOU'RE HER HUSBAND?" THE NURSE ASKS SKEPTICALLY.

Rightfully so.

Because I know fuck-all about Faye.

And I don't think me telling the nurse that she has Wine Nights with the neighborhood ladies and works from home would help endear me to him.

"Uh, yeah?" I say, even though it's definitely phrased like a question—but me flashing my ID and pretending to be Faye's husband meant that I was able to ride with her in the ambulance, and it allowed me back into the emergency department so she wouldn't be alone.

Not that she *knows* she's alone.

She's still unconscious.

"I thought you were married to that blonde chick."

I freeze, stomach starting to churn. Hockey players aren't in the news all that often, but over the years, Courtney has enjoyed parading our drama across social media—which means my life is far more *out there* than I'd want. Hell, a few times her posts have gone viral enough that I've been asked about it during post-game interviews.

Fun.

Not.

I grit my teeth together, shake my head. "Nah," I say, forcing my tone to stay light. "Don't believe everything you read online." Especially when I'll be giving my attorney the divorce papers (thank fuck, Courtney *finally* signed them) to file as soon as possible.

Once a judge approves them, Courtney and I will be officially done.

So why is there a niggling in the back of my mind, telling me it will never be that simple?

Probably because it's Courtney.

"Right," the nurse says dryly.

Fuck, he's not going to let this go.

"Okay, I'll level with you. We're not married—" He opens his mouth, expression going fierce. "I didn't—*don't*—want her to be alone," I add in a hurry. "I'll leave as soon as her family gets here. I promise."

He falls quiet, studying me while I do my best to look innocent.

Something that's hard to do when the memory of looking out my kitchen window and seeing the flames bursting through the roof of her house is still blazing through my mind. Right along with the abject terror that gripped me as I ran across the grass separating our houses—

As I looked in through her front door, saw her sprawled on the floor.

Not moving.

With flames erupting, their heat so intense it felt like they were singeing my skin.

It wasn't even a thought to kick her door down, to carry her out.

There was absolutely no way I could leave her.

Can leave her.

After a long moment, the nurse sighs. "We didn't have this conversation."

"What conversation?"

Mouth twitching, he turns his focus to Faye—the right move considering she's still unconscious with an oxygen mask strapped to her face. "Is Ms. Sullivan allergic to any medications?" he asks.

I glance at her, as though her prone body will give me a hint. Well, shit.

"Right," the nurse says dryly, correctly identifying my silence as not knowing. "Any surgeries in recent months?"

Double shit.

"Injuries or illnesses we should know about?"

Fuck.

"Pregnancy?"

"No," I hear, the word rasped out.

I freeze, eyes flicking to the no-longer-unconscious woman on the bed. Her eyes are open and fixed on me, cheeks having gone from pale to bright pink.

"Not pregnant," she rasps out. "No surgeries or illnesses or allergies." A long, wheezing breath. "Injuries?" She shifts carefully, as though testing her limbs. "I don't think so—aside from my lungs feeling like they've been rubbed raw on the insides with sandpaper."

I wince.

Because her voice sounds exactly like that.

Raw and painful and uncomfortable.

"Don't try to talk," I say watching as her eyes come to mine. Then go wide.

As though she's only just now processing that I'm here.

"But—" she begins.

I move to her side. "Don't talk," I order.

"I—"

I squeeze her hand. "Your lungs hurt, and it hurts me to hear you trying," I murmur. "So, just rest and let the doctors and nurses take care of you."

"Gray—"

Stubborn.

I didn't expect that from my shy, quiet next-door neighbor—especially when we've spoken all of a dozen words to each other over the last four years.

"Baby," I murmur. "I'm going to need you to stop hurting yourself."

Her eyes go wide again, her cheeks now bright pink.

But she falls quiet.

I take advantage of that and turn to the nurse, asking, "Am I right?"

He's slightly less distrustful than five minutes ago when I was considering imparting my Wine Night knowledge instead of her allergies. "Your..." A pointed look in my direction, telling me that even less distrustful, he's still going to be watching me. "*Husband* is right."

Faye jerks in the bed, mouth opening again.

But he talks over her, saying, "You need to rest." His eyes come back to mine. "I'll grab the doctor. Then you'll need to step out so she can be examined."

I nod.

A trickle of relief trailing across his face—likely because I'm not going to make this shit difficult—then he's stepping from the room, flicking the curtain shut behind him.

"Husband?" she asks quietly.

"It was the only way for me to ride with you in the ambulance."

A blip of humor in her eyes before they grow serious and she lifts the oxygen mask from her face. "You saved me."

It's still mostly a rasp but when I go to tell her to save her voice, her fingers wrap around my wrist, squeeze lightly. Fuck, but her eyes are pretty, a warm brown with flecks of gold and green, and so full of emotion my lungs seize for a moment.

Then her words slam into me.

"Thank you," she whispers.

"You almost made it out," I whisper back.

She had.

But she also *hadn't.*

Something I know she knows when she shakes her head. "I tried. But I wasn't going to get there."

"The firefighters were on their way."

"They wouldn't have made it in time. Not with how intensely the fire was burning."

"They would have." But I'm not so sure. They arrived not long after I carried Faye out, the ambulance on their heels, but her house was already completely engulfed.

I don't know how the fire started.

I do know it burned furious and hot and *fast.*

I'd only gotten there in time to save her because I was awake and chastising myself about being an idiot about Courtney.

I fucked her again.

And she had enjoyed herself then smiled sexily as she crawled out of bed, not bothering with clothes as she retrieved her bag from the kitchen and came back, handing me the manila envelope with the divorce paperwork I'd served her time and time again.

Only finally, *this* time—I checked—the papers were actually signed and notarized.

Freedom.

Then more shame.

Because *then* she was showing me the diamond engagement ring and I shouldn't give a damn that the woman who made my life a living nightmare for fucking *years* was engaged to another man and happily cheating on him.

But I did. *Do.*

I felt like shit—and it wasn't *just* guilt that I fucked an engaged woman whom I didn't know was engaged.

It was shame because a sick part of me was jealous she'd finally found someone else.

Fucked up?

Totally.

Completely.

I sat in that shame after she left, my shitty action movie playing in the background, my popcorn untouched...wondering how I'd gone so fucking wrong for so many years.

Until the glowing orange pulled me from my thoughts.

For a minute, I was confused, not understanding the sudden brightness in the depth of night.

Then I put the pieces together, was sprinting out of my house, bursting through the front door of hers, the wooden panel in splinters before I truly processed what was happening.

A heartbeat later, she was in my arms and I wasn't thinking about the cuts on my arms and face from the wood and glass, wasn't thinking about the way my side burned, my back as flaming debris fell while I was carrying her out.

It was just—

Faye in my arms and fresh air merely feet away.

"Maybe the firefighters would have made it in time," Faye whispers. "But you were the one who saved me." Another squeeze before her fingers run lightly over the bandage on my arm. "And you were hurt because of it—"

I still. When has a woman ever given a fuck I was hurt?

"—I'm sorry you were injured."

I shrug, heart pounding for absolutely no reason. "It's barely a scratch."

"I think—" Her tongue darts out to moisten her bottom lip, drawing my gaze to that plump, pink mouth of hers that gives a man—okay gives *me*—thoughts of different parts that are pink and plump. "I think," she says again, "it's much more than that." Another brush of her fingers. "But thank you for being there and saving me, anyway."

Before I can reply, those words rippling through my insides, the curtain slides open with a screech and the nurse is back, a doctor on his heels.

I gently free the oxygen mask from Faye's other hand, settle it carefully over her nose and mouth.

Then I start to stand, but pause, some insane urge stopping me so I can smooth back an errant bright red curl.

Her lips part.

My cock twitches—

Shame slices through my middle.

I pull back.

"I'll give you some privacy."

Six

Faye

I SMILE AT THE NURSE—THIS ONE A CURVY BLOND WITH burgundy scrubs, a badge decorated with a Grizzlies pin, and thank her.

She winks, taps a few keys on the computer next to my bed. "I should be thanking *you*." She taps the breast pocket of her top, where she carefully stowed the autograph she'd asked for, and sighs happily. "You're the one who introduced me to none other than Gray Roberts."

I know exactly how she feels.

I've sighed a time—or hundred—over Gray Roberts.

He's gorgeous, friendly...and rescues damsels in distress from blazing fires.

What's not to sigh over?

Being stuck in the hospital, I think dryly.

"You spring me from this room and I'll see about getting you tickets to the next home game," I tell her.

"Nice try," she teases, pausing at the door to look back at me. "But doctor's orders are to keep you overnight."

I scowl.

"That's cute. No wonder Gray likes you so much." She waves a hand at me, smiles widely. "I'm just so glad he's moved on from the other one—"

"Oh"—my face smooths out—"it's not like that. He's..."

But I don't get to finish before she's disappearing out into the hall and I'm left completing the sentence on my own.

"...just my neighbor," I whisper.

A neighbor who saved me from being burned alive.

And how the heck can I possibly repay him for that?

I wonder if he likes banana bread.

Then I think I could probably bake him his body weight's worth of banana bread and I still wouldn't come close to repaying him.

He broke down my door. He carried me from my burning house.

Yeah, banana bread isn't going to cut it.

Neither is my homemade fudge cake with rich double chocolate buttercream frosting.

Nor my pretzels with jalapeño cheddar dipping sauce.

Or my salted caramel filled sugar cookies or my zucchini muffins or my peanut butter fudge.

I could even pull out my most finicky and also my most impressive recipe—my chocolate soufflé—and it still wouldn't be nearly enough to repay him.

Not that I'm going to be baking any time soon.

Not with my house...well, I don't know what the state of my house is, really, but I can't imagine it's going to be soufflé ready anytime soon.

For a second, that thought threatens to overwhelm—God, it hurts *so* much to think of what I've lost—but I push it down, slap a lid on the emotions.

There's nothing I can do right now.

Not from here.

And in the meantime, I'm wide awake.

I'm alive.

I need to sit in that, *remember* that, and not be grouchy because I can't peck away at my keyboard—or really, enjoy the fact that I finished a book yesterday (and seriously, thank *God* I emailed it to Gerta before my house burned down and I lost all that work). I can replace plates and wine, my laptop and Kindle. I can replace my paperbacks (though maybe not all of my signed special editions, which sends a pang through my middle). I could —even if it would have practically killed me—recreated the final version of my book.

I have backups on the cloud.

Would I have lost the final day's worth of tinkering and that really sexy scene with the sprinkles, chocolate syrup, and the can of whipped cream?

Probably.

But I would have been okay.

I will *be* okay.

Because I always am.

Because my fictional main characters—and the side ones too —always find their way to their happy endings. Oh, and the bad guys (or gals or gender non-conforming baddies) always get their comeuppance.

That's not to say it's easy for my fictional friends.

In fact, I've had many an accusation on social media (and in my inbox) about my penchant for putting my heroes and heroines through the wringer.

Bad exes? Oh yeah.

Horrible, abusive parents? Definitely.

An evil druid out to destroy the world? Abso-freaking-lutely.

Sexual trauma? Loss of loved ones? Bosses that should be arrested? Yup. Yup. Yup.

I've written car accidents and broken bones, magical deaths, and yes, even a house fire or two.

But my main characters are always saved by a fantastic posses-sive and protective man (or occasionally—because my girlies need their turns too—by my kickass heroines).

Anyway, I should be thanking my lucky stars I was rescued by the hot hero (hello inspiration for future books) and also that I've done enough research on what to do after a house fire to know what my next steps are.

Get out of the hospital.

Get a hotel room.

Contact my insurance company.

Or, well, items two and three may be reversed depending on whether I can drum up some sort of payment method to guarantee the reservation.

Either way, I have next steps.

Then I can see about paying back one Gray Roberts for his heroics.

I reach for the remote that's attached to the bed, the long cream-colored cord wound through one of the holes on the side rail, and jab at the buttons until the TV turns on and I find some sort of game show to pass the time.

It's not long before my eyes start drifting closed, but my sleep isn't restful.

My nurse comes in to check on me and run vitals; I meet the doctor taking over my care when she rounds with the new night shift nurse. I'm finally cleared to eat something—though that *something* is broth and some green Jell-O (clearly the best flavor).

In between all those interruptions and me finding out what the survey says repeatedly, fatigue creeps back in and I nap.

And I've just allowed my lids to slide closed again when I hear the door to my room glide open with a soft *whoosh*, the sound of footsteps on the industrial-grade tiles.

Ugh.

What will it be this time?

Blood work? Making me pee to prove those parts are functional? The social worker who popped by earlier and promised to come back to discuss what support is available?

That would be really helpful, actually.

Since my house is...well, whatever my house is right now.

I open my eyes, tuck my elbows under me and start to sit up—

A warm palm lands on my shoulder.

"Just me, Faye."

Tingles spread all along my skin. Heat blooms in my belly. My head goes a little woozy.

Right. Not the social worker.

It's Gray.

He drops into the chair next to the bed, reaches for the remote and turns up the volume.

"What are we watching?"

SEVEN

GRAY

FUCK, HOW MUCH OF A SICK PERVERT DOES IT MAKE ME that the befuddlement on Faye's face when I ask her what we're going to watch makes me want to kiss her.

She almost died last night, for fuck's sake.

And yet the tiny crease between her eyebrows, the wide brown eyes...

Cute.

Really fucking cute.

Except, I can't think about how cute Faye looks—

The only reason I'm here is to make sure she's okay, that she's settled and comfortable until her family comes in to take care of her.

I turn toward the TV, focus on the show...

For about two minutes before I realize it's shit.

"You're really watching this?" I ask.

"Um..." she says and her next words have me straightening and focusing more fully on her. Because they're laced with sass— and I sure as shit wasn't expecting one Faye Sullivan to be sassy or sarcastic. Sweet, yes. Gentle and kind, absolutely. But all of that along with the hint of an attitude—a hint that well, *hints* at more than just attitude underneath the quiet—and I know...

I'm so totally fucked.

"It turns out there's not a lot of options on hospital cable."

Simple words.

But spoken tartly? And paired with a small smirk and dancing brown eyes?

Yup. So *totally* fucked.

Then she keeps talking, unwinding the ancient-looking remote from the bedrail and handing it over to me. "Want to try your luck at finding something better, hot shot?"

Oh fuck.

More tart. More smirking.

More danger.

"Or not," she says and I realize I've been staring at her, not answering, same as I haven't taken the remote from her, haven't done my best to find something that isn't the stupid ass game show I should have just sat here and watched in silence in the first place.

Sat here smoothing over my conscience, the nagging emotions that filled my last hours.

Worrying about her being here.

Alone.

"You don't have to be here, Gray. I'm fine." Her lips curve up into a smile, but I have the distinct notion that it's fake.

And I hate that.

I don't know why I hate the idea that she's pretending with me, that she's hiding parts of herself from me.

She's my neighbor.

I know nothing about her.

But...maybe I want to?

"I think you should go," she murmurs. "I'm sure you're exhausted."

Goddammit.

Now I feel like a dick.

I *am* exhausted. And I have a game tomorrow. I *should* go.

Visiting hours are over—something the nurse advised me of when I first came in. Shift change had occurred and no hockey fans I could win over with smiles and autographs were around. In fact, I had to sweet-talk my way in so I could come and make a mess of this conversation with Faye.

Christ. Why do I always fuck things up?

I grind my teeth together, shame rippling—

And watch her body tense on the bed.

She opens her mouth (and I know it's to tell me to go again).

"I'll find something better," I blurt, snagging the remote and starting to click.

Spoiler alert: I *don't* find anything better.

First, there's like ten channels.

Second, there's like *ten* channels, so for all my clicking, I don't manage to drum up a great Liam Neeson or Jason Statham action flick.

Instead...I end up back on the game show.

Which, I find after about five more minutes, doesn't *actually* suck.

It's weirdly intriguing.

Is it the pressure that makes the answers so bad? Or should I really start worrying about the state of education in America?

Likely both.

There's a loud buzz on the screen and I hold my breath as the other team finally gets a chance.

The number one answer is still not up on the board.

And it's not like the category is difficult.

I glance at Faye, see she's watching as avidly as I am. "Is not one person on either of these teams unable to come up with tent?"

"I thought you didn't like this show," she says quietly, barely any rasp in the words, though she's still pale and the dark circles under her eyes are intense.

I clench my hand at my side, resisting the urge to brush my thumb over the spots marring her skin.

"The category is Things You Bring on a Camping Trip," I point out.

"I'm not saying *I* wouldn't say tent." Her lips twitch. "I'm just saying that if the show sucked, you wouldn't be invested in it after five minutes."

"So you're a Family Feud fan?"

"I'm a whatever's on TV or hot on social media at the moment fan. And today with my ten hospital channels, that's Family Feud." Her eyes flick to the TV screen at the sound of another buzz. "For the record, I would have said tent, sleeping bag, and flashlight instead of portable latrine, matches, and bug spray." One slender shoulder lifts and drops. "Though I can see the merits of all three of those."

"I'll point out that *matches* was the only one of those guesses to make it in the top five."

"That's because the number four answer is pillow." There's that sass again, the adorable little smirk that has a hand reaching into my chest and wrapping around my heart.

Or maybe it's skipped my chest all together and gone straight for my cock instead.

Either. *Both.*

I lean closer, hand settling on the bed near her hip. Not touching her, but giving in to the urge to *almost* touch, thus soothing the ache inside me.

"A pillow?" I murmur. "Do I need to remind you that the category is things you bring *camping?*"

"Yup. And you need somewhere to rest your head when you sleep in that sleeping bag, inside that tent at night."

"I'm not sure that's a necessity."

"They're not saying it's a necessity...necessarily. The point of this game is to discern what one hundred people would say they'd bring camping with them."

I stare at her.

She stares back then lifts her brows in challenge.

Fuck.

"Touché, baby," I say softly, leaning a little closer.

Her inhale is sharp and fuck if my fingers don't shift of their own accord, brushing lightly against her side.

Another rough inhale.

God, I'd love to see her do that naked.

"Your lungs are better," I say softly. "How about the rest of the bumps and bruises and"—I gently tap the splint on her left wrist—"this bad boy?"

"I'm fine."

Why do I have the feeling that she would say the same thing, even if she hadn't just survived a house fire with minimal injuries? Even if she *wasn't* fine?

"Faye," I murmur. "You don't have to lie to me."

"No offense," she replies quietly. "Considering you saved me and all, but I don't really know you."

I *want* to know her.

I'm desperate for it, salivating like a dog waiting for his dinner bowl to be filled.

"We can change that," I point out.

"By bonding over game shows?"

"By passing the time and talking. You've been my neighbor for a couple of years now and I barely know more than your name and the fact that you work from home."

"There's nothing to really know," she says. "I do work from home and I'm boring. I like staying in and reading or watching TV or having my friends over."

"I like staying in too," I tell her.

"You do?"

"Yup." I stroke my fingers over the slender curve of her hip again. "My drugs of choice are cheesy action flicks and a giant tub of popcorn."

"I make a really great caramel popcorn."

"Yeah?"

A nod. "Yeah."

"Can I tempt you into making it for me?"

Can I tempt you into doing *other* things for me?

Her cheeks go pink, as though she's plucked the thought from my mind. "I was going to make you banana bread as a thanks for saving me."

Sweet, adorable, *tempting* Faye in the kitchen wearing just an apron and baking for me.

Yeah, I know exactly what I'll be thinking about as I stroke myself to sleep tonight.

"I wouldn't turn down either," I tell her, daring to stroke her hip again.

She shifts marginally, leaning into my touch, and swear to fuck, I feel that lean in my soul. "I'll make both then," she whispers.

"Deal."

We fall silent, the show still playing behind us, but I can't bring myself to focus on it. Not when Faye is right in front of me.

"You work from home doing what?"

Her expression is...interesting. It goes from embarrassed to recalcitrant in under a second.

And I feel my interest in her increasing exponentially.

Fuck.

"What do you do, baby?"

"I'm a writer."

Everything in me stills because that's...perfect. Everything about *her* screams author—the cute little skirts she wears, the blouses, the glasses (though she's not wearing them right now because they were lost in a fucking fire). But it's more than the outside—it's her quick wit and quiet, observing nature.

Cataloguing everything and storing it away to use later.

Yeah, I can totally see her writing some sort of cozy mystery or a thriller, diving deep into the plot and getting lost in her characters.

"What kind of books do you write?"

Her chin comes up, the recalcitrance increasing by an order of magnitude. "Romance novels."

My brows fly up. "Romance novels?"

"That's what I said." It's a pert rejoinder.

"Wow. Faye Sullivan is a secret romance novelist."

"It's not a secret."

"Then why am I just finding out about it?"

"Because we've barely spoken?"

She has a point, but I'm enjoying teasing her too much to acknowledge it.

"Wow," I say instead.

"What? You think your shy, homebody of a neighbor doesn't know anything about love?"

"No," I tell her, my teasing fading as I think about what my love life has looked like for the last years. "I think that writing about love is one of the hardest things a writer can do."

Her face smooths out. "What?"

"Love is universal and complicated and one of the things people want most in the world. To be able to write about it and make it feel sincere, make it something that readers want to root for has to be tough."

"I—" She swallows and shakes her head. "I guess I never thought about it that way."

She's befuddled again, and it's fucking cute.

And soft, her eyes coming back to mine, her words quiet. "Thank you for saying it that way instead of reacting how people normally react."

It's dangerous how easy it is to talk to her, dangerous how much I want to know every part of her. Yet, I find I'm unable to not touch her, so I stroke my fingers along her side again. "How do people normally react?"

She sighs. "By asking if I try out my sex scenes before I write them. Or asking me if writing love stories is just a little hobby and one day if I'll write *real* books."

"Seriously?"

"Unfortunately, I am."

I scowl. "That's bullshit."

"Maybe so, but that's the world we live in right now." She exhales again. "I provide for myself. I pay my bills. I do something I love, but I think because most romance books are written by women *for* women, they're still seen as less." Her nose wrinkles. "Gotta love that my job writing fiction mirrors the real world sometimes."

"That sucks."

"I'm lucky to do what I love," she says. "So, I'm not complaining." Her lips curve up into a self-deprecating smile. "Or not much, anyway."

"I get it," I tell her and fuck if my hand doesn't shift of its own volition again, this time tucking a lock of hair behind her ear, the silky strand almost tempting me into stroking. "My job is great, but sometimes people judge it from the outside, turn it into something it isn't."

"I could see that."

I nod, give in to the urge to stroke, gently running my fingers through her hair.

"Do you like it?" she asks quietly. "Does hockey feed your soul?"

"It does," I murmur. "So much so I can't imagine doing anything else. I know everyone says it's just a game, but the truth is, it's the only place I've ever belonged. Losing it would mean losing the only family I have left."

"Your parents?"

"Alive," I say softly. "Just not at all interested in their son."

Her eyes go sad. "I'm sorry." But before I can say it's okay, she says, "But I'm happy you get to do something you love."

"Me too."

Her lips twitch, curling up the slightest bit at the edges, cutting through my guilt for being here, for invading, for allowing myself closer when I should be pulling back. "Did you know I've written a hockey romance series?"

My brows fly up. "That's a thing?"

She grins and fuck it's pretty. "Oh yeah, it's a thing. A *big* thing."

The pull toward her intensifies, searing into me, and it's so intense that it's hard to breathe, to think.

All I can do is feel.

And right on the heels of that, is the need to yank myself back into reality.

"When's your family coming by to take care of you?"

It's an abrupt question, almost harsh.

Her expression clears, going completely blank, any of the teasing in her smile, her eyes disappearing like a puff of smoke.

And I know I've fucked up.

I just don't know how big.

EIGHT

FAYE

WHEN'S YOUR FAMILY COMING BY TO TAKE CARE of you?

One second, I'm thinking about my two favorite things: books and my favorite fictional characters.

And don't tell anyone, but even though I don't like watching it—like *really* don't like watching it—my hockey boys are my favorites.

They're sweet and strong with wicked minds and very skilled...parts.

And then they're whooshed right out of my head...

By my past.

So suddenly it feels as though my torso has been flayed open, my insides torn out, leaving my wounded heart to bleed out on the floor.

Because it hits me right then.

What the fire means.

What I've *lost*.

Not just my computer or my favorite pair of cozy lounge pants or my special edition hardcovers.

But Nana's recipe book and my baby album and the pictures of my parents and the necklace my mom had intended to put on me just before I walked down the aisle at my wedding but never got the chance to because instead she gave it to me on her death bed.

And Fluffy's—my grandma's pup, who really became *my* dog when I moved in to take care of her after Nana got sick—collar and her ashes because she passed not long after Nana did and the tiny clipping of hair the vet saved so I would never forget the exact golden shade of her fur.

I didn't just lose my home.

I lost *everything*.

I close my eyes against the sudden onslaught of emotions, the tears burning the backs of my lids, clogging my throat. I clench my teeth, trying to hold back the sobs, and I don't even realize I'm clenching my hands into fists too until I feel warm fingers on mine.

"What is it, Red?" he murmurs.

"Red?" I ask quietly.

"Your hair." He tugs a strand, and my eyes fly open to see him wearing a rueful smile. "Not very original, I know."

Baby had phantom fingers sliding down my spine.

But Red...Red is more.

Red is different.

Red is a nickname personalized for me (however original or not). But it's not just a token endearment.

It's...

Yeah, it's more.

"What is it, baby?" he presses.

There those phantom fingers go again, stroking, caressing, drifting carelessly up along the insides of my thighs.

"Why do you keep calling me, baby?" I ask, ignoring the sensation.

Definitely ignoring the shiver that wants to skate over my skin in response to his husky question.

Instead—and I'm not saying this is remotely healthy—I slap a lid on my past and stare up at him, waiting for him to answer me.

Waiting and watching.

There's an interesting play of emotions crossing his face.

I'm not sure I can tease them out—maybe a bit of guilt, maybe some fear, perhaps some resignation. But there is *one* I'm certain of...

Heat.

And that seems to be the emotion he settles on.

Mostly because he murmurs, "You know why."

I mean...I know why one of my MMCs might be here, might have heat sliding through his emerald-green eyes.

But it doesn't make sense.

I'm me.

He's him.

And...maybe something that makes me feel even worse than the fact that I'm me and he's him is—

"Aren't you with someone?" I ask quietly.

He withdraws his hand and the loss of that contact, that closeness is...

Well, I don't want to think about why it hurts.

"No."

Okay, so the ex is the ex.

Something unfurls in me...at least until I remember what I saw in the kitchen just yesterday.

"A woman then?"

Something else crosses his face—and it's not heat. "No," he says. "I don't have a woman."

"Right," I mutter, that piling on, adding to the wealth of shit-tiness currently swirling around my insides, setting the lid I'd slapped on it earlier rattling, threatening to bounce itself free, to allow those emotions loose again.

"What?" he asks, and I don't miss he's looked away from me, his gaze dropping to his lap.

There's all the proof I need.

He's lying.

He has a woman in his life and yet, he's here with me.

What. A. Jerk.

And I know I should focus on keeping that lid secured, on keeping myself together.

Especially when he's asking dangerous questions and I'm close to the edge, close to losing it in front of this man who is *him*.

While I'm me.

But I don't.

Because instead, when he orders, "Tell me, Red," the fire inside me bursts free.

That tone.

Him presuming to order me around—

The lid flies free.

Hits the floor with an ear-shattering *clang*.

"I saw you!" I snap. "You were with that woman in your kitchen just last night! And now you're sitting beside me, making no sense and you're touching me and calling me *baby* and looking at me with heat in your eyes like she didn't exist."

I know what it's like to feel that way.

To disappear so completely no one sees me.

I felt it when my dad died, when my mom lost herself in her grief.

I felt it again when my mom passed, Nana doing her best to go through the motions for me, but knowing that with just the two of us, we wouldn't ever be the same.

Then I felt it again when she was diagnosed, when she slowly wasted away, when I eventually lost her too.

And I felt it...

No, I *feel* it right now.

This beautiful man sitting next to my bed, touching me then not, and lying to me.

His eyes spark with anger and I brace.

Because the emerald depths have flash frozen.

He opens his mouth.

But his words are so damned far from what I expect—which, for the record, is a harsh retort designed to shove me firmly back in my place—that I can't breathe for a second.

I can't *think*.

Then I absolutely lose hold of the sadness inside me.

So when he says, "That woman is my wife," I burst into tears.

Like a complete and total psycho.

NINE

GRAY

I'M RIGHT IN THE MIDDLE OF CORRECTING MYSELF—OR rather adding, "My soon to be *ex*-wife," even while knowing that doesn't have a snowball's chance in hell of making me sound any better when I hear a strange noise.

I unclench my fists and look up.

Faye has her face averted, her chin lifted so high I can see the outline of the tendons along the column of her throat.

"Red?" I ask.

Her body jerks and terror punches a hole in my middle because at first I think she's having a seizure or something, like the doctors were right in worrying about her enough to keep her overnight.

Because something has gone seriously wrong.

Then her chest hitches.

And I see a single tear emerge from the corner of her eye, slide down her cheek.

Fuck.

"Baby," I murmur.

Another hitch, more violent this time, and more tears fall, faster now, cascading down her cheeks, soaking into her pillow.

I reach for her hand, but she seems to anticipate that, yanking her arm away, curling it around her middle and rolling to her side, away from me.

Hiding from me.

But there's no hiding what's happening to her.

This isn't an adrenaline letdown, the events of the last day finally hitting her.

This is...something else.

Something that has nothing to do with me (or Courtney).

Something that has her crying with such intensity—huge, wracking sobs that tear through her slender body, a body that seems all the more fragile and vulnerable lying in that hospital bed.

I'm frozen for a heartbeat.

But I can't withstand the sounds of her pain.

I react without really thinking, standing and toeing off my shoes, shoving the remote aside, and...

Crawling into bed beside her.

She goes stiff for a moment, the sobs halting.

Then, as though she can only hold them back for a brief blip in time, she curls herself into an even tighter ball and cries. *Harder.*

"Fuck," I whisper, carefully slipping an arm under her shoulder and drawing her back against me.

She fights me, but only for a second.

Then she turns and melts against me, pressing her face against my chest.

Tears soak into my shirt, her uninjured hand clenches at the material—no, *clawing* at it. Scratching my skin through the fabric.

I wince, but don't let her go.

Instead, I draw her more tightly against me, smoothing a hand lightly up and down her back.

I don't shush her, don't tell her to get it all out.

At this point, I don't think she could even hear me if I did.

So, I just hold her and wish there was something I could do to take this pain away.

Eventually, she quiets, the tears subsiding, her body slumping against mine as though she's used every bit of energy her body had left and even continuing to breathe takes effort.

I still don't speak, just keep stroking her back.

Mostly because I don't know what *to* say.

Maybe also because if I *do* say something the spell will be broken and I'll be forced to release her and get out of this bed.

I like her where she is.

Another reason to stay silent, to pretend she needs me here, *right here*, that me holding her isn't about fulfilling some fantasy.

She's just a woman taking comfort in my arms.

Needing me.

And not for a sick, fucked-up sexual connection, for some weird push-pull power play of a relationship that means neither of us can truly let go. Not for a relationship I ruined, a woman I turned into a monster—

"I'm sorry," she whispers, shifting as though she's going to pull out of my arms.

I don't know why I do it, but I lock them tighter, hold her closer. "It's okay," I murmur. "You had a long day and quite a scare," I add, giving her that out if she wants to take it. "The emotions were sure to hit eventually."

"Yeah," she whispers. Another shift, firmer now, and I find that as much as I like her against me, I can't ignore it.

I release her, crawl out of the bed.

Her face is averted again, body tense.

No more tears.

But clearly ready for me to go.

I should do exactly that.

Should leave.

But I don't.

"She's not my wife," I say and her head pivots back, brows lifting. "I know I said that. I—" I shove a hand through my hair, sigh. "The truth is that she brought me divorce papers yesterday."

Something happens in Faye's eyes then she reaches over and takes my hand in her uninjured one. "I'm sorry," she says again.

"Don't be."

"I acted like a psycho," she whispers. "Yelling at you about a woman when I have no business knowing about your love life then losing it and crying in your arms because I—"

"First," I tell her, turning my hand over and lacing my fingers through hers when she tries to draw back, "don't be sorry. I've been trying to get Courtney to agree to a divorce for years now. We're...not good together and for a long time I was too young and naive to recognize that. By the time I did, she decided to hate me and refused to sign the papers I sent her. Repeatedly. I was actually starting the process for a no-fault divorce when she showed yesterday."

"Oh," she whispers.

"Later, I found out she showed not only with those divorce papers...but also an engagement ring."

Faye's fingers tighten around mine.

"I wouldn't have done"—I wave my free hand, watch her cheeks go pink—"what I did if I knew she was engaged. Hell," I mutter. "I shouldn't have done what I did in the first place."

"She's beautiful," Faye says softly. "I'm sure that's irresistible to lots of guys."

There's something in her words that prickle through my mind, but when I can't tease out why, I just say, "Yes, Courtney *is* beautiful."

Too bad it's only on the outside.

Too bad I was dickmerized by her perfect body and shining hair and the way she exudes sex appeal.

Because once again, I had an orgasm, but it wasn't all that good of one.

Not when she was her usual pillow princess and I was hating myself for being a fucking moron.

Again.

Faye falls quiet.

I squeeze her hand, prompt when her pretty brown eyes come to mine. "Well?"

"Well what?"

"I shared mine, Red. You gonna share yours?"

TEN

"I'm tired," I lie.

Well, it's not exactly a lie since I'm exhausted, especially after crying like that.

I feel like I can close my eyes and sleep for a thousand years.

"I'm sure you are," he says, leaning in and lightly brushing his thumb over my cheek.

This being with his *free* thumb, since he's using his other one to trace light patterns on my palm, the rest of our fingers still intertwined.

"But," he goes on. "You said you lost it and cried in my arms because..."

My throat goes tight. "Because why?" I squeak.

One big shoulder lifts and falls. "I don't know, Red. You didn't say. So, why don't you tell me?"

Shit.

I walked right into that one.

"I don't know if you remember," I say, going for light and failing miserably, mostly because my voice is still mostly a squeak, "but it's kind of been a really long day."

"I would have given you that out, baby, had you taken it the first time I offered it up." He flattens his hand against my cheek, slides it down to gently cup my jaw. "Or if those tears didn't sound like they were ripping you in half."

I suck in a breath and tense.

And because he's cupping my jaw and holding my hand and leaning close...I know he doesn't miss that.

Doesn't miss *any* of that.

"You can talk to me."

I close my eyes.

"I told you about my ex, who's a nightmare, and not just because *she's* a nightmare, but also because I hate the person I am when I'm in the same room as her."

That has my lids peeling open. "Why?" I whisper.

"Because I regress into a dumbass twenty-two-year-old who married his college sweetheart when neither of us were ready for something that serious, let alone all the difficulties that come with dating a professional athlete." He sighs. "And that was *after* I was already a dumbass high schooler dating the prettiest but most toxic girl in high school. Though, it was before Court and I separated and I thought that Tara or Alicia or Hannah or Devon were the right women. Of course, Tara was just like Courtney and the rest of them I didn't have a chance with because I both couldn't get rid of and couldn't let *go* of Court and—" He shakes his head, a lock of hair falling over his forehead, his eyes sliding closed.

"I..." I say when he doesn't go on. "I feel like I need to tell you I've seen a few of the news stories about you two."

He exhales, lids peeling back, the depths of his eyes heavy with old pain. "Unfortunately, you're not the only one. The reporters got so bad after the story about us went viral last year, Coach told them to stop asking about her or they wouldn't get another interview." A muscle in his jaw flickers. "They used to love me—until they didn't. Now everything they write is like they're goading me to fuck up, to give them something tweetable."

My heart twists. "Gray—"

"Some captain, huh? Bringing all the drama," he says. Another shake of his head. "Courtney fed them the stories but I provided the ammunition. The fight, the suspension, my post-game meltdown—"

I bite back the urge to interject, wait for him to go on.

"I gave her—*them*—an easy target," he finishes quietly. "Now I've learned that silence is safer than trying to get them on my side."

"I can understand that."

His eyes come to mine, hold, as though searching them for any sign I might be lying.

When I just stare back, something in him relaxes—the line of his jaw or maybe the set of his shoulders. "Anyway," he says, "we're fucked up. We're toxic. I've realized that and been working to be in a place where I can let it go for a while now. And finally, it's done. The papers are signed. I dropped them off with my attorney this morning. I can finally close the door on that toxicity and move on."

"That's really great."

"Yeah." He nods brusquely. "Now, it's your turn."

It's only fair.

He shared...a lot. So much my heart hurts for him. So much I know I should give something back.

It's just...the lid I slammed down to keep my feelings in check is nowhere in sight now, even though I scramble to find it, to clamp it onto the pot of emotions inside me.

I would have thought I cried them all out.

But, nope. The fire's going, and they're threatening to boil over again.

"I lost my house," I whisper, and God, how is it I have any tears left?

It's probably the fucking tube in my arm, its cannula pumping saline into my body.

Making it possible for my body to keep producing the salty fuckers.

Making it *im*possible for me to ignore the way his face gentles as more tears to slip free when he says, "I know you did, baby."

"No," I whisper. "I lost my *house*. Which means I lost *everything.*"

"I know," he whispers back.

But how can he know?

Because—

"No, I mean...I lost N-Nana's banana bread recipe and my baby pictures and the photo of my mom and dad on their honeymoon." My lungs hitch. "And I lost the necklace my mom had bought to give me on my wedding day and Fluffy's collar and N-Nana's perfume and my mom's sc-scarf and...they're not here!" More tears sliding down my cheeks. "They're not here and they're not coming back and I can't just go buy another scarf because it won't smell like my mom and they don't make Nana's perfume anymore and I can't remember if her banana bread calls for one egg or two a-and I'll never be able to properly remember what my dad's handwriting looked like or be able to use my mom's special deviled eggs platter again."

"Red," he murmurs.

I use my free hand to angrily brush aside my tears, the Velcro on the splint catching in my hair. "I don't have them anymore. I don't have *anyone*. And I don't have any way of getting all that I had left of them back. So, *that's* why I lost it. Because I remembered I didn't just lose my laptop and my collection of signed special edition hardbacks. I didn't just lose my purse and credit cards and passport and who knows what else. I lost *them*, all over again and..."

"It hurts." Kind green eyes on mine.

"Yes," I say, looking down at the thin weave of the blanket. "It really hurts. Because I don't *have* a family to swoop in and take care of me when I'm in the hospital. I've had to learn to live without them and that sucks and"—I gently extract my hand from his—"I'm really tired of being alone, of having to do it all by myself."

That's the truth.

But I also realize how that sounds.

How *pathetic* it sounds.

I slam the brakes on the emotions churning in my belly, clamp down that lid tightly again.

"But that's the way it's been since Nana died," I tell him. "Which means I'm used to it. So, thanks for being kind and understanding while I got my good cry out. But I'm good." My lips curve into what I hope is some semblance of a smile, but I know I've failed when I gather the courage to flick my eyes toward his for a heartbeat.

Still, I press on.

Because that's what I do.

"Luckily," I say, running my fingers over the edge of the blanket as I dare to take another look at him. "I've written a book about this same thing happening to a character. The house burning down part," I add when his brows drag together, confusion in his green eyes. (I *don't* add that the love of her life, the other half of her soul, the man who saw her as the most precious object in the universe saved her, thus starting them on their path to happily-ever-after because...fiction versus real life and I don't need to feel any more sad in this moment).

"Anyway," I go on into the silence that's fallen, "I'm just saying I know what my next steps have to be, so as soon as the doctor springs me from hospital jail, I'll get on with them."

I smile, pretend this is fine.

Everyone says healing takes time—but no one mentions how lonely it is to start over.

It's quiet. No fireworks. Just slow, stubborn grind to the new normal.

"In the meantime," I say, pushing the forlorn down deep as he remains silent. "I'm going to eat as much green Jell-O as they give me and yell at the TV about the failings of people to properly guess the categories of Family Feud and pretend that this is some sort of really shitty hotel."

Finally, I stop talking.

My chest is heaving, my pulse pounding through my veins.

My muscles taut with the intensity of trying to keep it together.

But he's still not speaking.

And...off I go again.

"So yeah, you're off the hook, Gray. Thanks again for saving me."

I nod to the door.

"You can go."

He's silent, staring at me, and this time I can't look away.

Not because his face is completely blank but because—spoiler alert—he doesn't listen to me and walk his ass out the door.

Instead...he stands up and crawls into bed beside me again.

Takes me into his arms.

And—

Fuck.

Because then *I'm*...crying again.

ELEVEN

GRAY

I WAIT UNTIL HER BREATHING EVENS OUT THEN SLIP carefully from the bed.

She looks tiny now that I'm not holding her in my arms, barely taking up much of the mattress, her slender body shrouded by the blankets.

Eyes closed, lashes splayed over the tops of her cheeks, bright pink lips parted as she breathes slow and easy and steady.

The relief that fills me at that sight...

Too much.

Too big.

But it's natural for me to feel protective about the woman I saved from the fire, right?

Natural to have a soft spot for a woman who's endured all she's endured.

Natural to slip from the halls and want to punch something.

Then to keep punching and punching until the skin on my knuckles split open and the rage burning through my insides is abated.

Unfortunately, I don't think that punching a wall is going to make me feel better.

Because I saw the remains of her house.

And I don't think her Nana's banana bread recipe survived.

"Fuck," I whisper, hands clenching into fists as I stop and breathe. I know I shouldn't give a fuck—or not more than a passing, empathetic fuck that any normal human would feel for another human who's been *through* it.

But I do.

And I'm not even officially divorced yet, not even out of the shit with one woman.

Yet I'm thinking about jumping right the fuck back in with another one.

Yup. I'm an idiot.

Sighing, I force my hands to relax then lean forward and rest my forehead against the wall.

Then I pull out my cell and hit a number, not thinking how late it is.

Not until Smitty's normally loud as fuck voice comes on the line...

And it's quiet.

"Hello?"

What the fuck?

I pull my phone away from my ear, process what time it is.

Shit.

"Gray," he says, still quiet, though I hear movement now, the rustle of sheets, the pad of footsteps, the soft click of a door closing. "Talk to me."

It's louder.

Firmer.

More like the Smitty I know.

"Sorry, man," I mutter. "I didn't realize how late it was. This can wait till the morning."

Even if that feels like a lie.

Even if it feels like I need to fix this for Faye.

Immediately.

Years ago.

"Is it Courtney?"

Fuck. I hate that things are bad enough with my ex that's the first place his mind goes.

"No," I say quickly. "Go back to bed. We'll talk later."

"Yeah, you're not gonna get off that easy," he says, "considering it's after midnight and your voice sounds like it does and this may be the first time *you've* called *me*, as in ever..." He sighs and I hear the sound of a fridge opening and closing, a beer being opened. "Quit being ornery and just lay it on me."

I sigh, considering ending the call.

But I've already opened Pandora's Box—there's no way Smitty will let this go now.

"Gray," he warns.

"There's this girl—"

"Not Courtney?" A cautious question that scours its way down my back.

"Not Courtney," I rasp.

"Fuck, yeah!" he booms, doing it so loudly I have to hold the phone away from my ear.

Hell.

I should have started with the fire.

"Don't stop there, man. Tell me more. Who's the girl and how can Uncle Smitty help?"

The glee in his voice...

Christ.

My temple throbs and I exhale, thinking this is both a terrible idea and also...the only one I've got. I know Smitty will help. I know he'll do it without a second thought—albeit with a fuck ton of banter and shit-giving and nosiness...

But I'm thinking that Faye needs that.

Thinking she needs the special brand of family that only Smitty can bring.

So, I explain about the fire and earn a "Our own Gray Roberts a hero? I'm positively fluttering my lashes, sweetheart."

See?

I grind my teeth together, bite back the retort that wants to slide free, and order, "Focus, Smitty. She's got no one."

"No one?"

Except me, I want to say. I don't though. I keep that thought carefully tucked inside my head and instead remind him, "No clothes, no food. No place to stay."

"Kailey and I have a guest room."

"She's staying with me," I say before I can stop myself.

Lie.

I don't *want* to stop myself.

Smitty laughs. "Seems like she's got a place to stay. When will she be out of the hospital?"

"Should be in the morning. I want to try to get her set up before the game tomorrow."

"Kailey and I will be on it. Text me when she's been sprung from hospital jail and we'll meet you over there with what she needs."

"You know you could just leave it on my porch," I mutter, knowing that's wishful thinking.

Smitty just laughs again. "You also know that's not going to happen, man."

Unfortunately, I do.

"I'll text you in the morning," I mutter, lifting my phone again, preparing to hang up when I hear his voice again.

"She okay?"

That right there...

The concern Smitty has for a woman he's never met paired with the fact that he's not pissed about my after-midnight call is why he's my friend.

My family.

It's why I'll take his loudness, his brashness, the shit he'll stir up, his nosiness.

Because he cares.

Because he's helping me make the Grizzlies what I've wanted them to be for a long, long time.

"She lost her grandma's banana bread recipe and her baby pictures and her parents' wedding photo," I whisper.

"So, she's not okay."

"No," I tell him, "she's not okay."

"You'll get her there."

I tense. "Smitty."

"Courtney isn't you," he says quietly.

"Court and I are finally done," I say just as quietly back. "She signed the papers, is engaged to someone else."

"Thank fuck for that."

Since I thought that very same thing, I don't comment further.

"She isn't you," he semi-repeats.

"Ten years of fucking around with her makes that hard to believe."

"Gray—"

"Need you to focus on Faye," I mutter. "She needs clothes and conditioner and moisturizer and all the other girl things I don't have at my place. Oh, and baking shit. Flour and sugar and baking soda and whatever I need to go with one of those Kitchen Aid mixer things—I already have that."

Smitty's quiet—a rare feat.

"She likes baking," I find myself explaining.

"Got that," he says after a moment. "We'll get her set up."

"Right," I mutter.

I push off the wall, turn for Faye's room.

"Smitty?"

"Yeah, bud?"

"Thanks."

I hang up, and maybe I should go home, let her sleep, should get some rest in my own bed.

But I don't do that.

Instead, I slip back into Faye's room...
And then slide into bed next to her.

TWELVE

FAYE

I WAKE UP WITH MY CHEEK VIBRATING.

Considering I've fallen asleep with my face pressed to my phone on more than one occasion, I don't really think as I blearily reach a hand up, searching for the button on the side of it, trying to stop the incessant buzzing.

But my hand doesn't encounter the rubber edge of my phone case.

Instead, it encounters something hard and warm and... rumbling.

My senses finally catch up with me and my eyes fly open, the last of sleep disappearing in an instant.

Because I'm in the crappy hospital bed...and I feel more rested than I have in years.

Gray is on his back, one arm around my shoulders, wrapped tight so I'm on my side, snuggled securely against him so his other arm can settle on my waist, long fingers resting on my hip, drawing nonsensical patterns over the thin material of the hospital gown I'm wearing.

And the vibrating?

It's from him speaking quietly to the doctor.

I don't move, don't dare to lift my head. Hell, I barely even breathe.

"All of her vitals from last night look good," the doctor is saying. "I'll finish my rounds and come back, do a quick exam for which, I'm sad to say, you'll have to vacate the bed." I hear the smile in her voice. "Then we do our best to get her out of here. Medically, if the exam is good, she'll be fine to go home, but make sure someone hangs close. These things can change and it's better she has someone nearby, just in case." A pause. "Also, you should be aware there may be other long-term outcomes of the event."

Gray's body goes tense. "Like what?"

"Nightmares," the doctor says and it takes everything in me to remain still. "PTSD. She'll need someone watching out for her."

"We'll have her covered."

I wish I could see Gray's face when he says those words because there's something in them that has my pulse speeding, my heart rolling over in my chest...and the insane urge to roll closer, to cling tighter to him.

To trust in that promise.

But how can I when everyone I've ever cared about has—

"I know you're awake, Red."

I jerk in his hold.

Which, for the record, is completely the wrong thing to do when it comes to trying to pretend to be asleep in my hot hockey-playing neighbor's arms.

He slides his hand along my side, fingertips drifting over my forearm, lifting goose bumps on my skin. Up, up they travel— over my elbow, the outside of my arm, lightly trailing over my shoulder. There he stops.

Or doesn't *stop*.

He just doesn't move any higher as he winds a lock of my hair around his finger.

"Can't imagine too many women would spend the day in the hospital, after barely escaping a house fire, and have hair that feels like silk," he murmurs.

"The nurse helped me shower yesterday."

He bends, presses his nose to my head, and inhales. "Apples," he murmurs.

"It's all they had."

"I like it."

"Oh," I murmur.

Why did I just vow to only buy hair products that smell like apples from now on?

"Sleep okay?" he asks softly.

I nod, and as I do it, I realize I'm still pressed to his chest.

Which has me going stiff again.

But his finger keep twirling, and he doesn't unwrap his other arm. "You're quieter in the morning."

I'm quiet most of the time.

I just...last night was an anomaly.

Like the universe had turned upside down and I was a different person. But today the sun is shining through the windows and I'm...me.

And Gray is...Gray.

"You heard what the doctor said?" he asks, still softly.

"Yes," I say quietly, pushing lightly against his chest. The question reminding me where I am and what I'm doing and what's destined to happen.

He doesn't budge.

"Which means you heard what *I* said."

Not a question.

It doesn't matter, though.

The words are ringing through my head.

We'll have her covered.

First, who's *we?*

Second...what the heck does he mean by covered?

Because I know it definitely can't be something like what I'd write in one of my books, can't be what that secret place in my heart wants, can't mean what it sounds like.

I push at his chest again.

Spoiler alert: he still doesn't move.

"Gray," I protest softly.

He releases the strand of my hair, and even as disappointment is coursing through me because he's not twirling it any longer, my breath squeezes out of my lungs.

Because he's sliding his hand up, cupping my jaw, diving his fingers into my hair and murmuring, "I like the sound of my name on your lips, Red."

"I—" But that's as far as I get.

Mostly because I don't know *what* to say to that.

"You feeling okay?"

"Y-yeah," I murmur.

Even though I'm far from okay.

I'm sad and raw and worried about what I'm going to do next.

I'm confused as to why Gray is still here, nervous about what he meant when he said *We'll have her covered,* and...

I'm lying in bed next to him.

So there's that.

His mouth hitches up. "You're not okay."

"I'm fine," I whisper.

Then his hand is dipping further into my hair, tilting my head down, and pressing his lips to my forehead. "You're not okay, and that's okay, baby. It's okay to not be okay."

My heart skips a beat at the gentle way he calls me *baby,* but I know better than to put too much stock into the endearment. Likely, some part of his brain needs to see me out of the hospital and on my two feet. I'll give him that.

And maybe it's also me giving myself just a little more time to bask in the warmth of his attention.

"That's a lot of okays," I murmur.

He chuckles, the laughter a warm puff of air along my scalp. "Author brain coming out?" he teases.

Oh, my author brain is out.

As in *out*, alert, clocking every bit of this interaction, of the last day.

Because this is the stuff of fantasies...

And heartbreak.

That has me closing my eyes, taking a long, slow breath.

Then I gently push against his chest.

To my relief—and it has to be said, disappointment—he releases me.

"It's a gift and a curse," I say, forcing my lips to curve when he dips his face down again, green eyes coming to mine, holding, *searching.*

Eventually, he slips his hand from my hair and gently touches his finger to the tip of my nose. "I bet it is."

My lips part, my exhale shaky.

And—oh, my God, am I clocking *this*, committing it to memory.

Because I also don't miss what my shuddering breath does to his eyes.

How they heat and shift, how his hand splayed on the middle of my back presses lightly, bringing our bodies even closer together.

I don't miss how his head bends further, his mouth coming close enough that I know exactly where this next moment is going...

And how much I want it to go *there.*

For his lips to find mine.

For him to kiss me hot and sweet and long.

Maybe I misread—

There's a knock at the door.

He curses softly, glances over his shoulder, and I follow his gaze, see a woman in a lab coat standing there.

Her eyes come to mine and she asks, "Ready to get out of here?"

Out of the hospital? Yes.

Out of Gray's arms?

No.

Unfortunately, I don't think I'll ever want that.

Thirteen

GRAY

SHE'S QUIET FROM THE PASSENGER SEAT, BUT I DON'T miss the tension filling her frame, ratcheting tighter and tighter as I navigate us closer to our street.

And, damn.

I should have thought of this.

I pause at the stop sign and consider my next move.

Then know I need to keep driving.

Because I think *not* seeing her house, not knowing what she's lost and what's still left is going to be worse than facing this head-on.

Her shoulders go stiffer and her hands clench together.

"Breathe, Red," I murmur, reaching over the console and snagging one small hand, loosening her fist, lacing my fingers with hers.

She exhales and it's shaky again, as shaky as it had been back at the hospital when those plump lips of hers parted, the tip of her pink tongue sliding out to moisten them, turning them slick and damp and...tempting.

I would have tasted her had the doctor not interrupted.

I want to taste her now.

A horn beeps, and my gaze jerks to the rearview, seeing the car behind me, impatiently waiting.

Probably because I've turned a stop sign into a stop light.

One that hasn't turned green.

I exhale and wrench myself back into focus.

Then I squeeze her hand again and start forward, rolling through the intersection and eventually—after two more turns—making it onto our street.

The fire is completely out, but if it's anything like yesterday, the smell of smoke will be lingering in the air. And since the sky is clear of any clouds, the sun bright and shining, the charred remains of Faye's home will be far too easy to spot.

Case in point?

She sucks in a breath as I turn into my driveway, her gaze pointed through the passenger side window, her body stiff and her jaw clenched.

Her fingers tighten around mine, hard enough to send a bolt of pain through my hand, but I don't say a word. "I talked to the fire crew yesterday," I say softly. "They need to have an inspector come out and clear the structure before you can go in, but they think it'll only take another day or two."

"Okay," she whispers, her hand still clutching mine. "Thanks."

But her gaze is still pointed out the window.

And her voice...

"Red," I murmur.

She jerks, head whipping toward me, eyes distant when they connect with mine.

I can practically see her building a wall around herself, slapping together brick and mortar in rapid movements.

Shutting herself away from me.

"Can I borrow your phone?" she asks, tugging at her hand.

I frown, don't release her fingers. "Yeah," I say. "We'll go inside, get you somewhere comfortable and you can make as many calls as you need."

"Great." Another tug. "Thanks."

I smooth my thumb over her silken skin. "You okay?"

"Yup."

Short. Clipped out. Her shoulders hunching ever so slightly.

Of course she's not okay.

"I need to make those calls," she says, pulling at my hold again.

Something about the way she's avoiding my eyes as she tugs has me asking, "Who do need to call?"

Another hunch of her shoulders but when she turns to look at me, her pretty brown eyes spark with irritation. "Does it matter?"

"That answer tells me it matters a whole lot, Red."

Her lips press flat.

I lift my eyebrows.

Her nose wrinkles—and fuck, that's cute, so cute I want to lean forward and kiss the freckled bridge.

I don't, though.

I just wait.

And eventually, she sighs. "I need to call a taxi." Her chin lifts. "And book a hotel room."

My brows drag together. "Why?"

She jerks her chin at the charred remains of her house. "I need somewhere to sleep, Gray."

The hint of sass in her tone has my dick twitching. "You're staying here, Red."

Her lips part on a shaky exhale, one that has me leaning a little closer, wanting to feel that puff of air on my skin, on my *tongue.* "I-I can't stay here," she whispers.

"Why not?"

"You've already done—"

"Enough?" I finish when she doesn't.

"Yes!" She tugs again and this time with so much ferocity that I think she's going to hurt herself.

So, I release her.

Then curse softly when her arm flies back and her elbow cracks against the opposite door.

"Easy, Red," I murmur, guilt rippling through me.

Why am I fighting so hard to keep her near when the smartest thing—the safest thing—is to let her go?

She's gone still, clutching her arm to her chest and I move again, reaching for her, this time to capture her elbow and gently run my fingers over the abused spot.

"Just take a breath, yeah?" I say when she remains like that statue, so damned still I need to know she's breathing, that the wall she's erecting around herself isn't complete.

Isn't so thick yet that I can't break through.

And...yup.

This is so totally fucked.

But right now I don't care. I just need her to stay.

"You just got out of the hospital," I go on gently. "You need somewhere safe to recuperate."

"A hotel is safe."

Soft and sweet Faye, who's hardly spoken five sentences to me in four years since I moved in next door is stubborn.

I snatch at the information, hold it tight like Gollum and his ring.

My precious.

Then I focus on the task at hand. "Please, Faye," I say, still gently, "don't fight me on this."

"I have to." It's a whisper.

I tuck a wayward strand of her hair behind her ear. "Why, baby?"

"I can't do it."

"Can't do what?"

A shudder, her chin dropping forward, her voice going so

quiet I can barely hear it. "I can't get used to it." Then she adds before I can push further, "I can't get used to not being alone."

It's another piece of her.

A heartbreaking one.

My lungs seize. "Aw, Red," I murmur.

Her head snaps up, eyes flying open, and it's impossible to miss the regret written into the lines of her face.

Regret for having shared that.

"I'll stay," she murmurs. "But just for a few days."

"Red—"

But before I get more than that out, there's a knock on Faye's window.

Fourteen

Faye

I gasp, hand coming to my throat, banging my elbow against the door a second time.

This time, already sore, already open and raw and completely confused (and also scared that if I let go, even a little bit, give in to this fantasy, that I'll lose myself...and end up alone—only this time with a broken heart) a gasp of pain escapes me.

"Fucking hell," Gray mutters, shoving open his door and unfolding his big, strong frame from the car. "Smitty, you scared her."

His tone is deadly, and even not directed at me, a shiver skates down my spine.

Then I'm cradling my splinted arm, watching, soaking up his graceful movements as he storms around the hood of the car, moves to the big, bearded man who knocked on my window, plants a hand in the middle of his chest, and shoves him back.

Hard enough that the big, bearded man who's several inches taller and definitely quite a few pounds heavier (this being from his strongly muscled frame) goes back on a foot.

Then straightens, his face going stony.

"What the fuck, Smitty?" Gray growls, apparently not worried in the least about the expression on the other man's— apparently Smitty's—face.

"Dude," Smitty says and it's so loud that I jump again. "Chill."

"Keep your voice down." Gray's gaze slices to me. "You're still scaring her."

Smitty's head whips in my direction and his expression goes blank for a moment, something flickering through his eyes. But his voice is softer, almost gentle when he dips his chin my direction and says, "Sorry."

"Great," Gray mutters. "Apology accepted. Now back up. Faye needs to get inside so she can rest."

Smitty nods again and retreats a few paces, giving Gray enough space to open my door. "You good?" he asks softly as he reaches over me and unbuckles my seat belt.

Good?

He's reaching over me, his fingers at my hip, his spicy male scent in my nose?

I'm firmly in fantasy land.

And I don't think I'm going to be strong enough to leave it any time soon.

He helps me out, starts leading me up the driveway and toward his front door without preamble...like formal introductions. "The asshole is nosy and gossips like an old granny—"

"Make that plural. As in *grannies*," Smitty says, and though it's slid in the category of speaking rather than yelling, it's definitely still much louder than a normal person would speak, thus, I jump again.

Which makes Gray scowl, also again.

Or maybe he's glowering because when I turn around I see there's not one big, bearded man behind me, but four.

Umm...

Before Gray or I can say anything, a hand appears from behind Smitty, pressing into his side, and though it's a delicate, feminine hand, one that seems almost breakable, the light touch it gives shifts him effortlessly.

Like the woman who's appeared behind him is parting the Red Sea.

"Hi, Faye," she says as softly as Smitty spoke loudly, "I'm Kailey."

We make our introductions and she smiles. It's sweet, so sweet I know why the big, bearded man adores her. It's clear in the way he looks at her, how he loops an arm around her waist, drawing her into his side, how he presses his lips to the top of her head.

More book fodder.

More fantasy world.

Because Gray's come close too.

And though he doesn't snake his arm around me, he does settle his palm on the base of my spine.

"Faye is going to rest now," he says. "Go away."

Kailey's lips twitch but she doesn't speak.

Nope, that honor is given to the woman behind her, a pretty brunette with a great smile and gorgeous gray eyes. "I'm Luna. You met Kailey, and that big brute—"

"Hey!" Smitty protests.

My lips twitch when Luna goes on, unperturbed, hitching her head over her shoulder at a gorgeous man with green eyes behind her. "My husband, Aiden." Another hitch toward another woman, or girl, really. She's in her late teens, at most, though her eyes put her as much older. As though she's seen far more than someone of her age should have seen. "That's Bri. And those two goofballs—"

More protests of "Hey!"—this time from the other men.

"Are Leo and Ryan," she continues, still not missing a beat.

I have the feeling this woman is a force to be reckoned with.

Then again, the men around us seem to be their own forces of nature too.

They need someone to *reckon* them.

Is that proper English? I think not. But I'd go to the mat with my editor about that one.

Leo and Ryan definitely need some reckoning.

Of the feminine variety.

Gray too, I suppose, could use a woman in his life, one strong enough to go toe-to-toe with him.

I bat away the thought...and the slice of jealousy it invokes.

But before I can speak, Luna keeps talking. "All the boys play for the Grizzlies and they're *all*"—a deliberate look at the men—"going to head out to the cars and unload the stuff we brought for Faye."

Gray stiffens. "I—"

Her brows go up.

He sighs. "Fine," he mutters, fingers stroking lightly over the base of my spine. "Make yourself at home," he tells me. "I'll be right back."

Then he's following the others out the door and off the porch.

While I'm standing, staring after him, wondering how much stuff these women I've only just met have brought and how the hell I'm going to repay them for their kindness.

And trying to ignore the fact that they'll be in line behind Gray.

Because he's already done so much...like saving my life.

"They really do have nice asses, don't they?" Luna says on a sigh, looping her arm through mine and resting her head against my shoulder for a moment.

"Luna!" Kailey says, exasperated.

"Ew," the girl mutters.

I turn to face Luna as she straightens, her mouth curved. "I was just saying what we were all thinking—well, all of us except for Bri, anyway. Though..." She lifts and drops one slender shoulder. "Who knows what might happen if a cute, young player joins the roster?"

Bri wrinkles her nose. "Ew." A beat. "Also, I told you. I'm bi."

"Great. That means you have double the dating pool, including the age-appropriate section of the Grizzlies' roster." Luna rubs her hands together. "Think of all the matchmaking possibilities that await you."

"Luna," Kailey begins.

"I'm not dating a hockey player," Bri grumbles. "Not ever."

"Damn right," Aiden says as he pushes past us, his arms laden with bags.

My pulse begins pounding in my ears as I struggle to keep track of the conversation.

"Why not?" Luna demands. "Aiden is a hockey player, and he's great."

"He's the exception," Bri replies. "Smitty is too," she tells Kailey, who shoots her a small smile.

"Definitely agree," Leo says, one hand gripping a mitt-ful of bags. The other he uses to ruffle Bri's hair.

Hair she quickly attempts to right.

Then fails because Ryan's a step behind Leo and he does his own ruffling.

"No dating hockey players," he says, carrying in his handful of bags.

Luna rolls her eyes, opens her mouth—

"Did I hear matchmaking?" Smitty booms, both arms laden with bags.

I jump.

Kailey sighs.

Gray growls as he carries his own load past me.

Meanwhile, I'm pin balling back and forth, trying to track the conversation, the bags, the entries and exits, the teasing and rela-tionships, and knowing an instant later, that I'll never be able to.

There's too much history.

No, it's just that it's *all* too much.

The voices blur around me, I waver as dizziness washes over me.

I can't do this.

I need to go.

Need my quiet.

Need my space.

Need to remind myself that I don't have a big, loud, albeit clearly loving family.

I'm alone.

Always. Forever.

And that's the only way this is going to end.

FIFTEEN

GRAY

"RIGHT," I MUTTER, DROPPING THE BAGS ON THE FLOOR and moving close to Faye, settling my hand on the small of her back.

She doesn't react to my touch, doesn't lean back into it like she did just a few minutes before.

Nope.

Right now she's trembling, her gaze having dropped to the floor, her uninjured hand clenched into a fist so tightly it's turning bright red.

"Time to go," I order my teammates and Kailey and Luna and Bri, sliding my hand to the side, wrapping it around Faye's middle.

It's too much touching when I hardly know her, and it's certainly giving the guys too much shit to gossip about, but I can't seem to stop myself.

Not when Faye is shaking.

Not when she's holding herself so fiercely it's like she's going to break apart with the softest breeze.

I step closer, speak louder when the conversation doesn't dim, when it, in fact, grows in volume, the chaotic back-and-forth typical of my friends.

But Faye's shy.

And she's been through too much, not just over the last couple of days, but throughout her life.

And she needs to fucking rest.

"Time to go."

It's as loud as I dare, not wanting to startle Faye again, but the hooligans around me don't hear it.

None except Kailey, that is.

Her eyes come to mine then drift down and I know she sees in Faye what I'm seeing and feeling because she moves to Smitty's side, lifts on tiptoe and murmurs something in his ear.

He stops mid-sentence—or really, mid-shit-giving of Leo—and flicks his stare toward me and Faye.

Then he looks down at Kailey and nods.

"Time to go," he booms.

Faye jumps and I tighten my arm around her middle, drawing her back against me.

Aiden gives me a knowing look but doesn't comment as he snags Luna's hand and says, "We'll catch up with you two later."

"But I don't—"

"Later, tiny tornado," he says more firmly.

Luna hesitates. Then nods, leaving without further protest.

Aiden doesn't comment—verbally, anyway—just flicks his gaze to the woman in my arms, his mouth hitching up, then he's out the door, Bri following. Leo and Ryan nod at me and make short work of getting the fuck out.

Assholes.

But the good kind.

Smitty's gaze locks with mine and he kisses the top of Kailey's head, voice pitched to quiet. "Meet you at the car, little bird."

She touches his jaw, fingers sliding through the bristles of his beard.

Then she moves close to Faye. "Nice to meet you," she says,

gently squeezing Faye's arm. A wave in my direction as she slips away.

Leaving us with just Smitty.

I open my mouth because fuck if this man is going startle Faye again.

But he doesn't frighten Faye by speaking loudly. He doesn't even touch her.

Instead, he crouches a little—or really, a lot—to meet her eyes. "See you around, Faye," he murmurs.

Yup. Smitty is murmuring.

Never thought I'd see the day.

Faye manages a nod and I watch the jerky movement radiate through Smitty, know it's doing the same thing to him that it does to me—triggering all sorts of *Me man. Me protect.* caveman bullshit.

But I don't rein it in.

Just dip my head to the door, silently telling my teammate to not let it hit him in the ass on the way out.

His mouth twitches, but he follows the silent order and beats it, closing the door behind him.

I make sure Faye is steady before stepping back from her and flicking the lock.

Then I shift closer again, study her face.

She exhales, lifting a shaking hand, pushing her hair away from her eyes. "I'm sorry," she whispers. "I-uh...that was really nice of them. I, um, shouldn't have—" Teeth press into her bottom lip. "I'm not used to..." Her gaze slides to the side. "I'm not used to all of that."

Because she's alone.

My heart convulses, and I grind my teeth together.

Because that thought makes me want to punch something.

But I need my hands for the game tonight.

A game I need to start thinking about.

Instead of a woman I barely know, who I want to keep close,

who I need to learn, who I can't seem to let go even though there are far too many complications.

She's my neighbor. She's soft and shy and dealing with trauma I'm not equipped to handle. And she's alone. And...I'm me. The interest is there, the beginning of an obsession. It's not going to go away, not for a good long time. Fuck, look how long it took me to get my shit together with Courtney. And God, my fucking ex. I say I'm done, but history has a way of repeating itself, old habits taking over...

Then there are my teammates who will get attached and interfere and give me shit I don't need and...

It's all wrong.

Faye's all wrong for me.

But I know myself well enough to know I'm still going to claim her as my own, anyway.

Even if I'm wrong for her too.

"Come on," I say, when she opens her mouth once more, probably to apologize for no reason again.

I don't have time to sit in my feelings right now. Faye needs me.

"Wh-what?"

"I'm starving," I tell her, unable to resist taking her hand after I bend and snag a few of the bags from the floor. The touch of her palm against mine soothes some ragged part of me, and when her soft fingers lightly stroke along the back of my hand, I think about them stroking other places.

Harder places.

Focus, Gray.

Food first.

But I know if I offer to cook her something she'll turn me down, tell me she's fine. But *I'm* hungry and she's eaten—well, in truth—she's *hardly* eaten only shitty hospital food over the last day and a half.

She needs real food.

Then she needs rest.

And maybe later, she needs to watch a hockey game.

Tension finally sliding from my shoulders, I start down the hall, dump the bags on the counter, and pull out the container that Bri brought.

Cookies.

Fucking good ones with a gooey salted caramel center and chocolate chunks and flecks of sea salt on top.

Bri works at Molly's Bakery, and she's definitely picked up more than a few tips and tricks from the bakery's namesake.

"Here," I say, popping off the lid and handing Faye a cookie the size of my hand.

"Um..."

"Salted caramel with milk chocolate chips," I tell her. "Bri made them."

I watch the nerves leave her and secure another bit of information about Faye as she brings the cookie up to her nose, inhales deeply.

She really loves baked goods.

And baking, I remember.

I lost Nana's banana bread recipe.

I can't remember if her banana bread calls for one egg or two.

"Bri made these?"

I nod as I take a huge bite of my own cookie, the delicious mix of salt and sweet hitting my tongue in an explosion of flavor. The remaining tension in my shoulders evaporates when she takes her own bite, murmurs through it, "They're really good."

"They sure are," I agree as I head to the fridge, snagging the ingredients for my favorite pregame meal—chicken breast, grilled peppers...and a peanut butter and jelly sandwich.

Don't judge.

When I turn back with my arms full of food, I see she's devoured half the cookie.

And that she has crumbs on her bottom lip.

I move before I'm really thinking, setting the food down and reaching out...

Then freezing before I actually make contact.

Her lips part, eyes going wide, pink creeping into her cheeks.

I close the final inch between us, brush the crumbs away. Then because I can't stop myself, I shift closer, cupping her jaw, my fingertips sliding into the silk of her hair.

"What are you doing?" she whispers.

Our faces are so close I feel the words on my skin.

I don't know what I'm doing.

Or I do, but I'm not ready to admit it out loud.

Because it's wrong—

But nothing this wrong has ever felt so right.

"Bri works at Molly's bakery," I say going for distraction.

It works.

"Really?" Another puff of air on my lips and the spark of excitement in Faye's eyes has me shifting even closer. "I love Molly's! I swear, their seasonal peaches and cream muffins are so delicious they should be illegal. Then they top them with that—"

"—streusel," I finish, having devoured a peach muffin—or several dozen—myself.

"I really love that streusel." She smiles. "I wish they sold it by itself. I've tried to replicate it dozens of times but I can never quite figure out the correct combination of spices."

"Maybe Bri would teach you."

Faye's eyes widen. "You think she might?"

"I think I can ask," I tell her. "And that Bri would really love to teach you. She's...well, she's spent too much time alone too."

A wave of emotion across Faye's face, warming her brown eyes, flushing her cheeks, plumping those pink lips.

"Fuck, you're beautiful."

Sixteen

Faye

The raspy words have my mouth falling open.

Which he takes full advantage of, dropping his head and closing the final couple of inches between us.

His lips hit mine and...he kisses me.

He. Kisses. *Me.*

It's gentle but not hesitant, something that has my pulse skittering and my knees threatening to buckle...and then *actually* buckling when gentle disappears with his rough groan and he deepens the kiss, plunging his hand into my hair, tilting my head back, his other arm banding around me, keeping me on my feet.

At the same time, he moves into me, pinning me back against the kitchen island.

He tastes of chocolate and salted caramel, sweet and salty and male and—

Mine.

God, I'd love for this man to be mine.

He's mine right now.

Mine in this moment.

Mine for as long as his arms are around me and his tongue is in my mouth and—

I moan.

And the result is...*fabulous.*

He growls, the sound vibrating along his tongue, from his chest through mine, sensitizing my nipples, sending heat down in a bolt of sensation between my legs.

Pleasure.

Need.

Mine.

His lips release mine, dragging along my jaw, down my throat, burying his face there and inhaling deeply.

I shudder, my hands diving into his hair this time, holding him to me, loving the roughness of the stubble on his cheeks against my skin, the hot, sleek dart of his tongue on my flesh, the soft yet firm press of his lips on my neck.

Then really *not* loving when he stills, curses softly, and lifts his head.

"Fuck, I'm sorry," he mutters, his eyes not meeting mine.

Then, worse, he backs away, and I lose the heat and strength of his body, the spice of his scent, the feel of his lips.

I pick up my cookie—which thankfully landed on the counter and not the floor—and take a huge bite.

All the better to stifle the words bubbling in my throat.

The apology that wants to follow his.

The embarrassment that has me wanting to sprint out the front door.

But where will I go?

No car. No phone. No credit cards.

The loneliness washes through me and I bite the inside of my cheek, willing it away, blinking back the tears that burn my eyes.

I shove another bite of cookie in my mouth, chew and swallow, but I'm not tasting the delicious salted caramel or the melty milk chocolate, not enjoying the crumble, the gentle crunch, the soft, ooey-gooey center.

No.

It's like I'm chewing sawdust.

"I'll rest up tonight," I manage to push out. "Get out of your hair tomorrow."

That done, I exhale and lift the cookie, intending on forcing myself to finish each and every bite, but I don't get the chance.

Because Gray snatches it from my hand, tosses it on the counter.

"No."

I blink. "No, what?"

"No, you don't get to think whatever it is that has your face looking like that."

I blink again, still reeling from the kiss, from his withdrawal, from that damned apology, and feel the edges of my temper begin to fray. "Now you're telling me what to think?"

"Yes," he mutters, cupping my jaw and tilting my head up at the same time he bends and takes my lips in a searing kiss that has my knees wobbling again. "Because *I* was apologizing, not expecting you to."

I frown, knowing I'm letting him take over, but unable to stop myself, especially when his hand shifts, thumb tracing over my jaw, my cheek, the sensitive spot behind my ear, and his voice goes gentle and teasing. "You're tired and you need food, and I shouldn't be kissing you." He grins. "Even if your lips are far too tempting."

My mouth falls open.

He groans.

And suddenly he's kissing me again—hot and wet and not pulling back until my lungs scream for air.

"See?" he murmurs.

Then he snags the cookie, shoves it back into my hand, but before I can take a bite or verbalize that I'm really freaking confused, he's scooping me up and settling me on the counter. "Eat," he orders. "I'll make us both something to eat and get you settled before I have to leave for the rink."

It takes me a bit to recover, but eventually I do, and I find I'm intrigued by the confident and capable way he moves, picking up the ingredients and bringing them over to the stove, getting out a cutting board and knife and spices with practiced hands.

Though the ingredients are a confusing mix.

Peanut butter and chicken breasts? Strawberry jelly and red pepper slivers? And garlic. And red pepper flakes.

My tastebuds are already protesting.

"Eat your cookie," he says, and I lift my gaze from the cutting board and chicken that's being efficiently sliced and seasoned to find him staring at me.

More of my temper frays. "You really like giving orders, don't you?"

"I like to see a woman I care about eating."

My nose wrinkles. "You don't even know me."

He sets down the knife, dumps some oil into the pan and turns on the burner with a click. "You know more about me than almost any other person on this planet."

I freeze.

"Gray," I whisper.

"Which means I'm going to feed you, going to set you up in my guest room—where you're going to stay in until you're settled and ready to go back home." He fixes me with a stern look. "And not because you feel like you're imposing so need to run out of here."

"Gray," I say, irritation blooming anew.

"Yes, that's another order," he replies without the least bit of remorse. "Argue with me about it later." He turns back, dumps the chicken in the pan then moves to the sink.

I nibble at the inside of my cheek as I mentally count to ten.

When that settles my temper—*somewhat*—I consider my options...

And know that they'll likely have me ending up right in his guest room.

By this time, he's washed the cutting board and knife and is snagging the loaf of bread and peanut butter and jelly.

"What exactly are you going to cook for us?" I ask, curiosity getting the better of my temper.

"My pregame meal." He starts slapping peanut butter and jelly onto two slices.

"Which is what exactly?" My eyes flick to the chicken on the stove. The pan is sizzling intensely, and I start to hop down.

"Don't move," he—yup—orders, pointing the jelly-covered knife in my direction.

"The chicken—"

"Will be fine for the next thirty seconds." He tosses the knife in the sink, slaps another slice of bread onto each of the other two and turns back to me, shoving a sandwich into my free hand. His eyes flick to the one still holding my cookie. "Thought I told you to eat that."

I glare at him. "You're really trying to make me mad, aren't you?"

He grabs the second sandwich from the counter then takes a huge bite. "Better mad than sad as far as I'm concerned." And as I'm still reeling from that, he adds, "And my game day meal is the perfect blend of nutrition—PB&J and chicken and veg. Protein. Carbs. Fiber. It's the right mix to succeed on the ice."

"This meal did not come up in my research for my hockey series."

I take a bite of the cookie—sweet and delicious and more than a little sinful...

Just like Gray.

Especially when he glances over his shoulder at me, beautiful lips turned up into a smile. "What exactly did you research, Red?"

SEVENTEEN

GRAY

THE BEFUDDLEMENT ON HER FACE IS FUCKING adorable.

And I want to kiss her again.

But I've already jumped the gun on that, giving in to the urge to taste her when I should be feeding her, should be taking care of her.

So, I temper the urge to keep pushing, to taste her again.

Instead, I relax, knowing I'm on this ride, that I've waited in line, boarded the roller coaster, and secured the restraints.

The teenager behind the controls is getting ready to push the button to send us off.

And I'm ready.

For better or worse, I'm gonna take this ride.

"Eat your cookie, Red," I order just to see the adorable scowl that forms on her face in response.

She really doesn't like orders.

I wonder if that's everywhere...or if she wouldn't mind them in bed.

If maybe she wouldn't *like* them there. I'd make them good for her.

I promise.

Heat arrows toward my cock at the thought of giving her sensual orders, at seeing how she'd respond, phantom fingers wrapping around the length of my erection, pumping once, twice, three—

"I researched lots of things," she says pertly.

A tone that doesn't help the whole phantom fingers thing.

Especially when I want to taste that *pert* on my tongue. In fact, I actually take a step toward her, intending to do just that.

Christ.

Too much, too fast—she doesn't need that shit right now.

Food. Rest. *Hockey.*

Willing my cock to behave, I flick a gaze over my shoulder, see that she's almost finished the cookie and something in me relaxes.

"Like what?" I ask instead of kissing her...or telling her to get going on the sandwich.

Her eyes come to mine and hold, and I love that there's not a hint of shy, that her pretty brown eyes don't drift away and aren't filled with shadows and hurt. Instead, there's excitement and intelligence...and suspicion.

"Why do you want to know?"

I lift my brows in question before turning back to the stove, giving the pan one more stir before finishing it off with a pat of butter and another dash of seasonings. "I think it's interesting. I haven't met an author before, least of all one who writes books about hockey."

"Only five of them," she murmurs.

"Ask me how many I've written," I deadpan, serving up the food and bringing the plates over to the island. Her cookie is gone, along with the PB&J. Good. "Your job is cool, Red, and I want to learn more about it. That's all. No other hidden motives."

She accepts the plate I hold out. "It's really not *that* cool," she says as I retrieve forks and napkins. "It's just me sitting like a gremlin at my computer, pecking away at the keyboard as I down far too much Diet Coke and try to pretend I'm healthy because I choke down a vegetable every once in a while."

"You don't like veggies?" I ask, mostly because she's forking up the pepper slices on her plate.

"I love them," she says. "It's just that my author brain wants to function solely on caffeine and junk food and not on anything with, say, nutrients in it."

I chuckle and her head whips toward me, cheeks going pink. "What?"

She waves a hand up and down my body. "You look like *you*."

"And how's that?" I can't help but tease, loving that her cheeks grow a little pinker.

Her eyes narrow, though, that gorgeous brain of hers not missing a beat. "Hilarious," she mutters. "But you know you're in shape."

I lift my tee—and yeah, I'm showing off. "I don't know," I say, still teasing, "these probably need some more time in the gym."

She chokes, and smirking, I head to the fridge, searching the contents for a Diet Coke. I don't drink them but I'm pretty sure there are a couple left from the last time everyone came over. It takes a few seconds, but I spot the silver and red can and snag it, setting it by her hip.

Her face goes soft.

"So, what kinds of things do you research, Red?" I ask, picking up my plate and starting in on my food.

She points at my food. "That, for one," she says. "Pregame meals. And travel schedules—making sure my characters aren't flying to a game in the middle of summer, for another. And that not all their games are home games or against the same teams. I made a whole schedule for my fake team, actually. I even padded in the days off and travel time and holidays and preseason and playoffs." She shrugs and takes another bite, but I wait, not daring to interrupt the flow of her words, still in full Gollum mode, wanting to soak up every piece of her she gives me. "And what happens after a trade," she says. "And how contracts work and what the various positions on and off the ice are that bring the team together."

"What do you mean?"

"Well, obviously, there's you guys," she says, "but there's also the coaching staff and the trainers and the equipment managers and the player development department and..." A shrug. "Well, I'm sure you know."

"Yeah, Red. I do know. It's definitely not just us guys. The organization as a whole has to be functioning and supporting each other to be successful."

Something that's generally easier when the team's captain isn't going viral for all the wrong reasons—

No.

I don't want to think about Courtney and me, don't want to think about all the ways I've messed up.

I just want to enjoy...Faye.

She nods, keeps eating chicken and veggies.

"What else?" I prompt after we eat in silence for a few minutes.

"I'm sure there's more," she says. "I tend to get a little obsessive when it comes to work."

I smile.

"What?"

"Nothing," I say instead of admitting that I really like how her brain works. Or that sitting here eating and talking feels... domestic. And *right.* I reach for the can of soda when she does, popping open the tab and handing it to her.

"Thanks," she murmurs. "But why'd you smile like that?"

Stubborn thing.

"It's just that I know what's like to be obsessive about work."

Her head tilts to the side, one half of her mouth curving. "Yeah, making it into the NHL, you'd have to be."

And maybe also…I know what it's like to be obsessive about a woman.

Though, I don't think I've ever met one like Faye.

Shy and steel; thoughtful, albeit with a brick wall surrounding her heart; fragile but only because she's been shattered and glued back together too many times to count.

And beneath all of that is…*fire.*

Passion. Smarts. Strength. A dash of temper.

We finish our food in easy silence, and I bring the dishes to the sink, refusing her offer of help. Instead, I lift her off the counter, grab some of the bags—the ones I know contain clothes and toiletries—then hitch my head down the hall. "Let me show you your digs."

She doesn't protest as she trails me, and I know it's because her energy is waning, the fatigue catching up with her.

Lucky, my guest room isn't far.

When we get there, I peek through the bags, snag one with toiletries, another with pajamas—I skip a bra, telling myself it's because they're uncomfortable to sleep in, but really, it's mostly because I like the idea of Faye without a bra—and pass them to her.

"Shower," I command, nudging her toward the attached bathroom.

"Orders," she says with a scowl, but she doesn't argue, just slips into the other room, closing the door behind her. A moment later, I hear the water turn on.

Faye naked in the shower.

Christ, what I wouldn't give to see that.

Not the time.

Shoving the image of her naked and wet from my brain, I make short work of unpacking and putting away the items everyone brought. Tees and sweats that are velvet soft, bras and underwear and socks, a couple of hoodies. And a few nicer items too—several pairs of jeans, some blouses, a few dresses and sweaters. Shoes too—everything from flip-flops to sneakers to a couple pairs of heels.

Altogether, it barely fills a quarter of the closet, one drawer in the dresser.

"This is too much," I hear and I turn, see her in pajamas that should be cute and cozy, but instead are all sorts of tempting, her hair bundled on top of her head, her skin pink and damp and tempting.

It's not too much.

It's barely enough to get her started.

But I know what she means.

My teammates and their women—my *family*—really thought of everything.

There's even a swimsuit.

And I hope to God I'll get to see Faye in it, laying out by my pool, her curves gilded from the sunshine or with slick, glistening skin after taking a dip in my hot tub.

She shifts beside me and I focus.

"This is what we do," I murmur, proud that despite the shit-show that's been my personal life over the last couple seasons, I've still managed to keep the locker room healthy. Hell, half the time, it's been the guys keeping *me* sane as I weathered Storm Courtney.

Something that stings my pride, I can't lie.

But...it's what we do.

I nudge her back so she's sitting on the edge of the mattress, fixing the Velcro on her splint she didn't quite manage to attach evenly. "Shower go okay with the bandages?" She has some stitches and burns that needed treatment.

"Yes," she murmurs. "Everything's clean and dry."

I want to check, but...

Rest.

And hockey.

And *patience*.

So instead, I snag the pair of socks I kept out, tug them on her adorable feet, pressing a kiss to the top of each afterward, and though I want to linger, she needs to rest. I move to the dresser and grab the remote, setting it and my phone on the nightstand next to the container of Bri's cookies, just in case she needs a midnight snack.

"For your calls," I explain when confusion flickers across her deep brown eyes. I give her the passcode then point to the cookies. "For your tummy. And—" I wink as I tap the remote. "Because you'll want to watch the Grizzlies game later."

She smiles and it's so beautiful, I know the right thing to do is to walk away, to distance her from the storm that's my life.

But even now, after so little time together, the thought of leaving her alone in the quiet aftermath of *her* life...

Is impossible,

Eighteen

Faye

He's gone before I recover from the wink enough to tell him that while I found the research portion of my hockey books fascinating, I'm still not a hockey fan.

Fan of the players and the behind-the-scenes, yes.

Fan of actually trying to track the puck on TV—or at the arena? No.

I've been to a Grizzlies game, having heard that the best way to appreciate the sport is watching a game in person.

And while I enjoyed the energy of the fans—and the adorable intermission games, one featuring tiny hockey players and the other adults trying to ride tricycles on the ice—I'd also learned that hockey wasn't really for me.

But I don't get to tell Gray that.

Because of the wink.

And...

The rest of it.

The kisses and the clothes, the meal and the questions. He even put on my socks.

And made sure I had cozy pajamas.

And left me his phone.

And the container of cookies.

So, now it's nearly game time and I'm curled up in a bed in Gray's house. Curled up in a bed in the house of the neighbor I've been in love with for four years...and that love formed solely from the fantasy of a gorgeous, seemingly sweet man whom I didn't know but secretly admired.

The real thing is infinitely better.

The real Gray is...incredible.

His phone buzzes on the nightstand and thinking it's my insurance agent who promised to call me right back, I snag it and swipe my finger across the screen.

"Hello?"

There's a long pause, long enough that I'm beginning to think that it's a spam caller, readying to hang up.

"Hello?" I say again.

"Who the fuck is this?"

I go stiff at the furious female voice, so cold and sharp that if she were here in person I'd be dodging flying spikes of ice.

"Um," I say through frozen lips. "I'm Faye."

"Okay, *Faye*," the woman says derisively, "Why the fuck do you have my *husband's* phone?"

Husband.

Fuck.

That one word burns through every fantasy I've built about him.

"Courtney?" I ask.

"Who else would I be?" she snaps.

Not the ex. Not the *awful* ex who finally signed the divorce papers and...who I saw in this very house doing all sort of X-rated things with Gray.

Beautiful. Confident.

A nightmare.

So yeah. *Fuck.*

"Right," I murmur. "Well, I'm Gray's next door neighbor." I

explain about the fire. "He's at his game but let me borrow his phone because mine is...well, you know, burned. But—" I clear my throat. "I can let him know you called?"

Warn him, really.

There's another long pause.

"His neighbor?"

I nod, though she can't see me. "Yes," I say into the phone when she makes an impatient noise. "And I don't want to rush you off the phone but my insurance agent is calling on the other line."

Not a lie.

I can hear the clicking in my ear.

"Your house really burned down?"

My lungs freeze. But I seriously need to end this call.

Mostly because it's a suspicious question.

"Yes," I whisper. "I lost everything."

Another pause.

And the other line is still beeping.

"I really need to grab that call," I murmur. "I'll pass on that you've called when he gets home."

"Home? Are you staying at his house?"

Shit.

"Gotta go. Bye!"

I hang up, stomach twisting because I know I've just stepped into Gray's world in a way I can't undo.

I've seriously messed up.

"Shit," I whisper.

Then I jab at the phone screen so I don't miss the call from my insurance agent.

It's not an easy conversation and it's not short—but Courtney calling back nearly a dozen times plus the copious amounts of texts she sends makes it even less bearable.

Every *buzz-buzz* has my tension ratcheting up.

Add that in to listening my agent, Carrie, telling me the next steps I need to take and internalizing everything I'm going to have to do—not just to replace my house and car and the personal belongings I can, but also navigating permits and zoning and adjusters...

It's overwhelming.

And it certainly doesn't help that I've triggered Gray's nightmare of an ex into sending several dozen text messages and calling his phone too many times (and don't forget the voicemails she's leaving).

I rub my forehead, listening to Carrie's final advice of, "Take a breath, let me handle this, and focus on yourself for the next few days."

"Right," I murmur. "I'll do that. Thanks, Carrie."

But I know I'm lying to her as we exchange goodbyes and I hang up.

How can I focus on myself when my house is in ruins next door?

How can I focus on myself when I've unwittingly unleashed Gray's ex?

How can I focus on myself when I'm wearing the socks Gray put on me and the pajamas his friends brought and the remote he left is right next to the cookies Bri baked who might share Molly's strudel recipe with me...all of which is reminding me how damned great Gray is?

I nibble at my lip. "Damn."

It's a mess all around.

His cell buzzes again and I sigh.

Talk about a mess.

Courtney's messages were filled with more and more vitriol as my call with Carrie went on, so much so that I stopped reading them. Right now, though, I can't stop myself from looking down, gaze going to the banner that's appeared at the top of the page.

Quickly scanning it, even as I brace.

But this time it's not from Courtney.

It's from Gray.

GRAY (via Smitty): Smitty let me borrow his phone.

Okay, right. It's from Gray *from* Smitty's cell.

GRAY (via Smitty): Getting ready to head out onto the ice soon. I just want to make sure you were good.

My eyes flick to my toes, covered in those cozy socks. And my heart squeezes.

FAYE (via Gray): I'm good. Just enjoying your guest bed. The mattress is great and the cookies are delicious.

I weigh telling him about Courtney.

Decide it's best to leave that for after his game. The last thing he needs is to be worrying about her nonsense.

GRAY (via Smitty): And the upcoming entertainment is going to be just as great.

FAYE (via Gray): Entertainment?

GRAY (via Smitty): The Grizzlies kicking the Eagles asses.

FAYE (via Gray): I'm thinking this isn't the time to mention that I don't actually enjoy watching hockey.

A pause.

Long enough that I'm thinking it was dumb to share that, especially right before he's playing, you know, *hockey*.

Long enough that when the pause ends, I find myself being reckless as I settle back on pillows that I swear smell of Gray's cologne.

(But not finding myself caring all that much about my recklessness because it *is* Gray).

Gray (via Smitty): ...

Faye (via Gray): I'm not so much a hockey fan as a fictional hockey hero fan.

Gray (via Smitty): I can't decide if I'm insulted or not.

Faye (via Gray): You're not.

Gray (via Smitty): I'm not?

Faye (via Gray): Because tonight is your chance to make me one.

Nineteen

GRAY

TONIGHT IS YOUR CHANCE TO MAKE ME ONE.

Christ.

I don't need to be thinking about that message, don't need to be letting my imagination run wild.

But all I can think of is those gorgeous lips curving up into a smirk, her pretty brown eyes sparking with challenge.

Beautiful.

She'll have been beautiful writing out that message and hitting send and waiting for my reply.

Which, for the record, was:

> Gray (via Smitty): Challenge accepted, Red.

And I wasn't joking.

The problem is, she hadn't replied.

Or maybe she had, but after I sent it, I had to relinquish Smitty's phone back to him, finish getting dressed, and focus on the game.

A game that's been fast and brutal and—

"Fuck!" I growl as Kingston Bang from the Eagles takes advantage of my distraction by crushing me into the boards.

My stick cracks, the fiberglass composite not able to withstand the big fucker's force and my ribs groan in protest. Because, like I said, King is a big fuck. I drop the two halves of my stick and shove him back, ignoring the pain in my side, the throb in my jaw, the way the asshole Eagles fans on the other side of the swaying glass are pounding on the plexiglass, shouting and cursing at me while, at the same time, cheering on King.

That's hockey, and I know our fans do it too.

I just—

"Fuck," I growl again, shoving him off and hauling ass toward the bench.

Our equipment manager, Ted, is already waiting at the end, stick extended toward me.

I snag it and turn back in a rush, rejoining Leo and Aiden, who've been holding down the fort for me in the offensive zone (and doing it while I was daydreaming about a certain woman at seriously the wrong time).

Leo's pinned against the boards, scrabbling for the puck with King, Cam Jackson from the Eagles giving him a shove to his back before joining the scrum.

I whistle, watch Leo flick his gaze in my direction and jerk my stick to the corner, trying to take advantage of the open space.

It won't last long, but when Leo pops the puck over King's stick, I'm able to swoop in and scoop it up.

The Eagles defense is on me a mere heartbeat later, but I brace and keep position of the puck.

Watching.

Waiting.

Grinding my way to the front of the net.

My stick is slashed. I'm shoved from behind. Pain radiates through my hands and my core, all the muscles in my body working hard to keep my balance.

But I stay on my feet, retain possession of the puck.

And I watch.

And wait.

Leo streaks toward the net, drawing the goalie's focus. One of the defensemen currently hacking the shit out of me curses and peels off, taking after him.

But I'm not trying to get the pass to Leo.

Nope.

I'm focused on Aiden...who's circling around behind me.

I fake the pass, pretend I'm going to loft it over to Leo.

And, instead, I use the back of my stick and flick the biscuit between my legs.

Aiden makes use of his extremely talented hands to scoop up the puck, and he doesn't hesitate, doesn't try to do anything fancy. He just takes advantage of his proximity to the goal and the mass of players—including Leo and myself—in front of the net and rips off a shot.

It's already in the back of the goal before the Eagles realize Leo doesn't have the puck.

The red light flickers on.

The crowd groans.

The opposing players around me curse and I earn another hard shove for my trouble.

I can't care less.

I turn to Aiden. "Fuck yeah!" I throw up my hands, knowing that his shot is going to hit the social media highlight reels.

Picking that corner...whew, it was dirty in the best possible way.

"Fuck that was nice!" I exclaim as we hug.

I pound him on the back, shove at his shoulder, Leo doing much of the same as we make our way to the bench and fist bump our way down the line.

Then we're through the open door, dropping down onto the metal bench. Smitty reaches over me to pat Aiden on the helmet it. "Nice fucking shot, man."

Aiden grins but nods toward me. "Eh, Gray's the one who did all the work and set it up for me."

"You mean I got an assist *along* with an Ass Point."

Smitty chuckles. Aiden grins. Leo shoves in beside me.

Because Ass Point is our newest inside joke—it can be from the puck literally (and this was where the term originated from) hitting someone's ass and then going in the goal. Or it can be from like what just happened—a screen.

As in, my big ass in front of the net, blocking the goalie's view.

In this case, it was my ass *and* others.

But I'll take it.

And the assist.

Mostly because if that goal—and the rest of the game before it —doesn't impress Faye then I don't know what will.

We're on another level tonight.

Passes are connecting. Shots are going in—even ones that aren't nearly as impressive as what Aiden just did.

Hits are brutal, happening along the boards and at mid-ice.

Our goalie is killing it, making incredible, gravity-defying saves.

It's like the entire team knows that Faye is at home, watching.

Judging.

And they're ready to kick some ass to show her how good we are.

For the first time in several seasons, I grin as the camera on the Jumbotron cuts to me, winking, hoping that Faye is watching, that she hasn't slipped out as the broadcast cuts to commercial, that my dumb face makes the feed.

I want her cheeks going pink.

Want her to wonder what the wink means.

Want her to be thinking about me as constantly as I'm thinking about her.

The whistle trills and I jerk my thoughts into focus.

Because I have a woman at home to impress.

I play my ass off, get another goal and assist on my tally and we win the game against the Eagles handily. The moment the buzzer goes and my press obligations are complete (mostly pain-less for a change—or maybe it's that, for once, I'm not thinking about Courtney but rather how quickly I can get home to Faye), I rush through my post-game routine, drive home (glad that the Eagles are in a neighboring city so it doesn't take long), eager to see what Faye thought.

Of the game.

Of me.

But when I peek into her room, I find she's asleep.

I linger in the open doorway as disappointment slices through me, watching her slow and steady breaths, wanting to crawl into bed beside her, but having no reason to.

She has no idea how much of that game was for her...

My only consolation is that the post-game broadcast is still playing on the TV.

TWENTY

FAYE

I DON'T KNOW WHAT WAKES ME.

Last I remember, I was watching the Grizzlies game, hard-pressed to remember why I didn't enjoy my previous attempts at hockey viewing.

I'm not saying that I'm going to seek it out or become a diehard, eighty-two-game-plus-playoffs viewer, but...

It's a whole lot more interesting when I know someone on the ice.

Someones.

Because my gaze hadn't just been glued to Gray out there—I'd also spotted Aiden and Leo and Ryan and Smitty.

It was fun watching them.

Not as fun as watching Gray of course.

But still different than before.

I guess I just needed the personal connection.

Because I'd been *glued* to the television.

I don't remember turning it off, though maybe I had after Gray's interview had finished and the commentators started droning on and on about line combinations and defensive metrics.

I'd been thinking about Gray's wink during that interview. A wink that had matched one he'd given the camera right before it cut away to a commercial break in the second period.

A wink that had my heart fluttering.

No. It was *two* winks that had my pulse skittering through my veins.

Gorgeous man.

Talented player.

Soft, sweet heart.

Sighing, I curl onto my side and deliberately push my thoughts down. It's early, the sun just beginning to peek over the hills to the east, to shine gently through the window, turning the room into soft shades of gold and pink and orange.

Pretty. But I'm tired. It's been a trying—more than trying, that's for damned sure—few days.

And I'm sure Gray is tired too. The game didn't end until after ten and he had the interview, had to change and shower then drive home.

And he probably had some sort of postgame routine.

All of *my* hockey heroes did.

Plus, the Grizzlies had won.

Handily.

So he might have gotten together with the guys and celebrated.

In which case, he'd have been out late.

So late it won't matter if I close my eyes against the growing brightness and go back to sleep.

Because Gray will still be in bed.

Smiling at that sensual thought, I draw the blankets up a little further, bury my face into the pillow and allow my lids to slide shut.

A deep breath.

A deliberate relaxing of my body.

Then my eyes flash open.

Because I hear it.

I smell it.

Rumbling.

Burning.

Gasping, I sit upright in bed, searching the room for smoke and when I don't find any, or none in the immediate vicinity, I take a moment to calm myself. Then I grab a sweatshirt from the closet, shove my feet into the sneakers, snag Gray's phone from the nightstand.

The scent of burning still lingers in the air and my stomach twists.

Smoke equals loss.

I can't let that happen to Gray.

A gentle touch of the doorknob.

Finding it cool to the beneath my fingers, I carefully turn it and pull it open, searching the hall for any sign of smoke.

I still don't see any.

But I smell it, stronger now.

"Shit," I whisper, hurrying down the hall. I don't know exactly where Gray's room is, though, presumably, it's upstairs.

I need to locate the source of the fire then find him and make sure we both get out, that we're both safe.

Like he did for me.

But even as I'm searching for flames and planning my exit route, I hear it.

The rumbling.

Only...it's not the flames burning through the floorboards, tearing through the walls, the foundation, the noise of destruction reverberating all around me.

It's a...stand-up mixer?

And Gray cursing—an impressive string I couldn't have come up with in a book, not even on my most creative day in Writing World.

I turn the corner, get a full look at him...and the mess that's the kitchen.

Flour is dusting the counters, the floor, the cabinets, even that mixer, like fresh snowfall. And Gray isn't immune to it either.

It's on his cheek, sprinkled throughout his hair, dotted on his beard.

It coats his bare chest, his abs, the waistband of his low-slung sweats.

Holy hot baking fantasy.

I tug at the neck of my sweatshirt, needing some cool air since my body is suddenly hotter than the oven.

He curses again as a cloud of flour blooms, the mixer going too fast, and now I know exactly how the snowfall of flour was created.

But I'm too busy watching to intervene.

Too busy taking it all in.

The mess.

But also fresh bags of groceries and several bunches of bananas, a tablet perched up on the counter, a video playing, describing how to make...

Banana bread.

My heart convulses.

Because I also spot the source of the burnt smell.

Loaves—at least a half-dozen of them—spread out on the counter.

All charred within an inch of their lives.

Like seriously, they could be bricks, could be used to build a wall.

"...add one egg and combine well..."

Gray opens the carton, pulls out and egg and tries to crack it on the bowl.

Tries because he makes a mess of it, the shell going everywhere, the white exploding, the yolk breaking.

"Fuck," he hisses.

"...then add your oil and—"

"Slow down," he snaps at the iPad, hurrying to the trash can and dumping the abused egg inside. He washes his hands then wipes them on a towel as he turns back to the mixer.

Which is still rumbling.

But he only makes it a step before his head flies up and his eyes come to mine and—

"Now pour your mixture into a buttered and floured loaf pan and..."

TWENTY-ONE

GRAY

"CRAP," I MUTTER, SHOVING A HAND THROUGH MY HAIR and promptly showering myself in flour.

When I woke up this morning, far earlier than I wanted to because I was worried about Faye and how she slept and if she had nightmares and if so, was *she* awake, I knew there was no hope of me falling back asleep.

And as I lay there, staring up at the ceiling, wondering if she was hurting or scared in a room just a floor below me, her words from the hospital came back into my head.

And wouldn't leave.

I lost Nana's banana bread recipe.

I can't remember if her banana bread calls for one egg or two.

She had my phone, but I just snagged my tablet and found myself searching YouTube.

For banana bread recipes.

No, for *the* banana bread recipe—the one the interwebs declares is just like their grandma used to make.

Apparently, there are a lot of those exact recipes.

Too many to scroll through.

So I figured...grocery store for supplies and trial run?

I like banana bread. The guys are hoovers who won't turn down any or all baked good offering, even if it's only mediocre.

And maybe it'll give Faye something to smile about.

A smile I could then taste?

Only, who know how goddamned hard it is to make banana bread.

First there's the flour—measuring by weight. Well, I don't have a scale, or not one that's useful in the kitchen, anyway.

(My bathroom one doesn't do measure in grams...ask me how I know.)

Then there's using the fancy mixer Courtney bought years ago but I don't think either of us ever turned on. Well, that bitch is a *bitch*—flinging flour in all directions, mixing too fast or too slow (hello fucking *lumps*).

And sour milk.

Isn't that a bad thing?

So why am I mixing vinegar into good milk to make it?

None of it makes sense.

And look, I can cook. I have a repertoire of meals at my disposal. I'm not one of those helpless males who has to run home to mom to get a decent meal. I've been on my own, cooking for myself for a good long while.

But baking?

Well, I obviously overestimated my skills because my counter is littered with absolute disasters.

Mostly charred loaves.

Some underbaked ones.

And loaves that are somehow both at once.

Then there's the mass of dishes in the sink...and elsewhere.

Measuring cups, spoons, and scrapers are intermixed with potholders and kitchen towels. And *paper* towels because I've been using those liberally as well.

It's a disaster.

And Faye's seeing it.

For a second, I don't breathe.

It's not so much the mess that undoes me—it's the look on her face...and the shame washing over me.

Christ, if Courtney had found me like this—hell, if Courtney had found me baking at all—the amount of shit she'd give me...

Astronomical.

My parents would give it to me too.

Not that they're bad people.

They just...have boomer-era views on the proper things that men and women should be doing.

To clarify:

Playing hockey—men.

Baking—women.

As for my teammates...

Their hockey captain baking banana—and *failing*?—yeah, that would be prime shit-giving territory.

And now Faye's standing in the opening to the kitchen, pajamas rumpled, hair sleep-mussed, mouth fallen open in surprise.

Looking fucking adorable.

And gorgeous.

And *mine.*

But I'm bracing, watching her face as she shifts, shoving her hair back from her face, and then starts forward, moving toward me, lips curving, mouth opening.

Fuck. Preparing to give me shit.

Only when her words come out, they're not that.

They're...completely different.

"I fell in love with you four years ago."

The mixer is still going and she reaches over, turns it off.

Leaving us in silence, the smell of burned sugar hanging in the air, something like triumph—and maybe a bit of discomfort—churning through my insides.

No one has ever said that to me before—not like that.

It's always *me* deciding to take the risk, the women in my life accepting what I have to give.

Or oftentimes, *not*.

"I saw you in this kitchen"—a nod toward the window—"right through there. Our houses were mirrors of each other and I looked up, saw you in this room and...fell in love. You were smiling, laughing at something and everything in me just realigned. And that fantasy, the fantasy of you was something I held tight to, something I wrote about and dreamed about." She sighs, closes the distance between us, and touches my jaw. "But you're even more wonderful than the fantasy I fell in love with." A chuckle. "Which is terrifying, I admit. But"—her teeth press into her bottom lip, cheeks flaring bright pink—"I think...if that doesn't completely send you running for the hills then maybe we could kiss some more?"

"Faye," I rasp, starting to reach for her.

Then stopping.

Because there's flour on my hands.

And bits of egg I didn't finish washing off.

And my fingers smell like sour milk.

"Wash up," she says, her lips twitching. "I'll start in on the counters."

"What about the kissing?" I ask, still rasping.

"Maybe we clean up and get the banana bread in the oven first and then do the whole kissing thing?"

"Maybe *that* might end with another burned loaf." I make quick work of washing my hands then turn back toward her. "Not that I'd care."

More pink on her cheeks, her eyes going hot, her body drifting toward mine as I come close. "And maybe," she whispers, "*I* wouldn't care if you put your hands—in any state—on my body."

I'm moving almost before her words are out, eliminating the last few inches between us.

I plunge my hand into her hair, tilting her head back and dropping my mouth to hers.

She moans, and it's the best sound on the planet.

But it's not nearly as good as her body melting against mine, her hands settling on my waist, her tongue tangling with mine.

That has my cock going hard—or harder.

It has my grip on her hair tightening, tilting her head back so I can taste her more completely, so I have her completely under my control, so I can kiss her exactly as I've been thinking of.

Dreaming of.

And now she's rested.

And *now* she's made it clear she wants this.

And now—

"Gray!" she moans, nails digging into my skin.

My control snaps.

Twenty-Two

Faye

I FEEL THE CHANGE COME OVER HIM AND I SHIVER.

But it's not because I'm cold.

Actually, I'm really, *really* hot.

Like scorching hot.

His lips work mine, tongue thrusting into my mouth in sleek darts I hope to God will mirror the rough thrusts of his cock.

"Fuck, Faye," he growls against my lips, his hand in my hair tightening, tugging my head back at the same time his other palm slides down my back, cupping my ass, massaging it...generally driving me freaking insane.

Hot and wet and deep.

Slow and steady and unhurried.

Meanwhile, I feel...

Needy. Desperate. Ready to strip all of his clothes off.

He releases my mouth, trails his lips across my cheek, my jaw, laving at my earlobe. Then down, along my throat, across my collarbones, using his nose to nudge at one of my tank top's straps. It falls and then he's kissing me there, the stubble of his beard the sweetest abrasion. He takes his time, worshiping the spot with lips and tongue and the barest flash of teeth. Then he's softly kissing along my skin, gentle presses of his mouth that lift goose bumps in their wake.

Until he's made it to the other side.

Until he's nudging *that* strap down.

My tank top drops a few inches, catching on the tips of my breasts, one tug, one deep breath away from completely exposing myself.

The thought has moisture gathering between my legs, need coiling in my belly.

My nipples tingle and I hold my breath, the material teasing me.

Or maybe that's Gray.

Because he's started kissing his way down the tops of my breasts, growing closer and closer to the hardened buds of my nipples, but never quite getting there. Down, down. Close, closer. Hot, damp air. Slick, firm tongue. And then away again.

Until I'm trembling.

Until I'm diving my uninjured hand into his hair, holding his mouth against me.

Or maybe...I'm nudging it down, coaxing him toward the edge of the material, silently urging him to get it out of the way.

"Red?" His question is a hot glaze on my skin.

"Y-yeah?" I run my fingers through the silken strands of his hair.

"You ever done this before?"

I still.

Then my fingers tighten and his head shifts, eyes coming to mine.

"What are you asking?" My heart is pounding, embarrassment is beginning to claw at my insides.

Does he—? Could he possibly—? Oh, God, he thinks I'm a *vir*—

"You kiss like sin, Red." A nip to the curve of my breast. "But you said you've been alone, baby. If you haven't done this, that's okay. I just need to know, so I can treat you right."

More embarrassment.

But that's quickly chased aside.

By affection.

"If I knew how wonderful you were," I murmur, cupping his jaw, "I would have worked up the courage to talk to you sooner." He leans into my touch and relief loosens something old and tight and ugly inside me. "But I'm not a virgin, Gray."

"Thank fuck," he groans, dropping his face between my breasts. "And you did talk to me," he says against my skin, lightly rubbing his face, side to side, side to side.

A gentle motorboat.

Only, it doesn't make me laugh.

It has sensation rippling through me, need coiling tighter.

"I-I talked to you?" I ask breathlessly.

"Yup." He leans back, eyes twinkling. "You asked me to pass the potato salad at Donnie and Laurie's thing, and then at Ron and Laila's, you said yes when I asked if you guys wanted refills."

I blush. "I'm really not that good in social situations."

"Liar," he teases, reaching for the hem of my tank. "I've heard you cackling with the girls during your wine parties." He tugs lightly and, yup, I was right.

That's all it takes.

And there goes my shirt, dropping to catch on my hips, bunching at my waist, exposing my nipples to the cool morning air.

And his gaze.

Which is very *not* cool.

It burns into me, causing my nipples to tingle and tighten, desperate for his mouth.

"It's not a wine party," I manage to push out. "It's Book Club."

He blows out a breath, and I gasp as the rush of warm air hits my nipple.

I want him to lean closer, to take it in his mouth, to suck it deep and a little rough and—

"Do you actually read the book?"

Gasping, I glare down at him, my fingers tightening in his hair again. "I'm an author."

"So you read the books," he says.

I nibble at the inside of my mouth.

He grins. "Such a beautiful liar."

"I read almost *all* the books."

He lifts a hand, palms my breast, massaging gently...thus continuing to slowly drive me insane. "What does *that* mean?"

"Laurie picked a Winston Churchill biography o-once," I say, words hitching when he traces his thumb over my nipple, sending lightning bolts of sensation between my legs. "Her dad recommended it ah-apparently," I finish as he leans in and flicks his tongue out.

"Sounds interesting."

"It was"—another lick—"drier than an overcooked pork chop."

A chuckle that does all sorts of glorious things to my insides. "I don't know." His lips drift closer and closer to the hard bud of my nipple. "I think history can be interesting." A long slow lick over the aching tip and my knees buckle.

But he has me, sweeping an arm around my middle and lifting me up onto the counter, the cold granite a shock of sensation against the backs of my thighs.

"Gray," I moan in protest as he continues with his gentle touches, playing with me, taking care of me, slowly driving me to the edge of reason—something that has me reaching for him again, fingers clutching at his shoulders, nails biting into his flesh.

He doesn't seem to mind.

"Fuck, these things are beautiful," he mutters as he palms my breasts, massaging them, running his fingers back and forth over my nipples.

Slow and easy.

As though I'm not on fire.

As though I'm not trembling from needing more of him.

More of his fingers, his tongue, his *teeth*.

But he just continues the slow, inexorable tease.

"Gray?" I ask, running my fingers through his hair.

Another flick of his tongue, one that has my grip tightening on those silken strands.

"Yeah, Red?"

I open my mouth, ready to demand we both strip naked so he can be inside me, but even as the words bubble up, he smiles wickedly...

And seals his mouth over my nipple.

Twenty-Three

GRAY

HER HAND TIGHTENS ALMOST PAINFULLY IN MY HAIR, but I don't stop.

Or maybe it's I *can't* stop.

Not now that I've finally allowed myself to taste her this way.

She moans at the first touch of my mouth to her nipple, whatever she'd been about to say cut off in that rush of beautiful sound.

Later, I'll ask her what had her cheeks going even more pink than normal, had shy mixing with sin, almost tempting me back to her mouth.

Almost because the gorgeous curves of her breasts need to be worshipped.

I roll my tongue, feel her grip tighten further, her body arching against mine. Since her ass is on the counter, I snag one of her legs, wrapping it around my waist, needing to rock against her. The angle's not easy, what with me having to bend to taste her, but it's still fucking perfect.

Two layers of thin material between us.

My body cushioned by the soft pillow of her thighs.

And her pelvis mirroring my movements, her hand holding fast, her silken flesh on my tongue.

I suck and kiss, nip and draw, finding what she likes, what has my name filling the air.

"Fuck, but I really love the sound of my name on your lips, Red," I murmur as I kiss my way over to her other breast, as I treat that one to the same focused attention. But this side is even more sensitive, her cries of pleasure louder.

Then louder still as I snake my hand down her body, slipping it between us.

A shove has it beneath the stretchy waistband of her pajamas.

"G-Gray!" she gasps as I cup her over her panties.

"Soaked," I rasp. "I fucking knew you'd be."

Her eyes are glazed, cheeks pink...just like those nipples I've been sucking on. But the slick evidence of her desire on my fingertips is the hottest thing I've ever felt.

At least until I'm nudging the material of her underwear to the side and—

"Fuck," I groan.

"*Gray*," she moans, hips bucking, head falling back, hand slipping from my hair, palm dropping to the counter.

"Wet. Plump. Mine," I growl, stroking my fingers through her labia, parting her and dragging my fingers up until I find the hard, sensitive bud of her clit and circle it.

More learning.

More teasing.

More wanting her as desperate for me as I am for her.

Because my control is running thin. Because sooner or later it's going to snap.

And I need to make sure she's right here with me.

"I—" She starts to protest when I pull my hand out, but I have other plans, other needs, other places I need to taste her.

I press her back into the counter and because those lips of hers are right there, so tempting and plump and pink, I kiss her.

Sparks coalescing into ropes of lightning, zipping around

every nerve in my body, threatening the dredges of my control, especially when her legs come around me, when her hips rock and grind and send me right up to the edge.

"Christ, Red," I rasp, tearing my lips from hers. "You sure can kiss."

Her cheeks are flushed and those brown eyes are melted chocolate and her lips are swollen, reddened from my beard.

I need more.

Need *her*.

But I need to taste her *everywhere*.

I retreat from the temptation of her mouth and kiss my way down her body, knowing that her tank top bunched around her middle is probably annoying, but not wanting to stop my southern trek to take it off. Not when I have much more pleasurable routes to take. Much more pleasurable destinations—for both of us—to arrive at.

I trail my lips along her abdomen, nibbling at the indent of her waist, dipping my tongue into her belly button, loving the way her stomach ripples and contracts, her breath catches, her hands find their way back into my hair.

Love even more the way she readily lifts her hips, allowing me to shimmy off her pajama pants and underwear.

Pink cheeks.

Teeth nibbling into the corner of her mouth.

Shy eyes.

"So fucking pretty," I murmur, loving the way those pink cheeks go pinker as I press my lips to the inside of her thigh. "But even prettier here." I drag my tongue through her slick folds.

"Gray!"

"That's it, Red. Say my fucking name."

It's not even about control at this point—though, I love the sound of my name on her tongue—it's about her letting go enough to trust me.

She gasps.

Because I've decided to stop talking.

Or maybe to let her do *all* of it—and she delivers, in moans and cries, in gasped-out exclamations. In my name tumbling off her tongue again and again as I explore every inch of her lush, wet cunt, as I suck at her clit and slip my finger inside her to feel the tight clasp of her pussy.

"Fuck, baby," I groan against her flesh. "You're going to clamp down around me so hard."

"I want..." A shaking exhale. "You... *Inside.*"

I slowly slide my finger out then press it back in. "What if I'm not done teasing you yet?"

"Gray," she warns, her hand tightening in my hair again.

I grin and blow out a stream of air that has her shivering, her hips bucking, grinding against my mouth.

"For someone who's shy," I say lightly, trailing my tongue through her pussy, "you sure are doing a great job of riding my face, Red."

"I may be shy, but I still have thoughts."

"Mmm"—I kiss her—"what kinds of thoughts, baby?"

Her cheeks go red.

Her hips buck.

"Gray," she whispers.

"Tell me."

Eyes on mine, shy, but not.

"Come on," I cajole. "You write about this stuff, right?"

A nod. "People have sex, so my characters do too."

My mouth curves. "Missionary? Boring Victoria-era sex?"

More red, her eyes sliding to the side.

Then back—again shy, but not.

I chuckle softly. "Not boring sex then." I slide my finger through her slick pussy. "What do you write about, baby?"

She lifts her chin. "Lots of things."

"Tell me *one* of those things."

"I want you inside me."

Heat coiling at the base of my spine.

"I want that too." I suck at her clit. "But I also want to know about those dirty thoughts of yours."

Her mouth opens. Closes. Then she exhales shakily. "I'll let you read one."

"Promise?" I ask silkily.

Her eyes narrow. "I said I would."

"Will *you* read it to *me?*"

Hot cheeks. Eyes gone shy.

Then she surprises me by saying softly, "Yes."

My dick twitches and I stifle a groan. "First," I say as I lean in and drag the flat of my tongue up to her clit, sucking firmly, "I'm going to make you come like this."

Because she deserves to be pleasured.

Well *fucking* pleasured.

"Then, Red, you're going to come on my cock." I kiss that sweet pussy again and groan. "I know you're going to squeeze it so nice."

"But if I...you know...*now*," she says, chest heaving, those gorgeous tits of hers bouncing with the movement, "I won't be able to...you know...*again* when you're inside—"

I blow again, loving the way she shivers. "No?"

A shake of her head. Her hair and mostly naked body are covered in flour and crumbs and fuck, maybe I should care, but I don't.

Because she's spread out on the counter for me like the finest three-course meal.

"Never?" I ask, flicking out my tongue, feeling her body shudder, her pelvis grind against me.

Another shake of her head, this one jerky.

"Hmm," I murmur.

"Wh-what?"

I nip at the inside of her thigh.

"I think, Red—" A long, slow lick. "That's a challenge accepted."

Twenty-Four

FAYE

CHALLENGE ACCEPTED.

Who the heck could know that *challenge accepted* are the two sexiest words I've ever heard?

But I barely have the chance to open my mouth to ask what he means by that before he takes the oral sex to the next level.

The next, *next* level.

Before it was teasing touches and sensual kisses.

Now the man has *focus*.

And hell, I've written all about sex in my books, about lights flashing behind closed eyelids, about pleasure coiling and spiraling out of control. I've written a scene very much like this, albeit without the side of banana bread destruction...

And without the hero saying *challenge accepted* in the husky voice.

Before he unleashed tongue and teeth and—

"Oh, God!" I gasp as he does something completely unholy— and glorious—to my clit.

"Not God," he murmurs against me. "Gray."

Then he waits, mouth poised over me, breath coming in gusts that tease.

I'm trembling, pussy wet and throbbing, aching, *empty*, so it takes a minute for me to recognize what he's saying.

What he wants.

"Gray," I murmur and for once, I don't feel shy.

How can I—displayed like I am for him? Thighs over his shoulders, his big, gorgeous body between my legs, his fingers and tongue and lips working miracles?

A flick of his tongue.

"Gray!"

He grins. "Damn right, Red."

And for as good as he's making me feel, annoyance is also beginning to flicker. Mostly because Gray Roberts is a fucking tease!

And maybe that's why the words come...

The *demands*.

"Gray Roberts, so help me God," I snap, tugging at his hair. "If you don't make me come already I'm going"—I look to the side, spot the proper implement, and pick up the butter knife, pointing in his direction—"to unman you!"

He grins, runs his thumb over my clit.

Then presses.

My hand—and head—fall back, the knife clattering to the counter.

"If you unman me then how will I pleasure you?"

"I thought—" I suck in a breath, trying to settle my pounding heart, my hitching lungs. "You talked...a big game...about orgasms." I lift my head and glare at him. "Only all you been doing"—another breath—"is teasing and talking and—*oh my God!*"

He's slipped a finger inside me and dropped his mouth and all hint of my temper disappears into a haze of pleasure.

It floods me, going taut, sparking every nerve ending, and when he slides his other hand up, cups my breast, rolling my nipple between thumb and forefinger, when he does that at the same time he sucks at my clit, flicking out his tongue...

I go taut.

Then I shatter into a million pieces, my orgasm not like the ones I've had before, just flowing through me in a giant wave, gently drawing me into bliss. Rather, it explodes inside me, bursting outward, reducing me to nothing but sensation.

But it's glorious sensation and it goes on for what feels like forever, leaving me suspended in that fog of pleasure, that fantasy of feeling.

I could be there an hour.

A day.

A month. A year. An *eternity*.

Or...it might be minutes before I slowly sink back down into reality, into myself. Into this moment.

Gray is still kneeling between my legs, a satisfied smile curving his lips. He's cocky as fuck...and I can't even blame him.

Because that orgasm...

Holy hell, I'm undone.

"Gray," I murmur and my voice is basically a rasp.

His smirk grows.

My pussy convulses.

Something he notices considering that his fingers are still inside me.

He flutters them as he rises, bending over me, lips coming to mine for a single blazing kiss. I can taste myself on his tongue and I like it, want more of it.

So, I kiss him back, not stopping until my vision starts to turn black at the edges and my lungs scream for air.

"Inside me," I demand.

"Read me *two* scenes?" he asks silkily.

Still with those fingers inside me.

Still fluttering.

"Gray," I warn.

"Hmm?"

"Inside. *Me*," I demand again.

"Will you read to me, Red?" he murmurs.

"I already said I would," I snap.

His lip twitch. "*Two* scenes?"

"Yes," I say sharply. "Now—"

"Will you write about me too?" He scissors his fingers and I moan. "About how good this is between us?"

I freeze, cheeks going hot.

"Oh, Red." He chuckles hotly, eyes burning into mine. "You already have, haven't you?"

"It doesn't matter—" I reach for his sweats, start pushing down the waistband, but he stops me with a blazing kiss.

"It matters, baby. It fucking *matters.*"

I shiver, hands stilling.

A nip to my bottom lip. "What'd you write?"

"I'll tell you after—" I moan, head dropping back when he works me with those fingers.

"*What*, baby?" he presses.

I'm on fire, aching for him. *Wet* for him. And when those fingers slide out, press back in, it's good—great, even—but it's not his cock, not him stretching me as his body presses into mine, not—

"Gray!" I exclaim when he adds a third finger.

"Still love my name on your lips." He leans in, kisses me again, leaving me a limp, breathless mess. "And fuck, this pussy"—he groans, fucking me with his fingers—"I want to feel you slick and tight around me."

"Then..." I pant. "Get...inside...me."

"Not until you tell me, Red."

Something snaps inside me. "I based one of my heroes after you, okay?" I snarl. "Not a surprise since I fell in love with you through a window, right? Now, I want you *in* me."

He grins, lets me reach for his sweats again. "You're reading from that book."

It's another order.

But I don't even care.

"Fine," I yank at the waistband of his pants, pushing it down. "Just get inside...*oh.*" I still. Because I've finally managed to free his erection and—

"Actually, I don't think that's going to fit inside me," I whisper.

A cocky—no pun intended—smile. "It'll fit, Red."

He takes my uninjured hand, wrapping it around the hard length of him, and God, but I can barely make it all the way around him, he's so thick.

Which is when my nerves go into overdrive.

He guides my motions, teaching me how he likes to be stroked, how tightly he likes to be gripped.

Then he releases my hand, placing his on the counter beside my hip, head dropping forward on a groan. "Fuck, baby," he rasps, "but I like it when you touch me."

I like it too. So much so, my dirty mind makes an appearance. "I want to taste you too."

He goes statue still.

Then he's kissing me and his fingers are moving in me and I'm stroking him and—

I have power here.

Power to undo this big, strong, gorgeous man.

Power to make him lose control.

Power to own what I want, what I *need*...and the power to tease him back.

And that's when things get a little crazy—we're a flurry of limbs, of measuring cups and the mixer bowl and bunches of bananas and burned loaves hitting the floor. We're flour flying into the air, sprinkling over our naked skin. We're lips and teeth, tongues and touch.

And then...

We're one.

Gray managing to find his wallet, extracting a condom, rolling it down the hard length of his cock.

He notches himself at my entrance, slowly strokes in...and he's right.

It does fit.

We fit.

"Good, Red?" he asks, when he's fully seated.

It's a rasped-out question, his body taut, all those gorgeous muscles of his on display. My heart pulses, knowing he's trying to go slow, trying to be careful for me, trying to take *care* of me.

But I don't want him to be careful.

I want Gray.

Every single inch of him.

"I'm great, honey."

A flicker of emotion in his eyes before he smiles. "Good." He draws out slowly, slides back in just as leisurely. And he repeats that slow and steady, over and over again, incrementally driving us both insane.

And I can feel it.

The leash he's holding fast.

"Gray?"

A rumbling groan. "Yeah, baby?"

"Now's the time to fuck me."

He jerks, eyes flashing to mine.

And I watch the leash snap.

He fucks me, hard and fast and deep, his thrusts so powerful he has to keep me in place with a hand on my shoulder and another on my hip.

It doesn't take long for me to feel it, to know that challenge of his is going to be accomplished.

It builds in my middle, bigger, bigger, *bigger*—

Until implosion.

"Gray!" I cry out, convulsing around the hard intrusion of him, grinding against his pelvis, clutching at his shoulders as it tears through me.

Not gentle.

Intense.

Incinerating.

And renewed when I hear him groan, "Fuck, Red," and his strokes go wild, his own orgasm taking him under.

He collapses on top of me, breaths erratic, his lips trailing over my ear, my throat, my jaw.

And I can feel his smile.

Know he's going to tease me about that challenge being completed.

And I so don't care.

Because that was...*good.*

I hold him close, the only sound the pounding of my pulse in my ears.

Only...the pounding doesn't go away, even as my breathing evens out.

And when I look to the side, I see why.

My heart lurches, embarrassment threatening, but I can't bring myself to regret this moment with Gray...

Not even when I see the furious woman standing on the other side of the kitchen window.

Twenty-Five

GRAY

ONE SECOND, I'M IN FUCKING HEAVEN.

The next, the nightmare that's my life has reemerged.

"Get up," I order, levering myself off Faye and yanking up my sweats.

Her head is turned away from mine, cheeks flushed in what, minutes ago, I would have said was because she was aroused.

Now...it's embarrassment.

And horror.

Because Courtney is watching us through my fucking window, pounding on the glass like a lunatic.

"Red," I say more sharply. "Get *up*."

Faye's gaze jerks to mine, but she still doesn't move. So, I scoop her up, cradling her against me as I stride from the room, ignoring the total disaster I've—and then later *we*—made of the space. Mostly because the total disaster that is my life has shown up.

Just when I was starting to think things could be different...

Courtney fucking reappears.

And if that isn't fate reminding me I shouldn't be doing this with Faye then I don't know what is.

"Gray," she whispers and I clench my jaw as I move down the hall to the guest bedroom, not wanting to feel her gentle hand on my cheek, the soft stroke of her fingers down my chest. "It's okay."

I shove into the guest bedroom, move straight through it, not stopping until we're in the attached bathroom.

Setting her on her feet, I crank on the shower.

"Wash up," I order.

Because she's covered in banana bread detritus.

But also so the sound of the water will hopefully drown out Courtney's screaming.

I turn and walk away from Faye, hating that mere minutes ago I was planning on taking her to my room, on slowly washing every inch of her body...then tasting her until I accepted the challenge of making her come on my cock again.

That's not going to happen.

Because of fucking Courtney.

"Gray."

I flinch. God, why does my name on her tongue feel like torture now?

A reminder of what I can't have.

Because, fuck, I *can't* have it.

"Shower, Red."

She slips in front of me, her hands settling on my chest, eyes coming to mine. I can't read what's in them, except that maybe there's a flicker of humor in the brown depths. "So many orders," she says lightly.

Despite the shit-show outside, I chuckle. "Clean up, baby. I'll deal with her and be right back."

She winces.

"It's okay," I say. "I'm used to Courtney's shit."

"No"—she touches my jaw—"it's just...I need to talk to you about that."

"Why?"

"Well, she called last night and..." Faye tells me about their conversation. "I was going to warn you when you got home but I guess I fell asleep and then this morning well..."

Our time in the kitchen.

Well, yeah, we'd both been a little otherwise occupied.

"I'm sorry," she whispers. "I should—"

"Don't apologize." I settle my forehead on hers. "How could you know she'd go nuts?"

"Because she acted insane on the phone?" she asks. "And because you told me about her. So, I'm sorry, honey. I—"

The doorbell goes.

I start to pull back. "I should—"

"Stay," she says, one hand lifting, settling on my jaw. Flour still dusts her hair, like the universe is giving me proof that what just happened between us was real.

And God, I *want* that.

But there's knocking and the doorbell going incessantly and every time I've tried to ignore Courtney into submission, she's just gotten more determined, more insane, more nightmarish.

"Stay," Faye says again, stepping close, her body going flush to mine. "Shower with me."

There's a thud and she jumps.

I start to pull back. "I need to take care of—"

"Gray," she says more firmly, perhaps even bordering on order territory.

"Red," I warn.

She steps back, shimmies out of her tank top that was still bunched around her middle.

And fuck, the shimmy does all sorts of glorious things to her tits.

"Stay with me. Stay in this moment. I haven't had too many good ones in the last few years and I'm thinking you haven't either." She takes my hand as I'm reeling from the truth of that, from what I've been too much of a coward to admit.

I'm lonely.

"Don't let her take it from you. From *us*."

And how can I possibly deny her that? Especially when I want it so badly.

So, I ignore the doorbell that's still ringing and allow her to pull me toward the shower stall.

And I think...

Maybe it might be my best decision ever.

―――――

"Taste," Faye murmurs much later in the day, the kitchen now filled with the smell of delicious banana bread and not burned loaves and spoiled milk and whatever nonsense I'd conjured up this morning.

It's also clean.

Neat as a pin.

Something I insisted Faye didn't have to help me with after I'd taken on the challenge of pleasuring her in the shower.

(And accomplishing that twice).

But she *had* helped me and together it hadn't taken too long.

Then we used one of the recipes I found, one that Faye thought might be closest to her Nana's recipe to bake up the batch she's just pulled out of the oven.

"Taste," she says again, holding the piece she's sliced off up to my lips.

I snag her wrist, press a kiss to the inside of it and eat the proffered chunk.

"Delicious," I tell her after I've chewed and swallowed. "Almost like Nana's?"

She flinches slightly before forcing a smile on her face. A smile I hate. Because it's fake. Because it's not Faye's.

Because I don't like that *I've* hurt her.

"We don't have to talk about it," I say, smoothing back her hair. "I didn't mean to poke a sore spot."

"It's not a sore spot."

"You flinched."

A sigh. "You're right," she says. "I miss her and I wish she was here and I hate—" A jerky nod to the window, to the remains of her house on the other side of it a painful reminder. "I hate that I lost what I had left of her, of them."

"I'm so sorry, Red." I draw her close, smoothing a hand down her spine, yet even as I do that, my eyes are searching for any sign of Courtney coming back.

Because by the time we made it out of the shower, she was gone.

Nothing left behind aside from fingerprints on the glass and scuff marks on the front door from her trying to kick it in.

And how long before she's back?

Before she's doing worse than knocking on windows and trying to kick in doors?

Faye's next words are as though she's read those exact thoughts ping-ponging through my brain. "About this morning..."

I tense.

She leans back. "You were going to tell me what happened between us was a mistake, weren't you?"

I force myself to continue looking at her.

And a second after meeting my gaze she nods, whispers, "Yeah, that's what I thought."

"Red—"

Pulling from my arms, she slices off a piece of bread and passes it to me, another for herself then bites off a hunk of hers. "I get it," she says. "The urge to run, to stop this before..." She exhales. "Before I get too attached." She shoves the rest of the slice in her mouth, chews, and swallows. "And maybe that would be smarter, safer, especially since we hardly know each other." Her voice drops. "But every time I think about walking away..."

"What?" I rasp.

"I've written almost fifty books," she murmurs after a long

moment. "And in every single one of them, there has been this exact moment—the past wanting to tear my heroes apart, coaxing them into remaining exactly as they were because the possibility of a beautiful future, of changing and growing and being vulnerable with a person—no with *the* person—who can hurt them most deeply is absolutely terrifying."

My pulse speeds, fingers tightening into fists.

"And even after fifty books, I don't think I've captivated that terror properly," she whispers. "Because living it"—her gaze comes to mine—"even thinking about the possibility of having it is..." A shake of her head. "I don't know if I have a word for it that's more intense than terror." She takes a breath. "Because that's what it is."

A beat.

"Abject terror."

Twenty-Six

FAYE

I FORCE MYSELF TO KEEP SPEAKING EVEN AS HE MOVES toward me.

"But this morning," I say. "Even though we've had days, not months or years together, the thought of you walking away was scarier than me taking a chance on us."

He freezes.

My stomach churns.

Because the rational side of me is screaming *This is insane! Walk—no RUN—away.*

But the romantic soul that has me making a living writing love stories with tough, emotional, *angsty* themes—albeit with guaranteed happy endings—is telling me this is all I've dreamed about, all I've fantasized about.

A man like Gray doesn't come around more than once in a lifetime.

And as scary as it is to think about what might happen if it all goes wrong, I already know what it's like to be alone, to not have anyone to share my life with.

So to not take this chance to see what might happen between Gray and me...

Unfathomable.

"Gray," I whisper when he doesn't move.

I'm suddenly in his arms, his lips on mine, his soft groan vibrating along my tongue.

"Fuck, Red," he whispers when his mouth finally releases mine, "I really like the sound of my name on your tongue."

"I really just like *your* tongue."

He chuckles.

Then sobers, running the backs of his fingers over my cheek. "The moment I held you in my arms, my life seem to realign."

My heart skips a beat. "Probably the smoke inhalation," I say lightly.

"It wasn't the smoke." He nuzzles at my hair. "Or the flames."

"The heat?" I tease.

He tugs a strand of my hair, shakes his head. "Maybe I'm pathetic for admitting this, but I'm terrified too. If I felt for Courtney a modicum of what I'm feeling for you..." Another shake. "I don't think I could have ever walked away from her."

"But?" I ask, seeing the word written into the lines of his face.

"But it's only been a couple of days," he murmurs.

"And I was in love with a fantasy."

His face gentles and I slip—or maybe I fall—a bit more in love with the real Gray. Especially when he gently tucks my hair behind my ears then draws me a little closer. "We hardly know each other, Red."

"I know." I lean back enough to meet his eyes. "But isn't it going to be a blast getting to know each other, no matter where that leads us?"

He inhales in a rush, that big, broad chest rising on the influx of air.

Then he exhales, but he does it slowly, his mouth curving.

"Yeah, baby, it is."

I smile, let him draw me into a long, slow kiss.

And when he releases me, taking my hand and tugging me into the family room, down onto the couch, then into the circle of his embrace, determined to make me a hockey fan once and for all, my heart is happy.

But as he searches for the remote, I can't ignore the quiet, *oh so quiet* whisper that even though learning Gray is going to be great fun...

It still might end in heartbreak.

———

"You're snoring."

I jerk, pulling myself out of the lovely warmth that is Gray's body—his chest is hard, intensely muscled, but it's also surprisingly comfortable to rest my head there, to have his arms wrapped around me.

"Hmm?"

"You're snoring, Red."

I feel my cheeks heat. "I am *not*. I'm awake," I lie. "I'm enjoying..." I trail off as I try to focus on what the hell is on the television.

It's—

"Are you watching people push shopping carts for fun?" I ask, aghast.

"Not for fun," he murmurs, turning down the volume. "For sport."

I look at the TV, watch the average-looking person crouching and straightening, leaning from side-to-side, as though they're trying to gauge the distance between themselves and the metal rack the cart needs to presumably be pushed in to. Then I roll over so Gray and I are face-to-face. "What are you talking about? This *is* sport?"

His eyes dance and I want to close the distance between our mouths, to taste the amusement on his face.

Beautiful man.

And I love that all day we've done nothing but hang out and watch hockey and bad action movies and eat my caramel popcorn. And talk—and make out and...well, also participate in *just* a smidge bit of deliberate touching (to very enjoyable outcomes for both of us).

If it wasn't for me having to answer the occasional insurance-related phone call and putting in an order for a new cell phone and computer—who knew that having several of my credit card numbers memorized because of my addiction to online shopping would one day be a godsend? Anyway, if it wasn't for all that, it would have felt like a lazy weekend day we've been whiling away together.

Because between the calls and polishing off the banana bread and ordering in pizza (and working both of those foods off with horizontal exercise), we've just *hung*.

He's told me more about his parents...and how disconnected he's felt from them for years.

"They don't have any clue about how my life really works," he told me. "Hell, the last time they visited, my mom asked if I could skip practice to drive them to some outlet mall, like I was a ten-year-old kid who could miss ice-time without any consequences. On a basic level, they get this is my job," he said. "They just don't have any idea what that truly entails. It feels...unreal to them." He shrugged. "And they don't care enough to make an effort to understand."

God, how *that* had resonated.

Which meant I shared how I grew apart from friends who thought writing was a silly hobby and from those who sneered because I wasn't writing *real* books and from those who didn't understand that being a writer entailed so much more than just jotting down stories in my spare time.

We also talked about Nana and her recipes, bonded over a shared love of cinnamon rolls.

And as we devoured pizza, we discussed TV shows (no

surprise, I love love stories and he's more of a sports, in any form —hence *shopping carts*—man).

It was normal and it was great.

But it also felt fragile—as though one knock on the door, one of Gray's furtive glances out the kitchen window, could send it skittering away.

And maybe that's why it felt so precious.

Why I didn't complain when he put on the Gold game.

Truthfully, it wasn't that bad. He taught me a few of the finer points of hockey, shared some fun behind-the-scenes stories that had me craving my laptop so I could jot down *all* the plot bunnies.

But when those stories ran out and he started analyzing the game for their upcoming matchup, I'd lost interest.

Turns out, I need to be rooting for or talking to a hot hockey hero in order to truly appreciate the sport.

"I think I'd take hockey over this," I say, having turned back to watch the *sport*, watching as one of the contestants misses by a mile.

A chuckle that vibrates through his chest and along my spine, teasing my nerve endings, melting me against him.

He smooths his hand up and down my side and I sigh contentedly.

I could stay here—*right* here—all day.

This is so much better than the fantasy.

Even *if* I'm just watching people push shopping carts into pens for...*sport*.

Though, in fairness, it's less watching and more soaking in the smell of banana bread in the air as I let my eyes slide closed, my body relax against his, my mind drift until shopping carts are very far away.

"Faye, baby?" he murmurs.

It's tempting to let sleep suck me under, but something about his voice has me rolling over.

Then pausing to study his face, trying to ferret out what exactly his expression is.

It's almost...chagrined, like he's a naughty little boy.

"What is it?"

"Want to..." He traces a finger down my throat, making me shiver, my body automatically arch against his.

"What?" I breathe.

"Want to bake something else together?"

And I think...maybe real love begins just like this.

With crumbs and cuddling and laughter.

And daring to believe it can be mine.

Twenty-Seven

GRAY

"AGAIN, THEY'RE WOMBATS! HOW THE HELL CAN YOU BE afraid of wombats?"

My head whips to the side and I'm already pushing to my feet, readying to intervene if Faye looks the least bit uncomfortable.

But instead of her being on edge, body trembling, eyes wide and searching for an exit, she's...

Fuck, it's *beautiful.*

She's beautiful.

Her head thrown back, her musical laughter filling the air, the sound hitting me hard in the gut.

Probably because Smitty is on his feet, gesturing wildly and going on and on about how wombats are killers who crush their *victims* (he's nothing if not dramatic) with their giant butts against their burrow walls.

He also loves an audience.

"Their murderers, I tell you!"

Faye isn't the only one who's laughing at my teammate. Luna is sipping her mocktail, reclining back on the couch, free hand rubbing lightly at her pregnant belly as she giggles. Bri is in full hostess mode alongside Aiden's mom, but since she's filling the platter of snacks in front of Faye and company, she has a front row seat to his shenanigans.

And she's laughing too.

Another woman (though really, while she may be over eighteen, she's still a girl) who's gone through too much.

And Smitty's making her happy too.

Along with Kailey, who's shaking her head at him, but doing it with a smile.

Annoying fucker to be so charming.

But he's a good guy to have on my side.

"Are you going to kill him?" Leo says lightly. "Or am I?"

I slide my gaze to my teammate. "Actually, I was kind of thinking I'm glad he's using his powers for good."

Leo lifts his brows as he studies the group. Then shrugs, mouth twitching as he snags some food off the platter near us. "Okay, so you're not wrong."

"Wrong about what?" Smitty asks expectantly, slinging a heavy arm over my shoulders and sending me staggering back a step.

"Never mind," I tell Leo.

He nods. "Probably for the best we keep that one to ourselves."

"Keep *what* to yourselves?" Smitty grumbles.

Leo grins then drifts off to the table with drinks, snagging a beer from the big metal bin there.

But I don't miss that his eyes slide to the side, to the attractive caterer Aiden's parents—okay, really his mom, Kathy—hired for the event. Luna wanted to have her baby shower here at the family house she inherited, and Kathy and Matt made that happen.

The house is full.

The Grizzlies are represented with me, Smitty, Ryan, Leo, Sawyer—even a few of the younger guys popped by with presents before moving on to greener pastures (read: getting ready to hit the area's bars and nightclubs rather than hanging with a bunch of old dudes playing baby-themed games). Aiden's siblings—Carrie, Ralph, and Dave are here. Luna's brother and dad are not (but that's for good reason—they're assholes), though Jean-Michel Dubois, his wife, Tiffany, and his friend Jace Henderson and his woman, Marie, have come.

The billionaire businessman and a bunch of hockey players plus co-workers from the shelter that Luna works at may not seem like the most obvious pairing, but Jean-Michel and Jace have gone to bat for Luns more than once.

So fancy suits and high-rise buildings or not, I respect the two men immensely.

And between the billionaire and the Grizzlies and her friends and co-workers, we've got Luna covered.

Especially because some of the kids who she's looked after showed—some for quick pop-ins, a couple to set up the cake, since they work with Bri at the bakery, and a handful to shyly hang around, make conversation, play games, and search for a slice of belonging they don't often get.

So yeah, Luna's family house is perfect for events like this one.

It's why we all end up gathering here more often than not.

Sure, we all take turns hosting so it's not a burden, but...Luna and Aiden's place is the shit. Big, lots of room to hang out, and not so fancy that you worry about spilling your beer on the white carpet or whatever.

And it's filled with memories of *Luna's* grandma.

Something I hope she'll share with Faye.

Maybe they can lean on each other to make the loss seem less intense, the hole they both have a little smaller.

I watch Faye snag a canapé and nibble as she continues talking and laughing with the girls and I want to freeze the moment in time, remember that *I'm* the one who's given it to her.

And that I might be responsible for it being snatched away.

"Food's good," Smitty says and I nod as I tear my eyes from Faye.

It's good. *Seriously* good—and not just because fancy catering isn't usually on the docket when we hang out. Typically, we're ordering pizza or Chinese or Indian or firing the barbecue up in the back yard. So, I haven't seen the blond girl-next-door with the striking hazel eyes who put together the platters—full of those canapés—before. The woman who's currently cooking up her next delicious confection in the kitchen with confident assurance.

And I've certainly never seen Leo look like *that*.

As though he can't take his eyes off the woman, as though he's looking for any and all excuses to hang near the kitchen, to hang near *her*.

Fuck, maybe Smitty's matchmaking nonsense is starting to corrupt me.

Or maybe it's just that I have a good woman in my life now and I want everyone else to have the same.

Fuck.

Because, yup, Smitty's matchmaking nonsense is *definitely* corrupting me.

"Yo, Leo!" he hollers on the heels of that thought, and everyone is so used to all of his booming that he barely warrants a second glance.

I can almost hear my teammate sigh as he turns toward us. "What do you want, Smitty?" he calls back.

"Grab me one of those sandwich things from the kitchen, would ya?"

Leo's already opening his mouth to retort even before Smitty completes his semi-question, semi-order (and yeah, now I'm wondering what Faye thinks of those...and how quickly I can implement them in the bedroom) when the rest of the words seem to process Leo's brain.

A heartbeat later, all the irritation clears from his face. "On it," he calls back, his focus already on the kitchen.

Or really, on the *woman* in the kitchen.

"You know there's a platter of sandwiches right there," I tell Smitty, nodding to the table, all of three feet away from us and currently loaded with food.

"I sure do."

I wait for him to explain.

He gets on doing just that. "But those sandwiches"—he nods to the platter—"won't get Leo near Harper."

I frown. "Who's Harper?"

"The caterer Leo hasn't been able to stop staring at." A jerk of his chin toward the kitchen, his mouth curving into a wide smile. "And now the one who he hopefully won't be able to *stop* talking to."

I watch as Leo sidles close and strikes up a conversation with Harper.

Damn, the man's good.

"You're devious, you know that, right?"

Smitty just laughs. "No"—a shrug—"well, yeah. But also, I'm a matchmaker at heart."

"You're still on that nonsense?"

"My track record speaks for itself. No matter what that Blue Line Matchmaker is doing." He scowls. "Don't ask. Someone's trying to overtake my kingdom is all. I'll sort it out."

"Right," I say and since I don't really care about Smitty's matchmaking endeavors, I allow myself to do what I really want... look back at Faye.

"She seems more settled today," he says, clearly following my stare.

"You fuckers take some getting used to is all."

A chuckle. "That we do. But it's more than that." He slants a look in my direction, lifts his eyebrows in question.

"It's more than that," I agree, Faye's laughter drifting through the air to settle on my skin, in my heart. Then a thought occurs to me—outrageous and terrifying. "You don't have an affinity for fire, do you?"

He frowns. "What? No. That shit's almost as scary as wombats."

Right.

That would be an insane length to go to in order to bring Faye and me together, despite how committed Smitty is to his match-making efforts.

He wouldn't risk her—wouldn't risk *anyone*—like that.

Something that's reinforced when he fixes me in place with a stare.

"You're going to take care of her right?" he asks. "She needs someone steady and committed. Not for you to let that shit with Courtney—"

And hell, as though he conjured up the she-demon herself...

The front door slams open.

And my ex strides into the house.

Twenty-Eight

Faye

"Oh, no," I whisper.

"Is that—?"

"Courtney," the woman next to me, Veronica, says. I just met her today and she came with her sweet son, Alex.

And also with Ryan.

Whose behavior is...well...

Protective.

And maybe a bit possessive.

Hmm.

But I can't let my author brain get ahead of me. There's something closed-off about Veronica, as though she won't ever—*ever*—be open to what Ryan wants to offer.

Yet, Ryan's still here. Well, he and Alex are in the back yard, kicking around a soccer ball.

So...hmm.

"*That's* Courtney?" Luna asks aghast, and something that had gone stiff inside me, a tight knot of unpleasantness, loosens. Partly because of her tone—the clear disbelief—but also because, even as close as these people all are, Courtney isn't part of them.

But I am.

Or maybe, more accurately, I could be.

My heart rolls over in my chest.

"That's Courtney," Veronica confirms.

"But she's so..."

"Beautiful?" I murmur.

Luna's eyes flick to mine and my heart rolls back the other way when she shifts a little closer, pressing her thigh against mine, silently comforting me. "Yes," she says softly, her gaze flicking to mine. "But also...very *not* Gray."

Veronica tilts her head to the side, but it's Kailey who speaks.

"They don't fit," she murmurs.

I study Courtney, the beautiful blond woman with a gorgeous body. Her hair is sleek, sitting in perfect beachy waves. Her clothes are sophisticated and compliment her slender curves. She could be on the cover of magazines, could have tens of thousands of followers on Instagram.

And though Gray is equally as gorgeous...

Kailey is right.

They *don't* fit.

Maybe it's the calculation written so clearly on her face.

Maybe it's because she doesn't seem to care that she's hurting Gray.

Maybe it's just...Courtney.

I'm internalizing that—and trying not to immediately discount the thought that *I* fit Gray and that's why I'm here right now, why I'm not fighting the growing connection between us—when Smitty, Aiden, and Leo move to intercept Courtney, ensuring they do it while keeping themselves between her and Gray.

And there my heart goes again.

Protecting him.

Looking out for him.

I should be there, should be beside him.

Even as those thoughts are sliding through my mind, I'm rising, moving over to Gray, lacing my fingers through his.

Think that—yes—he and I fit.

He glances down, expression drawn, eyes full of shame, that gorgeous mouth of his pressed flat.

Retreating.

I shift closer to his side and his lids slide closed for a beat, his big body moving on a breath. "Red," he murmurs, and yup, the shame is riding him hard.

"This isn't your fault," I murmur.

"I'm the one who—" He seems to catch himself. "I'm the one who married her."

"Faye is right," Luna says, coming up on my other side, her hand on her belly. "She wants to make a scene." A shrug. "Let her have her scene."

Gray blanches. "This is your shower. My shit—"

Luna ignores him, cutting off the rising conversation in front of us by calling, "Aiden, honey?"

Aiden turns concerned eyes her direction.

"Do you want to make the introductions?"

He sighs, but his lips curve upward. "Luna, this is Courtney. Courtney, my wife, Luna."

Courtney sniffs. "Do I care?"

"Considering you barged into my house, you should," Luna replies, so sweetly, it seems to take a moment for Courtney to process the words.

Her chin lifts. "I need to speak to Gray."

Luna turns to Gray. "Do you want to speak to her?"

"Considering I dropped our signed divorce papers off to my lawyer a few days ago," he says tersely. "Fuck no."

"There," Luna chirps. "See? You came. You saw. Now you're going to walk your much-skinnier-than-mine-currently ass out the door."

Another pause, as though the wheels are slowly turning, as

though Courtney had a plan for exactly how this would proceed and now that it's out the window, she doesn't know how to react.

I'm learning that Luna is the type of person to always keep everyone around her guessing.

So, Courtney doesn't stand a chance.

Especially when her only response is to lift her chin, cross her arms, and—yup, seriously—stomp her foot. "I'm not leaving."

Luna shrugs her shoulders. "Suit yourself." A nod to the nearest platter of food. "You hungry?"

"Tiny tornado," Aiden warns.

If that isn't a fitting nickname for the other woman...

My lips twitch and I don't miss Gray relaxing next to me.

"What?" Luna asks, shrugging her shoulders. "We have plenty."

"I'll not leaving until I talk to Gray!"

Smitty interjects before Luna can—or maybe, it's that the two hooligans are pulling a one-two punch that not even the most determined shit-stirrer can top. He twists his big body our direction. "Say hi, Gray."

"Hi," Gray parrots.

"There," Smitty says. "You talked to Gray. Now"—he grabs a sandwich, shoves it in her hand—"you can go."

He doesn't touch her, but he somehow manages to shepherd her toward the door.

A door which she grabs the edge of, halting everyone's progress.

Leo sighs. "Why does this shit always happen here?"

"I have a gift for drama," Luna quips.

"I'll get her out of here," Gray says, taking a step forward.

"Nope." A wave of her hand as Smitty and a couple of men in suits that scream *expensive!* (I think someone said their names are Jean-Michel and Jace) maneuver her outside, the front door miraculously closing behind them. Courtney's protests grow loud enough to be heard through the wood. "Trust me on this," she says. "There's no need to engage and give her what she wants. You stay here while she has her scene. The boys will make sure she hits the road when she's done."

"Luns, she's my problem—"

"And we don't do solo shit," Aiden says firmly, as though reminding Gray of something (like, perhaps, words they've exchanged before). "Right?"

Gray sighs.

But, likely because Aiden and Luna are making sense, he relents—albeit begrudgingly.

"All right," he grumbles.

"Good," Luna chirps. "I'll leave you in the very capable hands of Faye..." Her head tilts to the side. "Wait, I don't actually know your last name."

"It's Sullivan," I tell her.

She freezes. "Sullivan? You're not related to Faye Sullivan, the author, are you?"

"Um..." Nerves beginning to twine through my belly, I glance at Gray then back at her. "I *am* her."

"Wait, you're *Faye Sullivan?!*" she exclaims.

The room grows quiet, all the remaining eyes turning to me.

Focusing on me.

And I just want the floor to open up and swallow me whole.

Not because I'm ashamed of what I do, but because everyone is looking and I've spent the majority of the last years with my fictional family, so this much attention is...uncomfortable.

Like a too-tight sweater.

Plus, there's always a weird dynamic when people find out I'm a writer, especially of romance.

The expectations, the snide comments, the offers to *inspire* me.

I don't think that Luna will be like that, but then again, I don't know her that well.

"Yes, I am," I say, lifting my chin.

There's a beat of quiet.

Then she's fist-pumping with a whoop, bouncing excitedly

on her toes. "Oh, my God! That is *so* cool! Would you sign my books?"

"Um"—I slant a glance at Gray, whose face has softened, the Courtney effect already waning, same as the scent of her perfume is fading from the room, the volume of her protests through the front door—"sure."

"Awesome!" She whirls around, hurries toward the hall. "I think I have almost all of them in the library. I'll go grab them."

"Wait, what about the shower?"

"Eh." She waves a hand. "There's plenty of time for games later. How often do I get to meet someone who writes killer books *and* will sign them for me."

Then she's zipping out of the room.

Gray and I follow her—a good thing, it turns out. Because she *does* have almost all of my books.

And since there are several dozen of them on the shelf, we don't let the pregnant lady grab them.

Gray pulls them down, I sign them, and he puts them back.

Thus, the chaos outside fades into laughter and the satisfying sound of pages turning as we chatter about Luna's favorite characters and I make recommendations to Kailey and Veronica about which books I think they'd like.

Then I do the same for Aiden's mom, Luna's work friends, and for the wives of the suited men who helped the Grizzly men escort Courtney outside. And carefully, for Bri, who is technically an adult, but a young one.

I even make recommendations for the caterer, Harper, when she brings in a tray of desserts because the guys eventually get rid of Courtney and join us in the library.

(FYI, signing fifty books along interspersed with chatting and reading expectations takes *a while*).

Still, even as I'm doing all of that, I make note of which books Luna is missing.

Not just because she has the others.

Not even because Gray is relaxed and smiling and right beside me instead of out front dealing with his ex.

And not even because she bought me pajamas and has done her best to make me feel included from the first moment I met her.

It's because in this book-filled room, I know I'm no longer alone.

For once, I'm not the quest observer taking notes—I'm part of the story.

And maybe because I think a few more love stories will make a perfect gift for a mom-to-be.

TWENTY-NINE

GRAY

SOMETHING DELICIOUS FILLS THE AIR THE MOMENT I push into the house after practice but as I walk down the hall and into the kitchen, there's no sign of Faye.

I move to the counter, lift the lid of the crock pot (another kitchen accessory I had but never used), and my stomach rumbles.

Fuck, that smells good.

Practice was brutal today—Coach putting us through our paces in preparation of the upcoming road trip.

We'll be out of our normal routine, on enemy ice—and Coach made sure we'd be ready.

I snag a beer from the fridge, know it'll soften the edges of my sore muscles, then go hunting for Faye.

She's not in the dining room, her supplies spread out on my table as she plots her next book.

Not in the family room—my lips twitch—watching a hockey game.

Not in our bedroom—and maybe *our* is a little presumptuous but that's where she belongs.

In bed beside me.

I make my way downstairs, a flicker of annoyance twisting with worry.

If she's next door at her house without me...

Click-click-click-click. Click-click-click. Click-click.

I frown.

Then relief ripples through me as I spy her through the window, her fingers flying over the keyboard of her laptop.

Ever since she was able to take the splint off, she's been doing that a lot.

Today, she's sitting on the back deck, hair bundled on top of her head, tendrils escaping and curling along her nape. I stand there and watch her work, studying her face as types then pauses, clearly stopping to think, nose scrunching, teeth pressing into her bottom lip, head tilting to the side.

Then she smiles and her fingers start flying again.

I stand there as though there's an invisible rope is connecting us, unable to look away but unwilling to interrupt her flow by going to her.

Not that I mind.

It's a really great view.

Eventually, she sits back in the chair, reaching forward and closing her laptop.

That's when I allow myself to finally open the door and join her on the deck.

Something loosens in me when she immediately smiles and pushes up to her feet.

My Faye.

Still sweet, still happy to see me. Still *mine.*

"Hey," she says, coming over and wrapping her arms around my middle.

I bury my face in her hair, loving the scent of her, then tug out the tie and tangle my fingers in the silken strands. Her soft curves press against my body and when I tilt her head back, she smiles before her lush lips mold to mine.

"Red," I murmur, brushing my thumb lightly over her collar-bone when we pull back.

"Gray," she murmurs back.

My mouth twitches...along with my cock, but I focus. Never do I want her to be uncertain how much I appreciate her. "Thanks for making whatever delicious concoction is in the crock pot."

Pink on her cheeks. "It's just chicken chili."

"Not *just*."

A shake of her head, dismissing the words. But I'm not going to stop appreciating her, not going to risk fucking things up between us.

"You hungry?" she asks quietly.

I'm starving.

Just not for food.

I'm starving for Faye—ravenous in my need to hold her, kiss her, *fuck* her.

But even more intense than that is...

The need to know every part of *her*.

"What were you working on?"

Her cheeks flare red. "Edits for the book I turned in a couple of months ago."

"What's this one about?" We've discussed the project she finished the night of the fire, along with the book she's just beginning to plot. But this is the first time she's mentioned edits for a previous novel.

Her eyes slide away. "A guy and a girl falling in love."

I lift my brows in question. Because that's the most bland description I've ever heard—she's passionate about her books, her work. I heard that at the baby shower, during our nights on the couch when we've done nothing but watch movies and cuddle and talk.

To equate *this* project to just a guy and girl falling in love...

Yeah, now my curiosity is seriously piqued.

"Why are you being shy?" I ask lightly.

"I'm just hungry." She takes my hand. "Let's go in and eat."

I draw her closer. "Is it because it's about me?" Her body jerks and I chuckle, stroking my fingers down her spine. "Oh, Red. This *is* the one about me, isn't it?"

Part of me expects her to back down, to keep playing shy, but to my shock—and pleasure—her chin comes up, a recalcitrant set to her jaw. "So what if it is?"

Something strange happens in my chest—fear, pleasure, and... an intense, all-encompassing curiosity. "*Red.*"

She studies my face...and then I get a glimmer of the confident, sexual, proud woman whom I'm falling for as she brushes her lips over mine, moves out of my arms, and sits back down in her chair.

She opens her laptop.

And begins to read.

"What are you doing here, Josie?" he demands as he strides across the empty locker room, his face a frightening mix of curiosity and need.

I straighten my shoulders, hold my ground, even as a glimmer of fear coils in my belly.

"You left before we got to the good stuff," I murmur as he comes close, the heat and strength of his body the most sinful temptation.

"There was a reason for that, baby," he rasps, his hand settling on my hip, scalding hot through the fabric of my clothes. "I can't control myself when I'm around you."

I press closer, my breasts against his chest, my thighs flush with his.

Maybe it's unwise to tempt him instead of listening to the voice inside me telling me he's very close to the edge, but I can't seem to stop myself. Not when I so want to see what happens when the leash snaps.

Hopefully he'll strip me naked and fuck me hard and furious against this wall—

I'm completely riveted at the sound of her husky voice, her intoxicating words.

"I don't want you in control," I say, tracing my hand down his chest, not stopping until my fingers are just above the waistband of his pants. "In fact, I think I prefer when you're very much out *of control."*

His hand flexes on my hip—

"What are you doing, Red?"

Her eyes come to mine, and though her cheeks are still pink, her eyes a little shy, the determination written into the lines of her expression wraps its fingers around my cock and squeezes.

Hard.

"I promised to read to you, remember?"

I remember.

Fuck, do I remember.

I just—

One moment, I'm confident. In control.

The next, I'm face first against the wall, his hands tugging me at the waist, guiding me until my palms are flat against the wall and my ass is in the air and—

"Oh, God," I moan as he cups my breast.

"Now think about how much better this will feel when you're naked."

"Faye," I rasp.

Her face is soft, but her eyes go wicked as she keeps reading.

And I'm completely entranced by everything about her—the way her lips form the words, the blush that lingers on her cheeks, the way she tweaks a line here and there as she reads out loud...this glimpse of how she sees *me*—

And how much I want to be the man from her book for her.

"Say my name, Josie."

I shake my head, unable to process all I'm feeling, all I need.

He pinches my nipple and I gasp, body arching against his. He takes advantage of my position diving a hand into my pants.

But he doesn't give me what I need.

Instead, he teases the aching bud of nerves that's my clit, circles the entrance.

"Please," I moan.

"Say my fucking name," is all he says in return.

She pauses, those wicked brown eyes coming to mine. "That's a new addition."

Heat blooms in my stomach and my cock is so hard it's a miracle I even have enough blood left in my brain to form the words, "I like it."

He rewards his name tumbling off my tongue by plunging his fingers inside me, by slowly driving me insane, and it's not until I'm shaking, until I'm fully wrapped up in everything that's the man I love, the man who's in every cell, every breath, every heartbeat, every thought that my clothes are gently peeled away, that he's notching himself at my entrance.

That he's slowly pushing inside. "You're mine."

"I love you," I whisper, my hands covering his as he bottoms out, shuddering as he draws back and—

Fuck, I'd be this woman's slave just to have her love me like her heroine loves her man.

"...and," she says softly, gently drawing me out of her story, "that's it for now."

I have to force myself to unstick, to move over to her. There's a vulnerability about her, a thread of nerves. "You're a great writer, Red."

Her face lights up and, fuck, but she's beautiful. "Thanks," she murmurs.

"But I do have to know..."

Nerves creeping into her eyes.

"...why'd you stop when you were just getting to the good part?"

Relief in her smile...and mischief. "Maybe I need to do a little more research."

"Need some help with that?"

"Nah," she says, lips quirking. "I need to find the proper inspiration." She stands, reaches for her laptop but I wrap an arm around her middle, drawing her flush against me instead.

"How're are you going to do that, Red?"

She shrugs. "Maybe I'll call Leo—"

I growl, hold her closer.

She giggles.

"Who's going to be your inspiration?" I narrow my eyes.

"Hmm..."

The impertinence.

I nip at her mouth.

"Hey!"

Taking advantage of her parted lips, I bend my head, kiss her until we're both breathless. "*Who*, Red?"

Her body has melted against mine, her eyes soft and warm. "You know you've been my inspiration for the last four years, Gray."

That truth slides through me, holds tight.

Fuck, but I like that.

"Well then," I say, lifting her into my arms, loving the soft squeak she makes, how her nails bite into my shoulders to hold on, "I think I'd better see about giving you even more inspiration to finish that scene."

"What about dinner?" she asks as I tug open the door to the house.

I kiss her. "I'm hungry for something else."

"Good," she murmurs, pressing closer, hand sliding down my chest. "Because I'm starving for you too."

There's a flicker of movement on the edge of my vision but when I turn to look, Faye's hand slips into my pants, her fingers wrapping tightly around my cock. I groan, bend down to kiss her...and that odd shadow is suddenly the last thing on my mind.

I slam the door as our tongues tangle, revel in the sound of her moans as I carry her upstairs, and when I drop her onto our mattress, strip her clothes off, and then part her legs, kneeling between them...

I see about being inspiring.

———

"Roberts!" Coach calls as I leave the ice the next day.

Something about the look in his eyes has my stomach churning.

"Yeah, Coach?"

He just tilts his head, indicating I follow him, so I do—through the maze of corridors, neither of us stopping until we're at his office.

He pushes open the door and I trail him inside.

"Shut it behind you."

Fuck.

What has Courtney done now?

"Grab a seat," he mutters, and I drop into the chair across from his desk, worry burning the back of my throat. "I need to warn you about something."

Fuck.

"What?" I rasp.

"The social media team came across this—"

He holds out the tablet and even though it's the last thing I want to do, I take it, I hit play.

"...and in other news, our own Gray Roberts is a bona fide hero. My sources confirm that he rescued a woman from a serious house fire at great risk to himself..."

"Fuck," I whisper, setting the tablet on the desk.

"Toni"—the team's publicist—"is already getting interview requests."

"No fucking way."

"I figured." He studies me closely. "I heard about you and..."

"Faye," I say quietly.

"Faye," he repeats and I don't miss the question there.

"She's my..." A beat. An exhale. Not fighting the truth. "She's just mine."

A nod. "I heard about you two in the locker room. I didn't realize you were serious."

"We are."

"Courtney?"

"We're done. Paperwork is filed. She's out of my life."

He leans back in his chair, goes back to studying. "Let's hope, for everyone's sake, that's true."

Isn't that the fucking truth?

"No interviews," I say as I push up to my feet.

"I'll pass that along."

"Thanks." I turn for the door.

"Gray?"

I glance back.

"Good luck with your Faye."

Why do I feel like I'm going to need it?

Thirty

Faye

"What about this one?" Kailey asks, holding up the wallpaper sample.

It's freaking adorable, a parade of forest creatures from foxes to bears to colorful little birds on a cream and sage green background.

Luna's nose wrinkles. "Maybe a little less...animal kingdom and a little more...*aesthetic*."

"How is it that she's both so lovely and so good at giving insults?" Harper asks dryly, flicking through the samples one-by-one, trying to find one with the right *aesthetic*.

"It's a gift," Bri says.

"Well, *I* think it's perfect," Kailey murmurs.

"Not for my nursery," Luns says as she continues flipping.

"No," Kailey agrees, "But it's going to be perfect for mine."

For a moment, nobody moves.

Then we're all moving at once. Luna get to her first, sweeping Kailey up into a tight hug. "Congratulations!" she squeals.

"I didn't think it would happen for us," Kailey says once we've all gotten our hugs and exchanged our good wishes. The wallpaper is forgotten as we gather around her. "We tried for so long that I thought it wasn't happening for us." Sadness in her pretty green eyes.

"Oh, honey," Luna says. "I had no idea. I'm sorry I—"

"None of this is your fault," she says firmly. "No one knew because I wanted it that way. I just...I wasn't ready to talk about it." A sigh. "And then when I finally was, I..." A tear slips free of her lashes, glides down her cheek. "I found out I was expecting."

Harper lifts her hand, pauses.

Kailey nods.

"How far along are you?" she asks, gently settling her palm on Kailey's still-flat stomach.

"Fourteen weeks," Kailey whispers. "I wanted to wait until it was a bit more certain in case..."

"That's completely understandable." I touch her hand. "I'm so thrilled for you."

"*We're* thrilled for you," Luns says.

"How's Smitty taking it?"

Kailey's face goes soft and it's so full of love, it sucks all the breath from my lungs. Beautiful—maybe the most beautiful thing I've ever seen. "He's thrilled." Her mouth hitches up. "I swear, it's killing him to not announce it to the world."

"I didn't think he'd have it in him," Luna says.

"He'd do anything for you."

My heart squeezes and Luna sniffs. "Sorry." She waves her hand in front of her face. "Ignore me and my pregnancy hormones."

But Kailey's sniffing too and then they're hugging, holding back tears as they murmur to each other.

I smile at them but when I transfer that smile to Harper, I see something like pain in her eyes.

Only it's there and gone so quickly, and Luna and Kailey are breaking apart and turning toward us, Luna demanding that we start shopping "immediately" that I'm distracted.

And I forget about it.

Until much later.

———

"Okay," my publicist, Marie, says, stacking her papers and setting them aside. She glances at her notepad then up at me through the camera. "There's just one more thing I wanted to talk about today."

I nod, finish up a note on my own pad, my mind more on the adjuster I met with this morning. My insurance company is dragging their heels and it's making me crazy.

I want to move forward.

Want to see something that's not the shell of my house next door.

Because as lovely and beautiful and soul-fulfilling as this time with Gray has been...my home, my memories, my past are all of thirty feet away.

And they need attention too.

"It's about the fire," Marie says and I snap to attention.

"I turned in my manuscript already," I say. "And I'm making good progress on my newest project, so it hasn't delayed me on that front."

"That's great, but it's not what I wanted to discuss."

I frown, but fall quiet, trying to read her expression through the video feed on my laptop. There's something in her tone that has my nape prickling.

"I presume you've seen the videos that have gone viral about Gray Roberts and you—though you haven't been named in them."

Small miracles, that.

Though, I suppose it's only a matter of time.

All it will take is one person looking into property records and putting the pieces together.

"I've seen them," I say, and I know Gray has too.

Same as I know he hates them, the tension ratcheting up

through his body every time one pops up on our feeds or someone mentions it during an interview.

"I don't comment on my personal life," is the only response he's given.

"I think we can use the videos to our advantage. Leverage them into some fresh coverage for your new release, see if we can't get the hockey romance fans salivating for the real-life story of the romance writer and the hockey captain."

My mouth falls open, surprise and disgust ricocheting through me.

I know Marie hustles for me, know she's good at her job.

But...

Ew.

And it feels even more disgusting after all the negative press Gray endured the previous couple of seasons, the sports bloggers and influencers taking pot shots at him, the media taking every opportunity to dissect his relationship.

"Think about it," she says, hands spreading through the air like she's one of those Hollywood producers trying to pitch a movie. "You'll be huge. You'll get all sorts of new readers. Gray is a household name and if you use that—"

Use *him.*

"No," I say.

"We might even be able to get a TV or movie—"

"*Fuck* no," I say more loudly.

"I can go back to the publisher, pitch a couple more books, see about getting a bigger advance—"

"Marie!"

She stops, mouth half open, eyes wide.

And I know it's partly because her brain is mid-exciting new book opportunity. But it's also partly because I don't think I've ever raised my voice with her.

"No," I say. "And I don't mean *no,* as in you'll be able to bring this up a dozen more times and wear me down," I add when it looks as though she's going to interject. "I mean *no,* as in *no* I will never *ever* use Gray that way. He saved my life and I know if I asked him to do this for me, he would—"

She inhales, eyes lighting up with publicist glee.

"But I will never—*ever*—ask him to do this for me. I care about him too much to ask that of him, and I'm warning you that if 'someone'"—I make air quotes as I fix her in place with my stare —"lets what happened *slip* then I'll be looking for a new publicist."

"Faye," she murmurs, horror drifting across her face.

I don't relent. "We've been working together a long time and I can't imagine not having you at my side...but there will be no using Gray—not for this book, not if we're going viral, not fucking *ever*." A beat. "Do you understand me?"

She nods.

"Good," I say. "I'll send you the stuff on my list as soon as possible and will send you a couple of dates and times for our next check-in."

"Faye," she begins.

I pause, lift my brows.

"I'm sorry."

"Don't be sorry. Just don't ever fuck with my man again."

THIRTY-ONE

GRAY

MY HEART IS POUNDING AS FAYE SLAMS HER LAPTOP closed and pauses, dropping her head into her hands, her exhale sharp.

"What the fuck?" she whispers. "What the actual *fuck?*"

"Red," I murmur.

She whips around in her chair with a gasp. "Gray."

Fuck, but I love the sound of my name on her tongue.

"Shit," she says, jumping up to her feet. "I don't know how much you heard—"

"I heard enough."

Her face changes, expression falling, but I'm already moving toward her, taking her in my arms, smoothing back her hair. "I heard enough, baby. Fuck," I rasp, dragging her more tightly against me. "I heard enough."

"I—"

I bury my face in her hair, inhale deeply. "No one," I whisper. "No woman in my life has ever stood up for me like that."

She jerks, then her arms wrap tightly around me in turn. "Gr-Gray."

Tears in her voice.

The only time I haven't enjoyed her speaking my name.

"Shh, Red," I say. "I didn't mean to upset you."

She sucks in a breath. "I'm not upset"—a shake of her head—"okay, well, I *am* but it's only because you should have that, Gray. And not just from Luna and company and the guys on the team, but from your parents, from the women you've loved!"

I draw back. "Baby—"

"Don't baby me," she snaps. "My head gets all mushy and then you distract me and—"

I kiss her.

Deep and long and with every bit of feeling that's twining around in my heart.

"That's worse," she says, breaths coming in rapid gusts. "I can't think when you do that."

"Good."

She pushes lightly at my chest, sucks in a breath. "Gray. I need you to know—"

"I know."

"But—"

"Red," I say, capturing her hands and drawing her toward the couch, settling on top of it, drawing her into my lap. "Baby."

She shudders.

I grin.

"I heard you."

"I—"

"I *heard* you."

And her words...fuck, it sounds cheesy as hell, but I can't deny they healed some part of me. Faye—my sweet, my kind, my shy Faye threatened to go to the mat for me.

Threatened to fire someone for me.

Threatened—

Don't be sorry. Just don't ever fuck with my man again.

Her man.

Yeah, I fucking love the sound of that. Maybe even more than my name.

"Gray—"

I kiss her again, one hand on her waist, the other in her hair, knowing I can't give her the words for exactly how much what she said, what she did means to me...but hoping that I can maybe tell her through my lips, my tongue, my teeth.

My *cock*.

I slip my hand under her shirt, trail my fingers along her side, up—

The doorbell rings.

I ignore it, draw her head down, kiss her again—

It goes again.

"We should—"

"Ignore it," I mutter, pulling her closer, my lips finding hers again—

Pound. Pound. Pound!

Faye stills, opens her mouth.

And I think of the videos currently circulating online. I think of Courtney...and how unhappy she's going to be when she sees them.

Unhappy enough to...

Come here and tell me all about her *unhappiness.*

Fuck.

"Red, I—"

She touches my jaw. "It's just Luna and the girls," she says, stroking her fingers along my jaw. "I forgot they were coming over."

Pound. Pound. Pound!

Right, that may be the case, but there's still no way I'm letting her answer the door. Especially when it sounds like the person on the other side is trying to bust through like the fucking SWAT team.

I set her aside, push up to my feet.

"Gray—"

I'm already moving to the door, already bracing myself for the nightmare on the other side.

I reach for the handle, twist.

Then tug it open...

To reveal complete and total chaos.

———

"You motherfucker!" Smitty shouts. "You blocked my train."

Leo just smirks and reclines back on the couch, dusting his hands together in a job-well-done fashion.

But I don't miss he keeps looking toward the front door.

As though he's looking for *someone*.

Luna's clocked it too. "She's not coming," she says as Faye bends and begins placing her train cars down.

The room goes still. Smitty opens his mouth.

Kailey settles her hand on his thigh and his teeth snap together so quickly I swear I can hear the *click* even from across the table.

His face softens as he glances down at her, the big man even gentler with his wife now that she's pregnant than before—something I didn't think was possible.

He touches her belly lightly, presses a kiss to the top of her head.

Then turns back to the board.

And scowls.

"Traitor!" he snaps, pointing his finger in Faye's face.

I lean forward, ready to break it off for being so near my woman, but as I've learned, Faye is no wilting violet.

"Hush," she says. "We're all trying to win—"

And we are.

Our *Ticket to Ride* showdowns get *intense* and today match is no exception.

Competitive fucks, the lot of us.

"—so quit bitching when someone makes a good move and deal with it."

Aiden grins.

Leo looks away—though he does it glancing toward the front door again (and maybe I'm channeling Smitty's inner match-maker, but I just *know* it's because he's looking for Harper...who, as Luna said, isn't here).

Smitty opens his mouth.

Closes it.

Then scowls and flops back on the couch. "You are all traitors."

"Traitors who love you," Kailey says.

"Speak for yourself," Aiden mutters, earning a smack from Luna, who's concentrating on her turn.

She places her pieces with a flourish then turns to Faye. "You're coming with us to the game next week, right?"

"What game?"

"The Grizzlies game. Kailey and I are going." A beat. "So are you."

Faye's eyes come to mine and there's something in the choco-latey depths I can't read. "We'll see. I might have some work stuff."

"At night?"

"You know my work doesn't abide by normal office hours."

Luna studies her, lips pressed flat, expression saying she doesn't buy that.

And neither do I.

But if Faye doesn't feel comfortable going then she's not going.

No arguments allowed.

"I'll let you know if that changes," she adds firmly when it looks as though Luna will protest.

"I—"

"She'll *let you know.*" I flick up my brows, hold Luna's gaze.

Of course, she doesn't back down. "But—"

"Luns," Aiden says.

She scowls, but after another pause, lets it go.

But that may only be because it's my turn to play...

And I block the hell out of her trains.

Thirty-Two

Faye

"You want to talk about it?" he asks, stepping close, his front pressing to my back as I brush my teeth.

Yup.

We've reached that level of domesticity—sharing a bedroom, brushing our teeth side-by-side.

Hell, beside the couple of nights he's slept away from me when the Grizzlies played away from San Jose, I've spent every night in his arms.

Dumb? Maybe.

A fantasy? Absolutely.

Too fast? Probably.

Gonna stop? No freaking way.

Never—*never*—has my soul felt more at home than when Gray is holding me, when his slow and steady breathing is ruffling the hairs on my nape, when his gentle voice is waking from a nightmare.

Less of those of late, less of an excuse to sleep next to him.

Except...that he's mine.

"I'm rested," I say after I rinse and spit, put my toothbrush aside. "That nightmare last night was a fluke. I think because I spent the morning at the house—"

Thinking about all the things I'm waiting for the insurance company to do.

Fire marshals. Engineers. Adjusters. Contractors.

And still cooling my heels while I wait for them to cut a check to reimburse me for my laptop and phone—not to mention the battle that's been taking place between my home owner's and auto insurance as to who's responsible for replacing my car.

Which is part of the reason I'm up early to drive Gray to the practice facility before he flies out for another game.

The other piece is that...I like spending time with him.

Especially when he does things like cupping my jaw and rubbing his nose back and forth against mine, saying, "I want to hear about the house, Red. And I fucking hate that you're still having nightmares—"

"*Occasional* nightmares," I correct.

His eyes are gentle. "*Occasional*"—his thumb brushes over my cheek—"or not, I still hate that you have them."

Warmth in my belly, spreading out through my body, coiling carefully around my heart.

I really, *really* like this man.

"Gray," I whisper.

Hot green eyes. Lips brushing over mine. "Hate it," he says firmly then lifts his head. "But that's not what I was talking about."

"Then what—"

"The game." He nuzzles at my throat, lips brushing over my skin. "I know you're still not the biggest hockey fan, but I'd love it if you would come watch." A kiss that has me shivering, my hands plunging into his hair, holding him close. "I'd make it worth your while, baby," he says earnestly, "I promise."

It feels so good to have him close like this I'm having a hard time focusing on his words.

"I know you will," I say, arching against him, trying to turn his head so I can kiss him.

He takes my mouth in a flash of tongue and teeth, leaving me breathless and limp and...slow to register the note of desperation in his words.

Of worry.

His lips trail to my ear, his tongue flicking out and making me shiver. "Come to the game, Red."

The game.

Why had I wanted to avoid the game again?

It's hard to remember now—with him so close, with his mouth on my skin, with his hands running over my body, lightly teasing my curves, drawing me flush against him.

"Okay."

Triumph in his eyes...until his phone rings.

We both still.

"Ignore it," he mutters, fingers slipping beneath the hem of my shirt, trailing up my side.

"You can't be late," I protest, though it's more sigh than words since his tongue is flicking out to taste the sensitive spot behind my ear again.

He spins me, bracing my hands against the counter. "We have plenty of time."

The phone cuts off.

Then immediately starts up again.

"Just answer it," I say, breaths coming in rapid gusts, "so we can get back to—"

A wicked grin as he snags his phone from the counter, swipes across the screen.

"Hell—"

"What the fuck are you doing, Gray?" Courtney snaps.

His hand drops away from my body and he steps back so quickly I waver on my feet.

Shame. Worry. Desperation. *Hurt.*

It spurs me into motion and I jab at his cell, immediately silence the next call that comes through.

Then block her number—a new one, I see, since the last time she's called.

Meanwhile Gray's turned into a statue, his gaze averted, the only thing that makes him appear slightly human the flickering muscle in his jaw.

"*That's* why I don't want to go to the game," I whisper.

He doesn't move, but his eyes fly to mine.

"I know you hate the attention"—I chew at my bottom lip—"and if I go, there's a good chance that people will put the pieces together about who I am to you or Courtney may see something and be even more triggered..." I shake my head, force my words through my tight throat. "If we wait until the news cycle calms down and people are moving on to different and more interesting stories, it will be easier for us..."

He just looks at me. And I...keep talking.

"But if I go now..." I exhale. "I know you just want to play hockey, honey. Same as I know you don't want more stories out there about you..."

Still silent.

And I just...keep going.

"I want to watch you play in person, Gray. I really do. I just..." I shrug. "I think it's probably safer to wait until..."

A thunderstorm across his face.

"...things settle," I finish.

And I don't have any more words, any more thoughts—

Because he's turning away from me.

"Fuck!" He punches the wall, doing it with so much force his fist bursts through the drywall, sending up a little puff of dust. "I hate this shit," he growls. "Hate that it keeps happening. Hate that she won't fucking go *away!*"

But when he goes to punch again, I grab his wrist, halting him.

"No," I rush to say. "You need your hands, honey. You need—"

He yanks out of my grip and I freeze expecting...I don't know what the hell I expect.

Certainly not what happens next.

Which is him spinning and wrapping his arms around me, burying his face in my hair, falling silent while holding me tight for a long, long time.

"Fuck, Red," he rasps and there's more in his voice I don't understand, pieces I'm missing, an incomplete puzzle. "What'd I ever do to deserve you?"

"Gray," I whisper. "We'll figure it out."

"That's what I'm afraid of." The words are so quiet I barely hear them.

But I *do* hear them, and so I ask, "What does that mean?"

He doesn't respond, just buries his face in my hair and holds me tight.

I open my mouth, wanting to demand he answer me—but the words won't come. I want to know what's scaring him, want to know every part of him. Want *him* to know he deserves everything, and certainly much more than he *thinks* he's entitled too. But I don't think he'll hear me if I say that, don't think he'll believe me.

And he has to be on a bus in an hour.

He needs to focus on work, not dredging up old drama.

So...I let it go as I hold on to him in return, as I do it tightly. Waiting. Hoping. Wanting him to talk to me, to give me the rest of it—why Courtney is so determined, what gives him the haunted look in his eyes when her name comes up...what the fear eating him up inside is.

Fear that has nothing to do with my nightmares or with my house or the videos currently going viral on the internet.

But...we're new.

But...we've shared so much already.

But...we're in deep—*deep*—in such a short amount of time.

So, I don't push.

I let him pull back and lightly brush his lips over mine, let him give me the soft, sweet words that are a way to gloss over what's just happened. "I appreciate you looking out for me, Red." He cups my cheek. "I appreciate *you*."

He seals his lips over mine.

"And you're right," he says when he pulls back, cupping my jaw. "There will be more games for you to watch."

I nod, hold him tightly again, hold him until he's releasing me, coaxing me to finish getting ready because he really *is* going to be late unless we get moving, and then I drive him to the practice rink, where the team's bus is waiting.

There are reporters outside, trailing him as he walks to the bus, calling out questions that have his shoulders going stiffer and stiffer.

As I watch him, I know it's the right call to skip the game.

I just can't know until later...

That *this* was the moment I should have pushed.

THIRTY-THREE

GRAY

"What's it like to be a real-life hero?"

"Will you kiss me after rescuing me too, Roberts?"

"I hear he's doing a fireman's calendar too!" A beat. "Will you stroke my hose good and hard?"

Shit talk from the players on the other team.

It's not unexpected.

Razzing is part of hockey, and it's smart to do everything in your power as a player to try to get your opponent off their game.

It's a sport of inches, of milliseconds, of grinding it out until the very end.

If you can fuck up someone's game so they're holding their stick a little too tight, so their shots are off, their passes don't connect...

It can work.

But the heckling wasn't why I played poorly.

Neither were the questions that continued to come up during media.

It was...

The disappointment in Faye's eyes when I didn't talk to her.

I spent the last couple of days remembering the flash of sadness through her brown eyes, the way she tucked it away and plastered on a smile as I deliberately moved the conversation on...and trying to ignore the sense that I'm seriously fucking this up.

No wonder my game was off.

Courtney wouldn't have let it go.

She would have pushed.

I would have pushed back.

And we would have ended up in a knockdown, drag-out fight that had me playing *mean.*

Brutal hits and sharp passes. Fights to blow off steam.

Maybe that's better instead of this guilt that's been my constant companion, swiping out it's talons to keep cutting me, over and over again, meaning that while I wasn't a deficit to the team, I certainly wasn't putting up points.

The guys noticed—of course they did.

But they thought it was the press, the attention, the shit the other team was giving me.

I didn't bother to correct them, to tell them it's because just when I was thinking I might be able to have something different, to truly make something different...

That phone call with Courtney smacked me back into reality.

And I froze.

And Faye had to deal with the fallout—I hadn't even been able to end the call.

Like the guys at the shower had to deal with Courtney's shit too—I didn't shove her out the door, throw the lock, and call the police to deal with her shit.

Because I'm pathetic, fucking *useless* when it comes to dealing with my ex.

And so my nightmare is going to continue to bleed into Faye's life, so much so, I might have to eventually let her go or risk my fucked-up world her turning into the one thing I can't bear for her to become—

"Christ, Roberts," I hiss, shoving out of my car and slamming the door. "*Enough.*"

I stride forward, push into the house, pausing to hit the button to close the garage, but when I start to swing the mudroom door closed...

It stops.

Of fucking course, it does.

Because nightmares in my head...and in real life.

A feminine hand grips the edge, pushes it open, nearly slamming the wooden door into me.

And...

Then I'm face to face with Courtney.

Her perfume wafts forward to fill the air, so forceful it almost chokes me. She's wearing a slinky dress that reveals far more than it conceals. My favorite outfit of hers...aside from her naked.

Or it *used* to be, anyway.

Because tonight I don't feel that burning need, the urge to rip it off or push it up or lay back and let her fuck me with the slender straps slipping from her shoulders, the material bunched up between us.

Tonight, it's just a dress.

She reaches out a hand, trails a finger down my chest.

And maybe I should have stopped her from touching me, should have shoved her back, but some sick part of me wants to test myself, to see if that need will reignite, to discover if I'm truly so fucking messed up in my head that I'll fall back into the same old shit. But...

To my surprise and relief, the contact does *nothing* for me.

That finger sliding over my partially unbuttoned shirt may as well belong to a teammate.

A stranger.

No, a really fucking annoying opponent.

There's no desire, no urge to divest her of her clothes.

I feel...*nothing.*

But because I'm processing that feeling, sitting in the strange and sudden disconnect after the turmoil I've been in over the last few days, I'm not focused on the fact that she's moving closer.

That she's taking me standing still, me pausing to think as a green light.

To press her breasts to my chest.

To lift on tiptoe and try to kiss me.

"What the fuck, Courtney?" I growl, grabbing her by the shoulders and halting her before our mouths can connect.

"Kiss me, Gray," she cajoles, her body arching against mine in a calculated move.

My name in her voice is wrong.

Nothing like my Faye who murmurs it like I'm that fantasy of hers, who forgets to be shy when I touch her, who's earnest and sweet and turns me on with a mere glance, with a soft smile, with her gentle hands on my body.

Not nails biting into my flesh, trying to force me into action.

Not a palm sliding down my torso, heading for the waistband of my pants, hoping to manipulate me into something that is acid on my soul.

"Don't," I say, brushing away Courtney's fingers, shoving her back a pace.

"You like it when I touch you," she says coquettishly, her mouth curving into a smile as she reaches for me again.

"*Don't.*" I stop her before she can make contact this time.

"Gray," she whines.

I snag her hand and hold it up—it's the left one, her ring glinting in the soft light Faye left on for me. Another piece of her. Another truth. Another way she cares. And another thing... Courtney never did for me. "You're engaged," I remind my ex. "Remember?"

She lifts a slender shoulder, lips tipping up. "My fiancée and I have an understanding."

"An understanding to fuck around on him?" I ask.

The truth flickers through her eyes.

"He doesn't know you're here."

"I—"

"Don't lie to me, Courtney."

"I'm not," she says, the bullshit palpable, her bottom lip sliding out into a pout. "He doesn't care what I do."

I sigh. "Then why are you marrying him?"

She looks away.

And I can tell by the set of her shoulders, I won't get the truth out of her. She has an agenda and she'll do whatever she has to in order to achieve it.

"You need to go," I tell her.

"I need *you*." It's a whine, that pout growing.

"Well, I'm not available. Not today. Not ever."

"We're good together."

"No, Court. We're not. We bring out the worst in each other and I'm done." I've said those words to her before—dozens of times, maybe even hundreds. But tonight is the first time I've truly meant them. "I found something better. *Someone* better."

Her eyes flash. "That dowdy little author who could barely even speak to you?" A sniff. "She'll never be to you what *I* am."

"God, I hope not."

I mean to think the words, not say them out loud.

And *fuck*.

I can see it in her face, in the set of her jaw, the venom in her eyes—she's going to snap. And I'm so worried about dealing with a Courtney-level drama after midnight while the woman who owns my heart is upstairs sleeping, I don't realize what she's said, what she's *revealed*.

Don't realize...until much, *much* later.

Yanking open the door to the garage, I grab Courtney's arm and drag her through it. "You need to go."

"Don't say that!"

I wince at the shriek, but jab at the button mounted on the wall, sending the metal door rumbling up.

"Don't say *that!*"

Fuck.

Her car is in the driveway, so I drag her over to it, pull open the door, and shove her into the driver's seat.

"I'm not going," she mutters, crossing her arms and making no move to buckle her seat belt.

And I just...can't find a fuck to give.

Spinning on my heel, I start for the house, but before I can shut the garage, Courtney is running up the driveway.

"Don't make me go," she says, plastering herself to my back.

I mentally calculate if I'll be able to get the garage door shut before she makes it inside, know that I won't.

Gritting my teeth, I move quickly, wanting this over as quickly as possible.

I stride through the garage, hit the button to send it rumbling shut again.

All while Courtney clings to my back like a limpet, tits pressed tight to my spine, nails digging into my middle.

Into the house and through the hall, the kitchen.

She starts to relax, to loosen her grip.

At least until I turn away from the stairs and head for the front door. Then she clings tighter, dragging her heels, trying to slow my momentum.

I undo the lock, whip open the door.

"Gray!" she whines.

"Let go," I grunt, reaching for her arm.

To my surprise, she does.

But she doesn't go quietly into the good night.

She jumps up and mashes our lips together.

"What the fuck?" I growl, shoving her back.

"I won't go!" she shrieks. "I won't leave you."

"You don't want me," I say as I plant a hand in the middle of her chest and push her out the front door. "You just want to be the one who decides we're over. But Courtney"—I bend, fix her in place with a glare—"that's done. *We're* done. I'm never going back."

Something's unlocked in me—

Maybe it's seeing her like this and feeling nothing but disgust and pity.

Maybe it's the time I've had with Faye—the peace, the calm, the sense of actually being seen, of having something different.

Maybe it's the tiny bud of hope in my heart that—no matter my part in the toxicity that was Courtney and me—this isn't all I get to have.

Maybe...I can have more.

More that isn't Courtney.

She opens her mouth, takes a step toward me.

And, proving I'm holding firm to my words, I shut the door and flick the lock.

My hands shake, but not from want. From what Courtney and I used to mean...and that it's finally loosened its grip on me.

Then she starts pounding on the door and I grit my teeth, know it's not going to be that simple.

But...tomorrow I'll deal with that shit.

Tonight, I just need some fucking sleep.

Thrusting a hand through my hair, I sigh and turn for the stairs.

Then freeze, every cell in my body tightening as panic knots my insides.

Because in the soft illumination of the lights she left on for me...

Faye is standing on the bottom step.

THIRTY-FOUR

FAYE

"RED," HE SAYS CAREFULLY, ARMS EXTENDED, palms out.

As though he's soothing a wild, panicked animal.

As though he's afraid I'm going to turn and run after that scene I just witnessed.

And considering that Courtney is now banging on the door, her shrieks echoing through the wood, maybe he's not far off.

She scares me, but more, I hate that he has to deal with her shit.

I don't love the idea of having to deal with her either.

But I want Gray. I want him in my life, in my bed, in my arms.

Because I like him.

No, I *love* him.

Not the fantasy. The *man*.

Burnt banana bread and scorching hot kisses. Red cheeks when I read him the scenes he's inspired and on camera winks and explaining the *sport* of shopping cart pushing.

So, yeah, I don't look forward to squaring off—however that's going to come—with Courtney, but I'm also not going to discount all the good Gray and I have together just because things might be complicated and messy. That's not me. Or it's not me any longer. Because...

That's not the woman I'm *going* to be.

I'm not giving Gray up.

I just wonder...why it seems like he's giving up on himself.

"It's not what it looks like," he murmurs as I'm processing my churning thoughts, the big feelings, as I'm registering his body language, the worry on his face, his slow careful movements toward me.

Why does he already think he's lost me?

"I think it's *exactly* what it looks like." I step off the bottom stair and onto the floor, releasing my tight grip of the banister so I can walk toward him. My pulse is pounding in my ears, but not because I'm afraid.

Because I need to protect him as he's protected me.

His arms drop, hands clenching into fists at his side. "Red, I didn't know she'd be here—"

I'm close, close enough to wrap my arms around him, to hold him tight. "I know."

He's still, stiff.

"She snuck in through the garage."

"I didn't think you'd willingly let her in, honey."

That has his arms lifting and wrapping around me in turn. But he's still tense and his words are full of pain. "If I was a good man, I'd end this—leave you to your life that's not filled with the shitstorm she's going to bring."

"Gray," I whisper, my heart positively aching for him.

Then even more so when he keeps talking...and Courtney keeps banging and yelling.

"I know you probably think that"—a nod to the wooden door that's being abused by his ex—"and the last few scenes were bad, but the truth is that you haven't seen anything yet." He slides his hand up my back, fisting it in my hair. He clenches the locks tightly after a particularly loud bang, as though they're a lifeline keeping him grounded in the here and now.

And though the grip is fierce, it doesn't hurt me.

Because I don't think this man has it in him *to* hurt me.

He'll bend over backward, take any amount of pain to stop someone else from enduring it.

And somehow he still thinks he isn't good, isn't worthy, isn't enough.

"When Courtney gets something in her mind, she doesn't give up." He exhales, drops his hand. "And she doesn't give a fuck who she has to hurt in the process of getting what she wants."

"And that's not your fault."

He goes still again.

Tense.

Then he pulls out of my arms.

I hate the distance but let him pace away, not missing the edgy movements of his body, the jerky thrusts of his hand through his hair.

But, *God*, I want to hold him, to find the right words to make him understand, to make this better.

I'm a writer.

That should come easy.

But there's no easy way to heal the wound inside him.

"Gray," I say softly.

He stops pacing, but he doesn't look at me. Instead, he stands there, hands fisted again, head tipped forward, gaze pointed at his toes. His big shoulders hitch up on a breath...then drop on his exhale.

"Will you..." I begin and his head lifts, his eyes finding mine. "Talk to me?"

Edgy is back in an instant. "About what?" he asks guardedly.

"About why you think you need to keep paying for something that isn't your fault."

He snorts, gaze flashing behind me as the banging continues. "It's me who married her."

"And"—I shift closer but stop short of touching him when his body goes stiff again—"you said you were both young, said you made a mistake. And clearly it's one you've tried to rectify many times over. So I guess"—I press my side to his—"I'm wondering why you have this need to keep punishing yourself for not being perfect?"

"You don't understand."

"Then tell me."

A muscle flickers in his jaw. "You don't need to hear this shit. It's over, and eventually she'll get the message."

Except...she's still knocking.

And screaming.

"Let's go up to bed," he says, reaching for my hand. "I wanted to talk to you about the engineer who's coming to look at your house."

"We can talk about that," I agree, allowing his fingers to wrap around mine. "But we also need to talk about the other thing too."

Because I let his avoidance slide the other day.

But...I don't think I can, don't think I *should*.

Not if I want more, want to love every part of him.

"Red," he warns.

It's not a caution I heed as he draws me toward the stairs...and up them.

Not one I heed as I push my nerves aside and give him words that are too big, too soon...

"The only thing that scene did was make me fall in love with you."

He falters on the treads, and maybe I shouldn't have started this on the stairs—for the fall risk alone.

Though, since I'm committed now, I keep going. "You're not perfect, and neither am I. But, perfect or not, Courtney doesn't define you—not back then, not now. You're Gray Roberts—captain of the Grizzlies, the man I fell in love with four years ago without knowing anything about you except that I liked the smile on your face and knew you had kind eyes and loved that you looked out for Mrs. Zander when she was ill."

He's quiet for a long moment. Then he tugs my hand again, coaxing me up the rest of the stairs.

"I'm not sure Mrs. Zander actually *was* ill."

"She wasn't," I says, lips twitching. "Something I know because she told everyone at Wine Club."

Gray's fingers convulse around mine.

Then he's chuckling and the sound soothes the roughest edges of my worry.

I can do this.

I can help him see.

"I miss the old bat," he murmurs as we walk into the bedroom.

"Me too," I say softly. "She gave me all the good recon on you."

"Oh? Like what?"

"Wouldn't you want to know?"

"I would." A beat. "That's why I asked." He wraps his arms around me, draws me flush against him, curved lips descending toward mine.

I know if he kisses me, I'll be distracted by all that's him and I won't push this.

Then he'll go internalizing all this hurt, this blame.

And who knows what kind of damage Courtney will cause in the meantime.

I need to tackle this head on.

For me.

And more importantly—

For Gray.

"I'll tell if you do."

THIRTY-FIVE

GRAY

ONE SECOND, I'VE FINALLY PUSHED COURTNEY—AND the noise she's making out front—from my head.

The next, my world's being rocked by Faye.

"Red," I warn again, straightening and stepping away from her. "It's late."

I just want her to drop this shit, to let me protect that small kernel of hope I've finally managed to cobble together, to trust in that before I tear myself wide open and admit what I've done, how I've fucked up, all I've ruined.

But one look at her face tells me that's not going to happen.

"Baby—"

"No *baby*"—she slices her hand through the air—"please just talk to me."

I waver.

Because I want to. *God*, I want that so fucking bad.

Because I know she'll be my Faye, soft and sweet and kind as she listens, but I just...*can't.*

Because if she looks at me like—

I grit my teeth together, shake my head, cutting my greatest fear off in its tracks. "Later, Red. Right now, I'm exhausted, baby. I need sleep."

I watch her waver before she sighs quietly.

Relief ripples through me.

She's going to let this go.

Thank fuck.

But when she speaks, her words are soft...and completely eviscerate me. "And if we get in bed right now, you'll fall asleep?"

I force myself not to flinch.

No, of course I won't fucking sleep.

I'll lie awake, convince myself that blip of hope is a lie.

That things will go wrong.

That I'll *ruin* another woman.

"Right," she says, her voice turning fierce as she plunks her hands onto her hips. "We're talking about this now. We're sorting it *now*."

My temple begins to throb.

"I need you to talk to me, Gray—"

My name on her tongue doesn't go straight to my cock this time.

Nope.

I may as well be a eunuch right now—or diving into an icy fucking pool, my balls retracting into my body.

"—not because you owe me answer, but because I'm tired of seeing you hurting, honey. Because you've held me as I cried and given me a safe space to be me and helped me realize that I don't have to be alone. Please trust me enough to talk to me, to be your safe space right back."

Her words are fair.

And so fucking tempting I almost give in.

In fact, I open my mouth, preparing to tell her everything when there's a huge crash against the front door.

And just like that, the past crawls up my throat and clamps its fingers around my windpipe, smothering the words. Instead what comes out is—

"Aren't you supposed to be shy and sweet and retiring?"

The asshole.

Confirming exactly what I've always known—that eventually I'll do this to Faye too, eventually I'll turn on her, *hurt* her.

And the evidence is right there in the flicker of pain crossing her face.

Only, Faye doesn't back down. Her cheeks go pink. Her chin lifts. Anger flashes through those deep brown eyes. "Don't you *dare* go there, Grayson Roberts," she snaps jabbing a finger into my chest and scowling at me. "I'm a nice person. I like you—"

"You *love* me," I can't help but interject.

(And yeah, I'm fully aware this isn't the right time to bring that back up.)

Her lids close and I can practically hear her counting to ten.

Then she peels them open and looks—okay, *glares*—at me.

But her tone is almost heartbreakingly gentle.

"Please don't do this."

I open my mouth to ask *do what* but she keeps talking.

Probably for the best, because her next words highlight how supremely stupid that would have been.

"Don't discount my emotions," she says more firmly. "Don't try to gaslight me into thinking that what you've been dealing with since I came into your life isn't going to be—or maybe already is—a huge gulf between us." She exhales, gentles again. "You've been perfect, Gray. Freaking wonderful from that first moment at the hospital and ever since."

"So what's the problem?" I ask edgily.

"You're keeping a huge part of yourself back."

"That's not fair," I say even though she's not wrong.

Her brows just lift in challenge.

"I've been more honest with you than I've been with anyone else in my life."

Her head cants to the side and she studies me for several heartbeats before she murmurs, "I believe that."

"Then drop this shit and—"

"I can't. I *can't.*" Teeth nibbling into her bottom lip. "I *want* to give you an out, want to let this go. But I love you, Gray and I can't stand by and watch you tear yourself apart—"

"I'm not—"

"Honey, I saw your face when Courtney came to the baby shower, when she watched us through the window in the kitchen, even when you locked her out tonight."

"Red," I rasp, heart seizing.

"So you can't possibly think I've missed that you thought I was going to flip out when you turned and saw me there at the bottom of the stairs, that it almost seems as though you're waiting for the other shoe to drop and things to go bad between us." An exhale, her voice gentling. "Or that I've forgotten you told me no woman in your life has ever stood up for you."

I close my eyes.

"And I definitely haven't forgotten how you react to the old stories in the news or the videos online or the way you look at me sometimes, as though half-expecting me to disappear."

My pulse is pounding through my veins, through the tightly clenched muscles of my jaw.

"I'm here," she says, settling her hand above my racing heart, my lids flying open. "I see you. I *love* you."

I want to say those words back.

But they won't come.

I can't do anything except stand there, frozen, as terror grips my insides.

"Why are you so afraid of her?"

"Courtney is—"

"Not Courtney. *You.* Why are *you* afraid of her?"

"I told you. We're toxic together and—"

"No, Gray. What are *you* feeling when she shows up?"

Bile begins to burn the back of my throat.

Fuck, I don't want to think about this shit. "It doesn't matter. Courtney and I are done."

"Are you?"

I grit my teeth together. "I think I've made that pretty damned clear, Red."

"Have you?"

"My attorney's filed the signed papers," I grind out. "The only thing that's left is for a judge to sign off and the divorce is final. I don't think I can make it any *more* clear."

"That's true enough."

"Good," I mutter. "That means I can finally fucking stop dealing with this shit and go to sleep." Unable to look at her, I undo the buttons of my shirt as I march into the closet, yanking the material off my arms when I've finished and tossing it into the hamper. I do the same with my slacks and socks then pull out a pair of sweats and tug them on.

Even though I'm annoyed, I expect Faye to have crawled into bed.

Because I want to hold her.

Want to smell her.

Want to feel the shame go away, the wounds heal over, the goodness come back into my life.

But she's still standing where I left her, arms crossed around her middle, legs locked, eyes laser-focused on me.

Fuck.

"Let's go to bed, Faye." I can't even pretend it doesn't sound like I'm begging.

Her lips part on a shaky exhale. "Faye?" she asks. "Not Red?" A beat. "Not baby?"

I rub at the ache in my temple. "It's late. I'm tired. We'll figure this shit out later."

"When?"

"Later," I repeat.

"When?" *she* repeats.

And I know she's just doing what she thinks is right.

But the shame inside me is twisting tighter and tighter, the talons of the past digging deeper and deeper.

So tight it's threatening to burst free and incinerate every-thing in its path. So deep it feels as though I'm bleeding out.

"If we can figure this out—"

That ball of tension explodes out of me, destroying everything in its path.

"Will you fucking leave it alone?" I snap. "I already have one annoying, lunatic of a woman who won't let shit go in my life. I don't need another one."

Her breath catches, those gorgeous brown eyes filling with tears.

"That's how you want to play this?" she whispers.

I can't answer her, can't do anything but stare at her knowing this was always going to happen, that I was always going to do this to her...and eventually, she does what she was always going to do.

She walks out the door.

And the worst part, is I just stand there and watch her go.

Thirty-Six

FAYE

I THOUGHT GRAY WAS THE KIND OF MAN WHO WOULD never cause me pain.

Boy was I wrong.

I curl my knees up, holding them tightly against my chest as hurt ripples through me.

As tears scald my cheeks.

As my stomach ties itself into knots.

As my heart *hurts*.

Then I exhale, shore up my spine...and I make a plan.

Pack my computer, my notebooks and plotting supplies. Then call for a Lyft—

No, hotel first.

Then computer and notebooks. *Then* Lyft.

I need a place to evacuate all this pain, all this grief, all this knowledge of what could have been...but now never will be.

"Focus, Faye," I whisper.

Hotel. Pack. Car.

I nod to myself, reach for my phone—

But the moment my fingers wrap around the case, the door to the guest room flies open, slamming into the wall, sending up another tiny puff of drywall dust.

And in the opening...

My heart squeezes hard.

Gray is standing there, eyes wild, hands in tight fists at his sides, breaths coming in rapid gusts.

"I'm a liar."

I blink. Then again.

Because that...I don't know what to do with that.

"You're a liar?"

He nods, lifting a hand, shoving it through his hair. "Courtney isn't—" A deep breath, his shoulders rising and falling before his soft words reach my eyes. "I put the blame on Courtney," he says, "but the truth is that it's my fault."

I frown.

"She didn't start off as the woman you've met."

"Okay," I say gently, waiting for him to go on, knowing there must be more.

"When we first got together, she was like you—sweet and kind, super smart and thoughtful. But the longer she was with me, the more I fucked her up."

I open my mouth.

Close it.

Because I don't know what that means.

But also because I think it sounds...like complete and total bullshit.

He's still talking, though, so I keep that thought to myself.

Maybe the rest of it will make the first part make more sense?

"It's like...the more intense hockey got, the worse we were together, and eventually...she became the person you met." A shake of his head. "I thought marrying her would make it better. Thought if she was secure that I was hers, things would calm down, but that didn't help. If anything"—he rubs his temple—

"things got worse until every time I'd leave for an away game, I'd have to spend the whole time I was gone managing her emotions."

Yeah, because she's an abusive, narcissistic psychopath.

Nothing Gray could have done would have made things better.

I'm not saying he's innocent in all of this...

Just that he's not the only one whose shoulders the blame needs to land on.

"I knew I shouldn't have started things with you, knew I'd do something unforgivable and ruin what we have. But I couldn't keep my distance, not once I got to know you. So fucking smart and beautiful and kind." He moves over to me, settles his hand on the side of my neck, squeezes lightly. "You deserve better than me, Red. But I just don't have the strength to stay away."

I wait for a couple of seconds to see if there's more.

When it seems as though he's done, I exhale then do something the old Faye never would have done.

I open my mouth and say, "That's complete and utter bullshit."

He blinks.

Then again.

"Excuse me?"

"You're not excused," I say backing out of his hold and tossing up my hands. "Because that is the biggest crock of bullshit I have *ever* heard!"

His mouth falls open.

"And you can be pissed at me or try to push me away, but you know what?" I glare at him. "I'm not going."

Forget the hotel, the packing, the car.

He needs to get this through his stubborn ass head.

And I won't go until he does.

"I thought you were going to say you cheated or God, *I don't know*, did something unforgivable like hit her or abuse her or rape her, but your big, soul-crushing secret is that you spent too much time playing hockey?"

His gaze slides away from mine. "My job takes me away—"

"So explain Kailey and Smitty and Luna and Aiden."

His mouth opens. Closes. Then he grits out, "What do you mean?"

"They're managing just fine and neither Luna nor Kailey has turned into a psycho."

"You're not Luna or Kailey." His body tenses.

"But I *am* like Courtney?"

He winces. "That's not what I meant."

"I know, honey. Except, you kind of did." I settle my hand on his chest, above his beating heart. "But your friends found partners who give and take, who make it work, who don't need their husbands to manage their emotions because they miss them. And maybe the Courtney of old and I have some things in common, but I'm not her. I've spent too much time alone, too much time without *you* to allow myself to be."

"Red," he whispers.

His expression makes my heart ache, but I press on. "So, newsflash Gray Roberts, neither of us are doing this shit anymore. I don't accept that you're solely responsible for Courtney's nonsense, same as I know you don't accept that sometimes *I* feel like it's better to be alone."

He scowls. "I *don't* accept that."

"Exactly," I snap. "Yes, sometimes I want to hide and sink back into being alone because it feels safer, because it means I won't have to live without you if it ever goes wrong between us." I lift a hand when he starts to interrupt. "But I spent too long being alone, too long being scared that if I wasn't, I might lose another person I care about."

"Red," he murmurs, face gentling.

"I don't want to lose you, to lose Luna and Kailey and the others, but I also don't want to give up on the beauty of what we can have *now*—even if someday it may all go away."

"Fuck, baby." He takes a step toward me, stops. "Let me hold you?"

My lungs seize.

Then relief pours through me.

I nod...and an instant later, his arms are around me, his big body holding me close. "I was an asshole."

"Yes, you were."

A rough chuckle. "I'm so damned sorry, Red."

My eyes burn and I nod against his chest. "Good. Because I love you and I think you love me too—and I don't love a man who'd turn me into something I don't want to be. I love the man who's given me the strength to be better, stronger, more confident. And you—" I blow out a breath because my throat has suddenly gone tight. "*You* love a woman who does the same for you. I love *you*, Gray Roberts." I lean back, hold his gaze. "Just as you are."

He closes his eyes for a long moment.

Then exhales and opens them. "Fuck, Red. How is it you make so much sense?"

"Because I'm smart?" I say, going for light, knowing we both need it right now. But it's hard because my heart is pounding and relief is a tsunami through my veins. "No more shitting on ourselves," I go on. "And if we catch each other doing it we'll... *we'll* cut off the other person from the banana bread stash," I finish in a rush.

He freezes.

Then bursts out laughing and after the last hour, it's the most beautiful thing I've ever heard.

Eventually, though, he sobers, taking my face in his hands. "I won't hurt you again." Piercing emerald eyes holding mine. "I swear."

"I know," I whisper.

I feel that promise in my heart, my soul.

"Thank you," he whispers back. "For believing me. For trusting me."

"Always." It's not even in question.

"Thank you," he repeats then tugs me against him again and holds me so tight I can hardly breathe.

But that's okay.

Because I'm exactly where I want to be.

Especially when he draws me back to bed, tucks me close, and murmurs, "I love you, just as you are, too."

THIRTY-SEVEN

GRAY

"ONCE THE CONSTRUCTION TEAM IS ABLE TO TAKE down these two walls," the engineer hired by Faye's insurance company says, "then you'll be able to go through and search for any items you might be able to salvage. For now, though"—he lifts the police tape back up, secures it over the skeletal remains of Faye's front door—"I'm asking that you resist the urge to walk through the space. Things are unstable and dangerous."

It's impossible to miss the pain rippling through Faye's face.

And the frustration.

This shit has been taking too damned long, but the amount of red tape we've—well, really, *she's*—cut through over the last couple of weeks has been insane.

But they've finally identified the cause of the fire—faulty wiring on her heater—and the insurance adjuster has come out, started the claim process.

And today, the engineer was here to survey the wreckage.

Though he hasn't brought great news.

Faye *still* can't search for her belongings.

I shift closer, some part of me still unable to understand why she lets me near her after what I've said, what I've done, but though what happened a couple of nights ago is still a sharp slice of shame that threatens to extinguish the kernel of hope in my heart, what I feel more is...her love.

And her strength.

This time will be different.

This time I won't waste it.

Won't allow it to be ruined.

Mostly because she won't let me.

On the heels of that thought, she straightens her shoulders and nods in response to the engineer, and fuck, that solid steel spine is beautiful.

"You have the list of contractors?" he asks.

"Yes, I'll begin meeting with them this afternoon."

"Good." He passes her a card, tells her to keep in touch, and then we're watching him walk back to his car, get in, and drive away.

"You good?" I ask, smoothing my hand down her back.

Another nod, but this time it's a little jerky, as though she doesn't need to have a shield with me, as though she doesn't need to hide her pain from me.

As though she doesn't always have to be strong with me.

That kernel in my chest grows.

"I've been avoiding coming over here," she says softly before her eyes come to mine. "And you've been letting me."

"You're living right next door. It's not like you can avoid seeing it."

"That's true enough." A breath. "But it's not the same as being right here."

Near the ashes, the scent of smoke soft but still seeping out of the charred wood.

"No," I agree, "it's not."

She exhales and looks at the remains of her life. "Part of it still doesn't seem real." It's a whisper. "It doesn't feel like my house any longer."

"It will again."

"Maybe." But her tone tells a different story.

She doesn't believe me.

"Want to take a lap?" I ask into the silence that falls.

She frowns as she looks up at me in question.

"Around the house," I explain.

Her frown deepens. "He said it wasn't safe to go in."

"We won't go in," I tell her, taking her hand and drawing her against me. "We'll just...look."

And hope to fuck I can find something that's not cinder and ash.

Something that reminds her she hasn't lost everything.

"All right."

As we walk, picking our way carefully through the broken glass, the shards of wood, I search for a way to relieve the tension creeping into her frame. "I was thinking about the game tonight..."

Her tension ratcheting up even further.

Dammit.

"Gray," she begins, shaking her head.

I touch her cheek. "No, Red. I just...I've been thinking about what you said, what you've helped me see. Courtney and I..." I shake my head. "My feelings aren't totally sorted on my part of what made us go so wrong, but I also know that I don't want to— *no*, I know that I can't keep living my life worried about what she's going to do."

She turns toward me, stepping into my arms, squeezing me tightly for a long moment.

"She's going to post on social media if she wants to, the stories are going to get picked up by the media if they get picked up. She might show at the house, might make a public scene, and..." I shake my head. "I can't do a damned thing about it."

Her arms spasm around me. "Oh, honey."

"I've spent a decade trying to prevent that from happening and it hasn't made a fucking bit of difference—"

"I didn't mean to make it seem…"

I cup her cheek. "*You* didn't do anything except make me realize I can't keep doing this." I sigh. "But the truth is, it's been easier to pretend I'm trying to protect you from her, to protect the team from the crap she brings. Because I'm scared, Red. What I feel for you…Courtney never had even a modicum of it."

Her eyes glimmer with tears.

I catch one as it slips from her bottom lashes.

"I don't want to keep hiding and avoiding and living my life to not trigger her. I just…I just want to be us, wherever that takes us."

Another tear falls before she buries her face against my chest.

"Gray," she whispers.

I hold her there, stroking my hand up and down her back, feeling her tears soak into my shirt, feeling my own throat grow tight.

But eventually, we pull ourselves together.

"So, about the game…" I begin.

"Yes."

"You don't even know what I was going to say."

She leans her head against my arm, smiles up at me. "And I'll still be there anyway."

Fuck, I feel that deep in my heart.

But instead of taking her back to my house and showing her exactly how much that means to me, I lace my fingers through hers and start walking again. She falls quiet as we round the corner and at first I think it's because she's processing—and likely going to be doing it for a good long while—all she's lost. But when I glance down at her, she doesn't seem to be in pain.

Instead, she seems a hundred miles away.

"What is it?" I ask.

She misses a step, then shakes her head, as though shaking off all those miles. "It's nothing, really," she says, but goes on before I can push her for a real answer, "I just…between the insurance stuff and Courtney, the stories in the press and my publicist..." A sigh. "It's been a lot."

"I know it has, Red."

I want to hold her close again, to find a way to make it all go away.

But we've had enough heavy over the last couple of days.

"You've had all of that *plus* having to bunk with a big, annoying hockey player who burns things on the regular." I tug at the end of her ponytail. "You've really been through it." A beat. "And I'm not just talking about the fire." Another pause. "Or the weird pregame meals."

She giggles. "You're incorrigible."

Not normally.

But it's easy with Faye.

Easy to laugh and joke and be myself.

"You like it," I counter.

"I do." Her lips twitch as she lightly touches my jaw. "In fact, I *love* it." A beat. "So much I forgive you for burning my banana bread."

Another thread wrapping tightly around my heart. Another piece I hold close.

But...keeping it light.

I tug at her ponytail again, laugh when she swats me away. "So, since banana bread is off the table, what are we going to burn next?"

"There's no *we* when it comes to burning." She lifts her chin. "And anyway, *we* didn't burn the sugar cookies we made last night."

Yup.

More baking commenced last night.

And we faired—well, *I* faired—much better at cookies than banana bread.

"Or the lemon tart," I point out.

"That's because we didn't actually have to bake that one," she says on a giggle that has my heart expanding.

True enough. It only required store-bought ingredients and time in the fridge.

I'm still counting it as a win.

We keep walking, picking our way to the spot where her kitchen window used to be and she exhales, laughter gone, the pain drifting back through her, hunching her shoulders, shrouding her eyes. "Nana used to love being in the kitchen," she whispers. "Said it was the heart of the house."

"I agree."

"You with your burning tendencies and chicken and PB&J pregame meal?" she asks and God, I love her strength, love that she tries to shake off the hurts, tries to keep looking forward.

But I don't want her to hide herself.

I'm not going to *let* her.

This shit hurts.

And she's allowed to hurt, allowed to express that pain.

I'm just...going to do my best to take it away.

Hell, I can think of any number of ways to kiss it and make it better.

But first, I think she needs something else. Cupping her face in my hands, I hold her eyes. "Red?"

"Yeah?" she murmurs.

"You need to know that my kitchen has a hell of a lot more heart with you in it."

Truthfully, my whole house, my whole *life* has felt that way.

Warmer.

Better.

Faye.

"Gray," she whispers, her eyes going damp.

"Shh," I say, smoothing back her hair. "You don't have to say anything. This is just us taking it slow and learning each other, remember?"

A deep breath. "Slow is you saying beautiful things and taking care of me?"

"Well, considering you fell in love with me in this very spot..."

She freezes. Then glares at me and pulls back. "If you remember correctly, this is where I fell in love with the *fantasy* of you."

"Ouch," I tease, rubbing a hand over my chest, pretending to soothe the ache there. "My ego."

"Gah, you're annoying."

"You like it."

"Maybe." She nibbles at her bottom lip, guilt sliding through her expression. "But I also feel that—at this juncture—I need to confess something."

"Confess what?" I ask, watching her gaze slide away, her cheeks go pink.

She wrinkles her nose. "It's embarrassing." A flash of eye contact. "Like *really* embarrassing."

"I think I've covered the gambit on embarrassing, Red."

She winces.

"No." I tap her on the nose. "No looking back. Now"—I draw her closer—"what's this confession of yours?"

Thirty-Eight

FAYE

MY CHEEKS FEEL IMPOSSIBLY HOT.

And I know they have to be bright red.

But I don't back down from the curiosity in his eyes—

"Tell me," he commands.

Or the order.

"I should refuse that, just on principle alone."

He grins. "You know there's no getting out of it now. You opened the can and the worms are escaping."

"I'm not sure that's how the idiom goes."

"*I'm* sure you'd know," he teases. "But quit trying to distract me."

"Gray—"

He bends and kiss me, not stopping until I'm limp against him, my body flush against his rigidly muscled form. My lungs work in overdrive, but he's steady, confident...

*Over*confident, his eyes lazy and half-mast.

"What do you need to confess, Red?" he asks quietly, and even as I try to summon some outrage for his cockiness, the orders, he strokes his hand along my side, dipping his fingertips beneath the hem of my shirt.

I shiver, his roughened fingertips the sweetest abrasion.

Distracting me.

Especially when his next question is as silky as his caresses.

"Tell me," he murmurs against my earlobe.

"I saw you and Courtney through the window," I blurt.

Holy shit.

I did not just say *that*.

I push against his chest, but he just bands his arms around me and holds me tight.

"Uh, we should keep moving," I say quickly. "Maybe I can find—"

He touches my cheek. "You saw Courtney and me doing what?"

Oh, dammit, there go my cheeks again.

I stare down at the ground, tap my foot on the charred blades of grass. "Hello? This is the time for you to open wide and swallow me up."

He chuckles then cups my cheek, eyes coming to mine, "Tell me, Red?"

And...ugh. I started this.

So dumb. Why am I bringing up Courtney when he's finally moving past her? And worse, doing it in a way that has me looking like a sick freak who peeps on people minding their own business.

"Um..."

"*Red*," he says again, tugging lightly at a strand of my hair before tucking it behind my ear.

"I saw you two kissing in the kitchen."

A pause, his eyebrows lifting. "You mentioned that in the hospital."

"Oh." Right. When I'd yelled at him.

"But it wasn't just kissing, was it?" he asks silkily.

"Um. Well..." My cheeks flame. "It was...*creative* kissing."

His brows fly up higher. "Creative how?"

"You and her...she—" I drop my head back and groan. "Okay. Look, I saw you go down on her. Well, less *down* and more lifting her up so you could lick her while you were standing and her legs were over your shoulders and her pussy—"

My throat dries up.

He's still.

Quiet.

Totally thinks I'm a sicko.

And yup, the ground could seriously do me a favor right about now.

Sink hole, anyone?

Gray laughs huskily. "So, you have a voyeurism kink, Red?"

"I—"

He grins and it's that's he's smiling—*laughing*—instead of being mad that undoes me the most.

"I've never done it like that before, okay?" I snap

"The stand-up oral sex or playing the Peeping Tom?"

"Gray!" I say, cheeks blazing. "It was hot—you two are gorgeous people. But it was seriously wrong!" I exclaim. "I should have turned away once I saw what you guys were doing. I mean, I *did* turn away. I just also turned back and—"

"First," he says, slanting his mouth over mine for a short, blazing kiss. "I think this once again proves that I need to invest in some fucking curtains."

Hysterical laughter bubbles up in my chest.

"Second, yeah it was wrong."

My gut sinks.

"Not because you looked, baby," he murmurs, rubbing his nose against mine. "But because it was Courtney and me." His mouth hitches up. "It was consensual. It was manipulative. It was seriously fucked-up." A sigh. "But most of all, it was wrong because I wish it wasn't with her, but rather with you."

My lungs hitch. "I was imagining it was me."

He nips at the hinge of my jaw. "Then I think I've just accepted another challenge."

I shiver.

"We'll make that fantasy a reality…" Another nip, the tiny bite of pain quickly soothed by his lips, by a flick of his tongue.

But before I can ask when exactly that will be, he's kissing me senseless.

"Red?" he asks when he pulls back, leaving me a limp, breathless mess.

"Y-yeah?"

"After curtains."

———

"What's that?" he asks a little while later, his eyes on the charred remains that I think are made up of my bedroom and the room that had been immediately below it—

My office.

"What do you mean?"

He releases my hand then moves toward the collapsed wall, stepping over the edge.

"Wait," I tell him. "The engineer—"

"I'm not going far," he murmurs. "I'm just—" He stops maybe two feet into the wreckage then crouches, shifting pieces of wood to the side as he searches for something.

Something that has my breath catching when he rises a moment later, his hands covered with soot, his expression unreadable.

Then I'm processing what's in his hands.

And it all bursts forward again.

Over the last couple of weeks, the raw pain has faded, the tears burning constantly at the backs of my eyes lessening, and somehow as I met with the insurance agent and the engineer, talked through the next steps with the contractors, this hasn't really felt like my house.

It was a project, a task list full of items to tick off, one after another.

Yes, there were moments it all welled up. Where I *remembered*.

But not like this.

My mother's soft hands braiding my hair for a dance recital.

Kicking a soccer ball around the back yard, cheering in victory when I "scored" by slipping the ball past my dad and between the two pillars of the porch we'd designated as the goal.

So many rounds of UNO that the cards were tatty, the colors rubbed off on the edges, their corners dog-eared, their middles rounded from being shuffled time and again.

Gray settles the metal box in my hands, and though it's not even remotely heavy, the weight of the memories inside have my knees buckling, my body collapsing to the charred ground.

He curses and drops down next to me, but I'm already wrestling with the partially burned and misshaped lid, nails scrabbling as I tear at it, seeking purchase. It's so swollen, it doesn't move, or maybe it's that my moments are so jerky that I can't *make* it move.

Either way, after a few more seconds of scrabbling, Gray slips the box from my now soot-covered hands and carefully removes the lid.

"Here," he murmurs, settling it back into my lap.

My gaze is on his face, on his gentle eyes, the concern in the emerald-green depths intense.

It's not until he nods slightly that I find the courage to look down.

The red cardboard of the UNO box is the first thing I see, and a sob hitches up in my chest as I carefully trace my fingers around the worn edges. I feel a tear slip free, slide partially down my cheek before dropping down, settling on something metal and shiny below it.

I lift the cards out then feel more tears come as I unearth the photo of my parents and me in a silver frame, the three of us smiling like loons, though I'm doing it upside down, my hair spread out below my head as my dad holds me by my ankles.

"You look like your mom," Gray says softly, shifting so he's sitting behind me, his legs on either side of mine, his arms wrapping around me.

Steadying me.

Because I'm trembling.

"I know," I whisper back. "Nana used to say that and I'd lie and say I didn't believe it."

"Why?" he murmurs, the word soft in my ear.

"Because then she'd pull out the family pictures, prove me wrong." I close my eyes, remember sitting with her at the kitchen table, paging through the albums, memorizing each and every similarity I shared with them.

My mom's hair and smile.

My dad's eyes.

Nana's nose.

Pieces of them in me...

And maybe I was never truly alone.

How can I be when they're always a part of me?

He laughs softly. "Sweet, sneaky Faye."

Smiling, I pull out the rest—my parents' wedding rings, the necklace my mom picked out for my wedding day. My first book that I wrote when I was in preschool, the tale about a misbehaving dolphin barely legible, and we're both laughing at what Gray calls my "truly inspired" crayon drawings that are very *not* dolphin-like.

"I think," he murmurs after we've both pulled it together, "that when you rebuild, this"—a finger gently tapping the cover I'd colored with un-ocean-like streaks of puke green and red and neon pink (so maybe I hadn't fully grasped continuity at four...*or* color theory)—"should get a place of honor on your bookshelves."

I carefully settle it back into the box with the rest of the mementos then turn in the circle of his arms, cupping his face in my palms, streaking ash on his skin, not that he seems to mind.

"I love you," I murmur, brushing my lips over his.

His mouth kicks up. "The real me or the fantasy me?"

I laugh, can't help but kiss him as my amusement is still vibrating off my tongue.

Then I settle my forehead against his.

"The good thing for me is that they're one and the same."

THIRTY-NINE

GRAY

"SO," SMITTY SAYS, SINKING DOWN NEXT TO ME.

"So what?" I ask as I tug on my socks.

It's T-minus thirty minutes until game time and the locker room is full of professional hockey players in various states of dress.

Some are completely geared up, ready for the game, including their helmets.

Others, like me, want a complete undergarment change after warmups before I pull my equipment back on.

And a few weirdos, like Aiden, are downing their pregame meal of a gas station hot dog (or maybe that's just Aiden).

Smitty is in between, dressed skates to waist.

"How's my favorite girl?" he asks.

I scowl at him.

But then I think of the tears Faye shed over the photo of her parents. I think of the laughter we shared over her first book.

I think about her soft words—

The good thing for me is that they're one and the same.

And I find myself sharing, "We found her memory box in the

ashes today." Soot on her hands. Pain in her eyes. And joy in her remembrance. "Fuck, but she looks just like her mom."

Smitty falls quiet—a rare feat. Then he slams his fist against his thigh. "I hate that she lost all she's lost."

"That makes two of us," I mutter.

"She okay to come tonight?"

"She wanted to."

"You okay?"

I think of Courtney's reaction and my stomach twists.

But I ignore it.

"I have to be," I mutter. "If I want to keep building something that isn't what I had."

He's quiet for a long moment.

Then he nods. "Yeah, I think you do."

Forward. Just keep moving forward like my beautiful, strong Faye.

"She going to be okay on her own when we fly out day after tomorrow?"

That sends another bolt of nerves through me.

Because—

"Fuck, I hope so."

Smitty goes quiet again, and I know his protective instincts have been triggered as deeply as mine.

Lost her parents. Her grandmother. Her house.

Too fucking alone in this world.

And now a good chunk of the family we're building, the one who's taken her under our wings, will be out of town for two weeks.

I love my job but, for the first time, I hate what it asks of me.

Faye is going to be alone and dealing with all the shit with her house and likely searching through the remains looking for more mementos and—

I won't be there.

And Courtney...fuck, I'm coming to terms with the fact that

I can't control her, but Faye's got enough shit to deal with—she doesn't need to take on mine either.

She should be baking banana bread and writing love stories, not fending off my ex.

She shouldn't have to deal with *any* of this.

My temple starts to throb and swear to fuck, I can almost smell smoke, smell Courtney's perfume, smell—

"Fuck you too!" one of the younger guys shouts across the room as he tapes his stick, not a care in the world.

Fuck, but a lot has changed since those days.

Hell, I don't know if I was ever that carefree.

Not with responsibility sitting so heavy on my shoulders.

Smitty claps me on the shoulder so hard it's a fucking miracle that my ass isn't shoved right through the bench. "She'll be okay."

I shake my head. "I know she will be."

I'll make sure of that.

And...she can take care of herself with that steely spine of hers.

"Luna's activated Bri and Kailey. She won't be alone."

Some of the tension knotting my insides loosens. Faye hadn't mentioned anything—then again, we spent the afternoon digging through ashes. "Yeah?"

"They have shopping plans and movie plans and Girls' Night In plans." He bumps my shoulder with his. "She'll be covered. And she won't be alone—not ever again."

Christ. He's an annoying fuck.

But he's also the best.

"Thanks, Smitty."

He shrugs one big shoulder. "It's what we do."

See? The best.

But even being the best doesn't mean he's off the hook when it comes to getting shit.

"I guess I'll have to cancel it," I say as I pull on my jock.

"Cancel what?"

"The wombat petting zoo experience I booked you."

He freezes as he's reaching for his shoulder pads, turns to glare at me. "Dude—"

I grin at him.

He shoves me so hard I nearly topple from the bench.

But he's laughing too. "I swear, one of these days, I'm going to figure out what terrifies you and I'm going to torture *you* with it."

I already know what terrifies me.

I thought it was getting close to someone else, thought it was falling into the same old habits with a new woman.

The reality is that now what terrifies me...is losing Faye.

I'm not going to let that happen.

Shoving that down, I strap on my shin guards and tug up my socks, "what do you make of Leo and Harper?"

"I *think*"—he drops his voice to a whisper, shocking the shit out of me—"that they went home together."

My brows fly up. "They did?"

"Yup. Aiden said Leo hung out after the baby shower after the rest of us left, *helping*"—he makes finger quotes—"her clean up and load her truck...and then she sent her staff back to the kitchen while she got into Leo's car."

My brows go higher. "Holy shit."

"Smooth, right?" Smitty's eyes slide to the other side of the room where Leo's tying his skates. "Truthfully, I didn't think the man had it in him."

"No, me neither." Leo isn't exactly a monk, but I've known him for a few seasons now and he's not the type to pick up a woman he's just met.

"Though maybe he actually doesn't." Smitty pulls on his jersey. "Because Kailey told me that Harper was supposed to come to Game Night but bailed and that one..." A jerk of his chin. "Has been in a foul mood ever since the shower."

That's true.

He missed a shot in practice yesterday and nearly broke his stick on the goal post.

Then there's the permanent scowl that's been etched into his face since the party.

Not to mention the look in his eyes—one I've seen in the mirror too many times since I rescued Faye from the fire.

Longing, worry, *guilt*.

I've been so distracted by everything happening in my life I haven't been paying close enough attention to my teammates.

I'm the captain, and though we don't have any real assholes on the roster, there are always behaviors I need to help manage, ruffled feathers than need to be smoothed, concerns that need to be brought to the coaching staff.

I've been in a holding pattern, Auto-Mode engaged.

Right.

I need to be better about that.

And—I study Leo a little closer—I need to watch out for him too.

Because if the expression on his face is any indication, something has seriously pissed him off.

And that *something* was definitely a woman.

FORTY

FAYE

"Thanks," I tell the sales associate as she passes me the bag.

She smiles at me, her expression a little harried, and I know it's because there's a line a dozen deep behind me, all of whom are eagerly—if not impatiently—waiting to buy their Grizzlies goodies.

I hurry away from the counter, letting her get on with it.

Kailey and Luna are waiting outside the shop, the brightly lit concourse filled with fans dressed in the turquoise, gray, and black, the Grizzlies' colors.

How a team with an angry, rabid bear (complete with the red eyes to prove it) has those colors, is beyond me.

But they sure are pretty.

"What did you get?" Luna asks, bouncing on her toes and clapping her hands together.

I pull out the jersey and hold it up.

Luna grins—one that widens when she peaks around to read the back...and the name emblazoned across the shoulders.

I like the sound of my name on your lips, Red.

I shiver, wondering if he'll like it on my back too.

Kailey smiles her gentle smile then winks at me. "You know how to play the game, Faye."

My own smile fades.

"What?" she says.

"I—" I nibble at the corner of my mouth. "I'm not trying to play games," I murmur. "I just really like him"—*love* him—and—"

I like the sound of my name on your lips, Red.

"Shoot, I didn't mean it like that," Kailey says softly, concern rippling through her green eyes as she presses a palm to her stomach, as though protecting the growing baby within her womb. "I only—"

"—meant these men seriously love seeing their name on your back," Luna chimes in, looping her arm through Kailey's and reaching her other one forward so she can snatch the bag from me with her free hand. "And she's right. Now pop that baby on and let's get down to the ice. Warmups are going to start soon."

I consider that. "Is she right?" I ask Kailey.

She nods.

Relief slides through me. "I guess you'd know since you've held the heart of your hot, hockey player the longest."

Kailey's cheeks go pink, but she nods. "Lucky for me, he's held mine—and kept it safe—right back."

I freeze. "That's beautiful."

Luna bounces again, her hand smoothing over her belly. "Maybe that will make your next book!"

Kailey's eyes slide away, but not before I see that the prospect excites her.

God, I really like these women.

"I think it just might," I say as I tug on the jersey then loop my arm through Luna's free one. "You two have any other gems for me?"

Luna laughs.

Then starts sharing *all* of her gems.

Which means that Kailey and I are both laughing the entire way down to ice level, the roar of the crowd growing with every step.

And not once do I think about Courtney...

Or what she'll do when she realizes I'm here.

I should have though.

I *really* should have.

———

"Here they come," Luna says, bouncing next to me.

I hold my breath as shadows form in the hallway behind the Grizzlies' bench, growing larger by the second until the first player emerges.

"Wow," I whisper.

Yes, I've been to games in person.

No, I haven't seen hockey like *this*.

And they're not even playing yet.

They're just hopping onto the ice, skating laps, picking up the pucks, taking easy shots on net before the Grizzlies' goalie moves to the crease and starts doing that thing goalies do, scraping their skates back and forth across the blue paint.

"I can't see!" I hear from somewhere behind me and the tiny voice has me glancing over my shoulder, seeing a little girl with pigtails jumping up and down. "I." A grunt. "Can't." Another. "See!"

Lips twitching, I shift to the side slightly, wave my hand at her. "Come in front of me," I tell her.

She slips between the metal bars, clambers over the chair between us and then she's right in front of me, adorable in her tiny jersey. She grunts again, lifting on tiptoe to see over the boards, sending her pigtails bouncing.

I glance back, see her mom, motion to ask her if it's okay if I pick the little girl up.

She nods, smiling gratefully, and then I'm bending, asking, "Want a boost?"

Another bounce of those pigtails as the little girl looks up at me. "What?"

"Want me to pick you up and help you see?"

"Yes!"

I hold out my arms and a moment later, she's in them. As I straighten, hearing the thunks of pucks colliding with the boards, the crunch of skates on the ice, my heart spasms.

Because Gray is there.

Right there on the other side of the glass.

And his eyes are hot, burning into mine, telling me...*a lot.*

That he likes I'm here.

That he likes the jersey.

That he likes I'm holding a little girl in my arms.

My lungs go tight because I'm picturing perhaps what *he's* picturing—a future that may someday lead to me holding another little girl.

Our little girl.

Our gazes hold for long moments, both of us saying a lot.

Too much for a short time together.

Not enough to encapsulate all I'm feeling.

Not a fantasy.

Real.

More real than anything I've ever had before.

The little girl wriggles in my arms, the moment broken, but Gray doesn't miss a beat. Just grins as he bends and scoops up a puck, waiting until we're ready to toss it over the glass. I catch it, pass it over.

"Whoa!" she says then wriggles again, spinning toward her mom. "Look, Mom!"

I set her on her feet, throat tight with yearning as I watch her clamber back over the chair, slipping between the bars, and holding up the puck.

Her mom bends down to admire it and I rotate back to face

the ice, stomach fluttering when I see Gray is still standing on the other side of the glass.

I used to sit on the sidelines watching life speed by.

Now I'm here, the chill of the ice hitting my skin, my friends' laughter in my ears, and...with my own hot, hockey player making me so damned happy I got in the game.

"Shouldn't you be warming up?" I mouth to him, knowing that he probably can't hear me over the din of the arena.

He watches my lips move, a furrow of concentration on his gorgeous face before he mouths back, "Probably."

I make a shooing motion.

He grins then winks at me.

But before he skates away, his eyes go hot again and he mouths,

"Like the jersey, Red."

FORTY-ONE

GRAY

"PERFECT," I SAY, LEANING BACK ENOUGH FOR FAYE TO see the number on the scale. "See?"

She grins. "Learning the difference between grams and cups, are you now?"

"Turns out grams is a more accurate measurement for baking."

"Hmm." She comes close, her breasts pushing against my arm, her scent in my nose, her lush body in the Grizzlies jersey with my name on her back.

Fuck, I'm a caveman.

I love the sound of my name on her tongue, her lips...

But seeing it emblazoned between her shoulder blades may be even better.

"Where'd you learn that from?" she asks, stroking her hand along my side.

"From a very smart, very *sexy*"—I turn, take her in my arms— "woman."

"And whom may that be?"

I nip at her bottom lip, dip my fingers beneath the hem of the jersey, trailing them up her bare thighs. "She's an author," I murmur, bending and tasting her lips, her jaw, her throat. "She knows all sorts of things."

"Like big words?" A breathless question.

"And proper comma placement."

She shivers. "Ah, Gray, you sure know how to talk dirty to a woman."

Laughter bubbles up in my chest, glazes her skin with the damp heat of my amusement.

Her hands dive into my hair, holding me against her as I suckle at the fluttering pulse point at the base of her neck, as my fingers drift higher and find that she's not wearing any underwear.

The burst of need at finding that slick pussy bare to me means I'm no longer thinking about banana bread, about the newest recipe we're testing out, trying to replicate her Nana's deliciousness.

Nope.

I'm only thinking about tight, wet heat, about my name in the air, about her nails biting into my skin as she—

"Gray!" she gasps as I lift her up in one smooth motion. And then she gasps again...probably because I haven't stopped to settle her on the counter.

No, I've kept going...

Higher.

Higher.

Until lush thighs are settled on my shoulders and that slick pussy of hers is bared for my lips.

"Oh, my God!" she cries as I drag my tongue through her.

Her hands tangle in my hair, her legs clamp tight...

And then I drag her even closer.

Then I see about conquering another challenge.

———

We're both naked and panting...and covered in flour by the time we finish.

"You're a menace," she says, panting as she sprawls on my chest.

"Please tell me I'm inspiring enough for another scene," I joke, slanting my mouth over hers and kissing her deeply.

Which means we get even further distracted from baking banana bread.

But I can't find it in me to care.

Faye doesn't seem to mind either, especially when we end up with no bread baked our naked bodies intertwined in the shower, our hands tangling as we take turns washing off the remains of the mess me made.

"Molly's?" she asks when we finally make it back downstairs. "I think Bri is working today."

"You're on." I tug a lock of her hair. "I'm pretty sure Aiden said peaches and cream muffins are on the menu this week."

Her face goes soft. "You remember?"

"That those are your favorite?" I touch the gentle edge of her smile. "I remember everything about you, Red."

"God, I love you."

I nuzzle at the hinge of her jaw, murmur the truth, "You're my heart."

Another kiss. Tight fingers in my hair.

But eventually, we make it out of the house and over to Molly's.

As is often the case, we find it full of Grizzlies—Aiden and Luna at the register with a tray full of goodies, Smitty and Kailey saving them (and then us) seats at a large table. Bri pops out from behind the case when she sees us, giving Faye a hug and then surreptitiously passing her a bag of what I find out later is Molly's famous streusel.

And Leo is there too.

Glowering at everyone as he eats an apple turnover.

I need to do something about him.

But not today.

Today, I'm enjoying good food and spending time with my family and...I'm enjoying time with the woman I love.

Especially when she settles her hand on my thigh, leans close and whispers, "Thank you."

"For what?" I whisper back.

"For making it so I'll never be alone again."

Those words hit me so hard they steal my breath.

So hard it takes me a minute to realize the table has grown quiet around me.

"What is it?" I ask when Faye and I finally pull back from each other, finally tune back into the rest of the world.

To find my teammates and their women looking at me with concern.

No.

More than concern.

With matching expressions of horror.

And then Smitty lifts his cell, pointing it in my direction.

"Fuck man, but you need to see this."

He taps the screen, hits play...and I watch the thirty seconds.

Thirty fucking seconds.

That's all it takes to go from loved and complete, secure and wanted...

And dive headfirst into destruction.

FORTY-TWO

FAYE

"I DON'T UNDERSTAND," I SAY TO MARIE. "YOU WERE just talking about how this would be a great thing."

A hot hockey captain to play inspiration.

A shit-ton of books being sold.

Social media gold...

Except somehow, it hasn't worked out that way.

Probably because the top headlines linked with Gray and my names on Google are—

Grizzlies Captain's New Flame Pens X-Rated Tribute—and It's All About Him

Fallen Hero? Captain Roberts Linked to Erotic Novelist Amid Divorce Drama

And maybe worst of all—

Love Scenes on Ice: Local Smut Writer's Real-Life Hero Revealed as Grizzlies' Gray Roberts

My fault. This whole mess is on me.

Marie sighs and the dark circles under her eyes tell me she's spent the last day since this broke not sleeping. Familiar, that. "Maybe if we'd pushed the fire and rescue angle before the chapter leaked, had gotten ahead of what was happening with you and Gray instead of it being turned into this weird, titillating story that's gone viral and now crossed into the world of sports bros..."

I rub at my temple, at the throb that's been there from the moment our impromptu family breakfast was shattered by a video.

And then another.

And then ten.

A hundred.

More.

So many it seems like the only thing the internet is talking about right now is me.

And Gray.

Twisting what we have.

Making me sound—

I clamp down on the sickening thought.

This has affected Gray far more than it's affected me. He's endured this before, barely allowed himself to believe we could be different...

And now my career is affecting his.

Because the Grizzlies have been distant, slow to return his calls, and the only statement they released...

They're "monitoring" the situation.

Is this the straw that breaks the camel's back?

Am *I* going to be his downfall? Not Courtney?

Stomach churning, world having been tipped so violently on its axis, I try to think my way through this.

But I don't have any good answers as Marie and my agent, Nalini, keep talking, as my gaze drifts toward Gray where he's sitting at the dining room table, out of camera view, but still here for me. No. He's here...but he's also not. His mind has taken him someplace else. His heart fighting him. The shame and embarrassment slicing his insides to ribbons.

Because of me.

Nalini draws me back into the conversation. "The optics aren't good, Faye. Especially after the controversy a few seasons ago—sexualizing athletes, the line between fantasies and TikToks and the real-lives of the players getting blurred." She shakes her head. "Now we're adding in your career and Gray's notoriety and the fact that your books are already being review bombed..."

I close my eyes.

"Not to mention, the trolls on your social media posts and your ads, and um...the unfollows."

My throat goes tight.

"The Grizzlies' publicity team has reached out and we're coordinating with them along with your publisher's team, trying to turn this into a positive," Marie chimes in.

"They have?" I blurt, relief a cool wash through me.

Gray's eyes come to mine, and the hope in them has my mind clearing, my focus returning.

We can get through this.

We *can*.

"They have, and we're going to combine efforts. But babe," she says carefully, "we're way behind the posts, and honestly...I'm not sure how we can possibly spin this into something good at this point."

That hope fades from Gray's eyes, and that cool wash of relief becomes a burning worry singeing my nerves.

Because there's something worse coming.

I can *feel* it.

"And there's also one other thing," Nalini says and it's not gentle...it's so *beyond* gentle I feel my throat close up, my pulse begin speeding through my veins, hammering behind my ears so loudly that I can barely hear her as she continues speaking. "The publisher's pausing your upcoming release."

"What?" I gasp.

"Just until things calm down and we can get ahead of the press," she hurries to add. "Then we'll—"

Screech!

Gray shoves back his chair and jumps to his feet, hands fisting in his hair, body going so still for a heartbeat, he's back to playing statue.

Then he's striding away from the table, pushing out through the back door.

"I'm sorry," Nalini says as it slams shut. "This isn't what any of us want—"

"Definitely not." Marie scowls. "Turning tail and running instead of fighting." She makes a sound of disgust. "It's pathetic."

I drop my gaze to my lap. "I should have listened to you instead of getting upset and defensive the other day. If we'd found some middle ground this might not have..."

Blown up in my face—the explosion so big Gray has been caught up in the crossfire I was trying to protect him from in the first place.

"No, Faye." Regret on her face. "I was out of line. And I was greedy, thinking about how to milk the situation for all it was worth. You were trying to protect your peace, to protect what you and Gray are building. If I'd had a care to that, we may have been able to figure out a way to avoid all this."

We all fall silent, and I know I need to end the call, to go after Gray.

I just...

There's one thing I need to know first.

"Will I have to pay back the advance?"

I haven't received all of it yet—some is paid out after release—but with my insurance company not yet cutting me a check and all the expenses I've incurred to purchase enough stuff to living my life...

Paying that money back will hurt.

I'll do it.

But it'll still *hurt.*

"Not at this point," Nalini says. "And if they try to cancel the contract, we're going to fight tooth and nail. You're not in breech; they're the ones delaying things."

I nod, try to hold on to that one small positive. "Okay."

Marie makes a shooing motion. "You need to get off this call and avoid social media for a few days. Hole up, do your best to be patient, to reassure Gray. We're all working on this and once we figure out a plan, I'll loop you back in."

"The book is low priority," I say, even though the words hurt my heart, even though I know it's the best thing I've ever written and shelving it would destroy a part of my soul. But— "Whatever it takes to make this easier for Gray, do it."

Because he's more important.

And it's my turn to protect him.

A long pause before Marie nods. "We're on it. But you're not a low priority, babe. We're going to make this right for *both* of you."

Heart full even as the worry churns my stomach, I thank them and sign off thinking...

Alone.

For so long I thought I was alone.

But the truth is I just never let myself trust in the people around me.

Until Gray showed me there's another way.

And now it's time for him to trust in that too.

FORTY-THREE

GRAY

THE BACK DOOR OPENS AND CLOSES QUIETLY BEFORE I'm ready.

Because I know what I have to do.

I just...I'm not sure I have the strength to follow through.

The stories.

The derision.

Her book being pulled.

Fuck. *Fuck.*

And worst of all—

I've had a taste of how beautiful it can be to have her...and I'm going to have to let her go, anyway.

"I know the articles are bad," she says. "But my team is good, and I know the Grizzlies PR team is equally as talented. We just..."

She keeps talking, but I'm not really hearing her.

Not when the headlines designed to provoke are on the fucking internet in black and white—

Pucks, Passion, and Porn: Has the Captain Gone Too Far This Time?

Grizzlies Captain in Hot Water (and Hot Scenes): Management 'Monitoring Situation'

From House Fire to Homewrecker: Author Behind Grizzlies' Newest Scandal.

Captain's Girlfriend Cashes In: Erotic Fiction Writer Profits from Private Passion

And the fucking videos.

Everyone having an opinion. A comment.

The derision being tossed her way.

If it was just me, it would be easier. But it's not just me. It's not just a media storm to ignore and "no comment" and wait until it dies down.

No, Faye's been pulled in right next to me.

And I know—fucking *know*—that Courtney is behind this.

My teammates, my *family* wouldn't talk to the media about Faye's job, about the fire—and certainly not about me being inspiration for her books.

But Courtney could have heard something or surmised enough to create this.

To hurt Faye this way.

To hurt *me.*

A gentle hand settles on my back.

"Don't," Faye murmurs. "Stay with me."

Those words kept me with her before, mere weeks ago. Fuck, that feels like an eternity ago, a lifetime.

And—God—I want them to let them keep me with her now. But—

"You know I can't stay," I rasp, turning to face her, wrapping my arms tightly around her, burying my face in her hair, her neck.

Taking this one final moment to hold her.

"You promised," she whispers, hands clenching at my shirt,

nails biting into my skin. "You *promised* you wouldn't hurt me again."

I did.

And this hurts—it fucking *kills*. But if I don't do this now, don't end this here today...

It will only get worse.

Until Faye is...

Until she's not my Faye anymore.

Until everything she is, everything she loves is ripped away from her.

So...better to hurt her today than ruin her tomorrow.

"I have to, baby."

"Why?" she asks, tears glimmering in her eyes.

"You know why."

Her throat works. Her chin lifts. "Tell me." A demand. An order.

One I can't ignore. "I ruin people." I smooth my hand up and down her back, knowing I have to let her go, have to step away... just not quite able to do it yet. "I can't do it again—not to you."

She touches my jaw, her expression swimming with pain. "You're not ruining me, honey. You've saved me."

"The evidence is there, Red. It's already begun and—" The video. Her book. I shake my head. "It has to be now."

Because if I don't do it now...

I won't have the strength to let her go later.

"Gray." She presses closer and I can't stop myself from wiping away her tears. "You gave me a family. Gave me safety and security and made it so I won't ever be alone." She covers my hand with hers. "Don't make me live a life with you not in it."

"I don't want that, baby."

"So, God, *why* are you doing this?"

A broken question.

One that eviscerates me.

Fuck, the idea of not holding her as I fall asleep, of not having her baking in my kitchen, of not seeing her smiles, hearing her beautiful laughter, touching that silky skin...

I want to tear my hair out, punch my fist into the tree that's sending patterns of dappled sunshine on her face and hair and body. I want to tilt my head back and scream until my voice is gone, until the *pain* is gone.

But I know it won't disappear that easily.

Know that this will be an agony I carry to my grave.

Yes, this will hurt Faye—it *is* hurting her—but she'll move on, she'll have Luna and the others, and she won't be alone.

But me...I need to let them all go, give her the space to build her life without the albatross of me hanging around her neck.

I can handle being separate, handle letting her go.

Because she'll have them.

Because letting them go for *her* is...bearable.

Barely.

"I have to," I whisper.

And then I step back.

The loss of her in my arms almost breaks me. But I manage to retreat another pace. Then another.

Until there are five feet between us.

Ten.

Until I'm at the porch, at the door, until I'm forcing my feet to keep moving even though I can see her reflection in the glass.

When she falls to her knees, I almost break.

But that will only prolong this torture.

So, I turn the handle, push inside...

And then I walk away from the only woman I've ever loved.

FORTY-FOUR

FAYE

I SIT IN THE BACK YARD, TEARS STREAMING DOWN MY cheeks for what feels like an eternity.

Waiting.

Hoping.

But Gray doesn't come back.

Not as the sun sets. Not as the moon rises and my tears finally cease.

Not even when the morning sky begins to lighten on the eastern horizon.

It's the sound of construction next door that finally snaps me out of my haze, and...I make my way on stiff, frozen legs inside.

It's quiet.

Silent.

The house feels empty, hollow...or maybe that's just me.

"No," I whisper, clenching my hand into a fist at my side.

I won't be the same Faye I've always been in the past.

I won't accept someone else deciding what my life will be, won't accept that this is all I can have—a taste of beauty only to have it ripped away from me because someone thinks they know better.

I love Gray, but I can't make him see me, want me, *keep* me.

If nothing else, this time with him has taught me that, and as much as it hurts me, as big as my feelings are...maybe he and I have reached our expiration date.

Maybe I can't be the woman he needs.

Maybe he can't be the man *I* need.

Maybe extreme circumstances brought us together and I got this beautiful gift of spending time with him, of love I've only dreamed about, of memories I'll hold tight to, right next to those of Nana and my parents...

And maybe that's all I'll *ever* have.

Because...I begged.

And he still walked away.

My chest hitches, a sob in my throat, and I stand there in his beautiful kitchen, memories all around me, the faint scent of banana bread in the air...and hopelessness in my veins.

"Talking a big game, Faye," I whisper.

Because if he walked in through the door right now I would throw my arms around him and tell him how much I love him.

If he called, I'd pick up the phone and beg him to reconsider.

As though fate is laughing at me, my phone buzzes on the counter and I launch myself toward it.

Only, when I see the name on the display my heart sinks.

Because it's not Gray.

> LUNA: The internet has lost its mind. Are you okay?

Disappointment.

But also...wanting to soak up as much time with Luna as possible.

Because who knows how much more of it I'll have?

When she finds out Gray and I are...

Well, I should just take what I can for the time I have it.

So, with shaking fingers and tears in my throat...I text her back.

———

"Come and sit with me," Luna murmurs as we walk into her house.

The warmth of the sunshine flowing in through the windows eases some of the chill inside me as I follow her into the library and sink down onto the chair next to hers.

There's a box on the coffee table, and when she notices me looking at it, she pushes it toward me, her lips twitching when I open the lid and see some of the delicious goodies she had at her baby shower. "Don't worry," she says. "They're fresh. Aiden picked them up this morning before he left for the road trip."

The road trip.

With the Grizzlies.

And Gray.

Throat tight, I avoid the slice of banana bread and instead select a cinnamon roll. "That was nice of him."

"Therapeutic carbs," she says with a small smile. "To keep me company while he's gone."

Gray's company.

My heart squeezes.

I don't have that. *Won't* have it ever again.

"What a sweetheart," I say, trying to smile back and knowing it must look pathetic given the way she reaches over and squeezes my arm.

I take a bite, try to pretend I'm enjoying it, enjoying myself.

But the truth is the cinnamon roll tastes like sawdust.

Because the last time I had them was with Gray—him feeding me small bites between kisses, licking frosting off my bottom lip, and kissing me with the scent of cinnamon and sugar hanging in the air.

"My Aiden *is* a sweetheart." Luna says, pulling me out of the memory. The misery. She tilts her head to the side, studying me closely, adds softly, "And so is Gray."

My lungs constrict.

"Though the look on your face is telling me that may not always be the case."

"It's fine," I say quietly. "He and I just—" I shake my head. "Well, it doesn't matter. But do you think I could crash here—?"

"Yes."

I blink.

She reaches over, pulls the cinnamon roll out of my hand, and sets it on a napkin near the box. "Yes, honey," she says, holding my gaze. "You can stay here as long as you need."

"But I don't know—"

"As long as you need," she repeats, squeezing my arm again.

"The baby. Bri—"

"It's a big house," she says. "We have plenty of bedrooms."

My throat goes tight, but I manage to nod, to whisper my thanks.

Silence falls for a beat before she asks, "Do you want to talk about it?"

Me begging him?

Him walking away?

My lungs spasm as I shake my head. "I know you guys are friends and I don't want—"

"Gray and I are *family*, and"—her soft eyes come to mine— "so are you and I."

My eyes burn with tears, and maybe I still should keep it to myself, not bring her into what Gray and I have become...but we're family.

And this is what we do.

Besides resisting further is pointless. If I wanted to hide, wanted to do this alone, I would have ignored the text, gotten a hotel room, and lost myself in my next manuscript.

Instead, I texted Luna, came here, and—

Now I just...let the words come.

"That jerk!" she cries, jumping up to her feet then freezing and smoothing her hand over her belly, as though her outburst startled the baby in her womb.

And maybe it did.

Then she's in motion again, cursing Gray's name, muttering about stupid, stubborn men.

"I should have listened to Marie," I say. "Gotten in front of the story breaking." Then I shake my head, immediately correct before Luna can jump in (she's already spun my direction, her lips parting, protest written into the lines of her face), "*No*, I couldn't have known what would happen, and it was important for me to protect him."

Like he protected me.

Like he's trying to protect me—however misguided his methods—now.

"Exactly." She scowls. "Because you don't owe the world an explanation for your love life."

"No," I agree, "I don't." I sigh. "And story or not, Gray should be here fighting beside me. Otherwise, we're both right back where we started."

Him taking the weight of the world on his shoulders.

Me alone.

"Yes," she says earnestly. "Aiden—" She clamps her lips together, cutting off whatever she was going to say.

But I'm an author.

I understand inference.

Aiden wouldn't have left her.

Not like Gray had left me.

My heart shrivels up in my chest, tears threatening again, and I can't look at her, can't look at the pastries, can't look at the bookshelves that had brought so much joy to me the last time I was over.

Because that's gone now.

He's gone.

"Hey," Luna says, rushing over and taking me into her arms,

squeezing me tight, "these men may be stubborn, but they have good hearts. He'll get his head straight." She pulls back, her mouth curved into a gentle smile. "Then he'll come back, groveling."

I shake my head. "I don't want—"

Apologies? Groveling?

To go back to how we were before?

Gray?

"I don't want..." But I can't form the words, the name.

"Glorious makeup sex and jewelry?" she finishes for me with a waggle of her brows. "Are you sure?"

I freeze.

Because who *wouldn't* want that?

Except...this is a hell of a lot more serious than jewelry and orgasms.

Levity of the previous moment gone, she nudges my foot with her own, her expression going back serious. "It'll be okay. I promise."

"How do you know?" I whisper.

"Because I know Gray. He'll get his head on straight," she says snagging my cinnamon roll and passing it back to me. "I promise. By the end of the day, he'll be groveling."

I nod, feeling a little better.

Maybe it's just because the pastry no longer tastes like sawdust.

Maybe it's because I want *so badly* to believe her—want to believe Gray's and my love won't end up in ashes.

More likely, it's just...

The Power of Luna.

FORTY-FIVE

GRAY

I DON'T WANT TO TALK TO ANY OF THESE FUCKERS.

Nope. No fucking way.

But apparently—for the umpteenth time in the last few days —no one gives a fuck what I want.

Not the media.

Not Faye.

Not my teammates.

I purposefully chose an empty row at the back of the plane when I boarded to avoid interacting with these fuckers, but Smitty ignores my silent signals to leave me alone and drops down next to me, pulling out one of my earbuds.

"Wombats," I growl, snatching it back.

He winces but doesn't go away. "What the fuck are you doing, man?"

"I'm not *doing* anything."

Except trying to listen to my music.

And pretending I didn't seriously fuck up my life.

"If you didn't do anything," he booms—of *fucking course* he does, drawing the attention of every asshole on this plane, "why is my wife telling me that you may have fucked up the best thing you'll ever have?"

My stomach convulses.

Shame ripples through my middle.

Ignoring that, ignoring *him*, I shove my earbud back in, crank up my music.

"Dude—" he booms.

I reach into my pocket, pull out my phone, tapping until I've brought up the album I created only to be used in very special circumstances.

Today is one of those *special* days.

I search through the AI renderings of Smitty (with wombats), trying to find the perfect image as he continues talking loud enough to penetrate my music.

"—you seriously don't want to fuck this shit up. Faye is—"

I don't need him to tell me all that Faye is.

Good. Sweet. Beautiful. In love with me.

Everything I've ever dreamed of wanting.

But fuck if I'll let my shit *ruin* her.

It's already gone too far, she's already been hurt too much.

I *had* to end it.

I grind my teeth together.

Because this shit is why I spent a sleepless night knowing Faye was in my house, in my bed, hurting, and that all I had to do to make it right was go to her and apologize, to take her in my arms and tell her that we'll be all right.

But I couldn't.

Because I can't promise that.

Because my head is fucked up.

Because I know eventually the hurts will be too big to come back from.

It *had* to be now.

Before we got in even deeper.

Smitty reaches for my earbud again.

I hold up my phone, pointing the screen in his direction.

Normally, the sound of terror that comes out of his mouth would have me busting up.

Today I don't laugh, though.

Because I've fucked up the best thing I've ever had.

He snatches my phone out of my hand, jerkily jabbing at the screen and shuddering. "Jesus, delete," he mutters then squeals, eyes going to half-mast as keeps tapping.

Probably deleting all my hard work.

I reach for my cell, but he holds it out of reach.

"Give me my phone," I growl.

"When I have the chance to search for dick pics?" He grins at me. "Never."

"Smitty," I warn. "You know I can just recover the images and torture you with them later, right?"

"No, you can't," he says with a smirk. "Because I deleted them out of the trash too."

"Hey!" I snap.

He tosses my phone into my lap and stands. "I know you're going to be a stubborn asshole and not listen to me. Same as you'll ignore Aiden and anyone else who tries to advise you to pull your goddamned head out of your goddamned ass."

I open my mouth.

"So, I'll leave you to your sulking and save my words for someone who wants to hear them—"

"Impossible," I mutter. "Because no one ever does."

He points his finger at me. "First, rude. Well, no. That's second and third too, rude and *rude*." He bends, his face in mine. "Fourth, don't wait until too long to *un*fuck this."

"Is that a word?"

He straightens, eyes flashing, mouth pressing flat. "Maybe ask the author in your life. Oh wait, you can't." A beat. "Because you fucked it up."

———

Later that night, my phone pings with a notification.

Not from Faye—and I can't lie and say the fucked-up part of me isn't desperate to hear her voice, to read one of her pithy (and well-punctuated) text messages.

It is.

I miss her—so fucking much.

But she hasn't reached out, though the notification is about her.

Still, I should ignore it.

Hell, it would be better for both of us if I canceled it outright.

Yet, even as my fingers descend, preparing to send a message to do exactly that...I can't bring myself to do it.

Instead...

I pay extra for expedited delivery.

FORTY-SIX

FAYE

THE CONTRACTOR FINISHED TAKING DOWN THE WALLS today, and I've spent the last few hours sifting through the remains of my house.

"I don't know, Nana," I murmur, running my hand lightly over the delicate blue bloom of her hydrangeas. "I don't know what I should do."

Luna offered to help, but I wouldn't risk her baby with the smoke and ash and who knows what other kinds of chemicals are still hanging around.

Plus, there are decisions to be made and—

"I think I needed to do this by myself."

"No, you didn't."

I blink, see Luna herself walking through my back yard, along with Bri and Kailey and...Harper.

The latter waves awkwardly. "I know I'm probably intruding" —her eyes slice to the side, toward Luna then back to mine—"but I brought food?"

"And also, Luns insisted," Bri says dryly.

Luna narrows her eyes at her. "Excuse me?"

"You did," Bri says.

An aggrieved sigh though her mouth curves up. "Fine. I did. But Harper works too much and she mentioned she needed some fresh air when we went over to pick up the food." Luna waves a hand around the back yard. "So...fresh air."

"With a side of barbecue," Bri mutters.

"Bri!" Luna exclaims. "You can't say that."

Maybe I should be upset, but I'm not.

Instead...I'm laughing.

And it's...like my ribs are cracking open, my laughter scraping against my grief until I can't tell which is which.

I bend at the waist and grab my middle, tears streaking down my face, my cheeks aching.

"Umm..." I hear and try to pull it together.

"Shh, Bri," Luna hisses.

But it's Harper who moves.

Maybe because my tears of laughter have turned into real tears.

She slips an arm around my shoulders and hugs me tightly.

I hug her back. Me, the shy, formerly distant woman who spends most of her life in front of her computer screen is hugging a woman I'm just starting to know.

But it doesn't feel strange or wrong.

It just...feels nice to be held.

"I'm sorry," Bri says when I finally pull back, dashing a hand over either cheek. "That was..."

"Funny," I murmur, reaching for her hand. "And it's not you. The last few days have been...a lot. Luna is right. I shouldn't have done this alone today."

"Did you find anything?" she asks, her gaze going back to the mess that used to be my house.

I try to put the brightest spin possible on it. "Yeah. I'm super lucky. I did find some stuff."

Just...not what I was hoping for.

Not Nana's recipe book.

And no pictures.

And none of my special editions or the copy of the first book I published.

But also...not Nana's recipes.

I hadn't realized how much hope I was holding out for them until I searched through the kitchen.

"We brought masks and gloves and stuff," Bri says as Kailey digs through her purse and offers me a napkin to wipe my eyes. "I'm really good at finding things."

"She is," Luna says earnestly.

I scrub at my face. "I bet you are," I tell Bri. "But can I have a rain check? I think..." I sigh. "Honestly, I think I've had enough for today. I'd really love to just eat some of Harper's delicious food."

Bri nods quickly.

Kailey moves close.

Harper takes my hand.

But Luna steps right in front of me, studying my face for a long, tense moment.

My pulse speeds...mostly because it's like she can see into my soul—and if that's the case then she knows it's not just the house, the memories, the videos and headlines still circulating the internet.

It's Gray.

Who hasn't gotten his head together.

Who hasn't called.

My throat goes tight. "Please," I whisper.

She sighs. Then touches my cheek before turning toward the others and commanding,

"If Faye wants to eat, then we eat."

———

"Oh, my God!" I gasp a few hours later. "You didn't!"

Luna nods and leans back on the couch in Gray's family room. Yes, it hurts—being here, remembering cuddling with him while watching bad action movies and eating popcorn, but we defaulted to his house because it was close and because, however painful (and likely ill-advised) I stayed in the guest room last night, having to be at my house bright and early to meet with the contractors this morning.

"I did," Luna says of showing up on Aiden's doorstep with a decade old marriage contract. "I was desperate, and not thinking straight—or maybe..." A grin. "*Maybe* my subconscious was operating on *all* cylinders for a change."

"That one," Kailey says. "Because you ended up with Aiden."

Luna's face softens. "Yeah. You're right."

"He's a sweetheart, always coming in and grabbing food for you," Harper says.

"I blame you for my cravings." Luna winks at the chef.

"Happy to take the blame for that one." Harper winks back.

I glance over at Bri, who's smiling...and chowing down on one of the delicious sandwiches Harper made. Then at Kailey, who's nibbling on a cookie, also made by Harper. They both grin at me and shake their heads—and I get exactly what they're silently communicating.

Harper and Luna have set about bringing the entertainment.

Doing their best to distract me, letting me sit back and just exist in the laughter and teasing and fun and the fact that I'm not alone.

Not any longer.

I may not have Gray, but I don't need him.

I'm okay.

Especially with a belly full of delicious food and a couple of glasses of wine. I finished my sandwich, downed a bag of home-made kettle chips with some sort of seasoning called Chicken Salt. It's apparently from Australia and not made of chicken, though it does have salt, along with a lot of other yummy spices. And then I ate two cookies.

Yum.

See? I'm good.

"And what about Leo?" Luna asks.

Harper freezes. "Wh-what?"

I jerk to rigid focus at her tone.

"Are you happy to take the blame for *him* too?" Luna presses.

"I don't know what you mean." It's an edgy response.

Luna fixes Harper with a stare that calls the words for the bullshit they are—it's in her guilty expression, her pink cheeks, the way she's looking toward the door, as though searching for an exit.

Except, Luna drove them all here, so there *is* no exit.

"Luns," Bri warns.

"What?" A shrug. "Leo couldn't keep his eyes off her at the baby shower."

Harper's pink cheeks go bright red.

"And then there's the fact they left together."

Now they go somehow brighter.

"I think we should talk about something else," Kailey says.

I nod. "Maybe Harper doesn't want to talk about it."

"So what?" Luna counters.

Bri groans.

Kailey goes for distraction. "Time for more wine."

"I'm not drinking," Luna says and makes a hurry up gesture at Harper. "So..."

Silence.

Then Harper shakes her head and sighs, glancing at each of us in turn before stopping on Luna and wrinkling her nose. "I know you well enough by now to understand you won't let this go. Not that it matters, anyway. Leo and I...well"—a shrug—"we had a night and then that night was over."

My heart squeezes.

Because there's hurt in Harper's words.

I reach for her hand, something healing in me when she holds it tight in return.

Luna's expression sobers, and she asks softly, "What does that mean?"

"Leo—" She slants a look at Bri, nibbles the corner of her mouth.

"I'm a vault," Bri says, miming zipping and locking her lips. "So's Kailey. And we'll make sure Luna is too."

Harper shakes her head. "You're too young."

"I promise you, I've heard a lot worse than the details of a one-night stand."

"Shit." Harper winces. "I didn't mean—"

"*You* didn't do anything," Bri says, channeling a little bit of Luna with the forceful redirect. "And, truthfully, it's nice being able to think about dates and Luna being nuts—"

"Hey!"

"—and men being jerks," she says without missing a beat. "Than..." She falters here for a moment then lifts her chin, presses on, "Than what was done to me growing up."

Kailey slips her arm around Bri's shoulder as we all fall quiet for a beat.

Then Luns, right on cue, breaks the tension. "Can I tell Aiden?"

"No!" we cry in unison.

She scowls. "But I tell him everything."

"Not this," Bri orders.

A sigh. A considering look at Harper. Then a grudging nod. "Fine. Then I guess I'm a vault too."

That promise secured, Harper's gaze comes to mine.

I lift my hands in surrender. "I don't have anyone to tell. But I'm a vault too."

She laughs softly. Then sighs and says, "It was...well, it was magic. The connection I felt. Our"—another glance at Bri, more pink cheeks—"*time* together. And when I fell asleep with his arms around me, I felt...safe."

I reach for her again, tighten my hand around hers, knowing the worst is yet to come.

"Then I woke up," she whispers. "And he was gone. No note. No text."

Luna scowls, lips parting.

"But he came by the shop just as I was closing," Harper goes on in a hurry.

Luna's mouth snaps closed.

"And then..." She shakes her head, finishes softly. "He made it damned clear that our night together was a mistake."

Her words slice through me.

Because it's heartbreak in a different disguise—instead of broken promises and running from what *might* be...it's an empty bed and magic that turns out not to be real.

"Oh, Harper," Luna whispers, clamping her hand over her chest.

"I thought it was something it wasn't." A shrug. "That's on me."

Luna's expression is thunderous. "No, it's not. He shouldn't have—"

"We were two consenting adults. We made no promises and had a really great night together." Her smile is forced. "I'm going to ask you to leave it at that."

They face off.

But Harper doesn't give in—and eventually (and to my surprise) Luna does.

"Fine," she grumbles. "But I need to make it clear to this room of intelligent women that Leo is being an idiot." Her gaze comes to mine. "Along with Gray, in case that wasn't obvious." Her nose wrinkles. "And all I can say is that this shit better not be spreading."

We're quiet again—and my silence is for a completely different reason this time.

And I know I'm not the only one feeling the same way when Harper says, "You're good people, Luns."

"I just—"

"You are," Bri says firmly.

"Yes," I agree, my heart shattered and still somehow full. Because I'm not alone. "The *best* kind of people."

"The best," Kailey semi-repeats.

Luns sniffs.

Then waves a hand in front of her face. "Ugh! Don't make me cry! Pregnancy hormones are the worst, and I don't want to spend the rest of the afternoon blubbering. Especially wh-when I th-think you guys are the b-best t-too—"

Kailey sniffs, dashes a finger beneath each eye, clearly struggling with pregnancy hormones herself.

Crap.

Now *my* eyes sting—and I don't have the excuse of growing a tiny human.

And Bri and Harper don't look far behind me.

"Want to hear about my idea for my new book?" I blurt in order to save us all from dissolving into tears.

And luckily, it works.

Luna's tears dry up, and she squeals, clapping her hands together. "Tell me everything."

"No, tell *us* everything," Harper says.

I look nervously at Kailey and Bri, but they both seem interested too (and further from tears)...so, I do.

And then we talk about other things—TV shows and books and food and...everything and nothing.

But eventually, Luna starts to wane and Bri has homework to do and Kailey has work to complete and Harper needs to go to bed because she has to get up early in the morning for a big event she's cooking for tomorrow.

I walk them to the door.

"Are you sure you don't want to come back with us?" Luna asks.

"I'm sure." I give her a hug. "I have another meeting with the contractors early tomorrow morning. No sense in me getting a ride there only to have to come right back."

"You'll call if you change your mind?"

I nod.

She fixes me in place with a glare. "And you won't go searching again without backup?"

My heart squeezes. "I won't."

Her eyes narrow. "Promise?"

"I don't want the wrath of Luna Black neé Maybelle now, do I?"

She pats me on the arm and smiles. "You sure don't." Then she starts to turn away, pauses. "It looks like Gray's got a couple of packages here."

"I'll grab it," Bri says when Luna starts to bend as though to pick the boxes up. "But they're not for Gray." She squints at the label. "They're for Faye."

I try to remember what I've ordered.

But truthfully, I've had to replace so much it could be anything.

"Thanks," I tell Bri as she passes them over.

"Oh!" Luna says as I set the packages in the house, just inside the door. "Don't forget your phone."

Frowning, I accept it from her.

"It must have fallen out of your pocket," she says, hugging me one more time before stepping back. Something flickers through her face I can't read, something that almost looks like guilt, but then the others are moving in and we're exchanging goodbyes and then I'm waving as I watch them drive away.

I step back into the house, see the boxes...open the first one.

Then freeze, right there in the hall, every cell in my body in agony.

It's a shadow box and within, professionally framed...

Is the first book I ever wrote.

Dolphyn's Advenchure

Preschool me couldn't really spell either, but even the cuteness of that doesn't distract me from the pain of knowing that Gray loves me enough to do this for me...

But that he doesn't love me enough to stay.

I hold the frame close and whisper,

"I hate you, Gray Roberts."

FORTY-SEVEN

GRAY

"YOU'RE NOT HERE," I GROAN, GRIPPING THE EDGE OF my hotel room door, preparing to slam it shut.

"I'm here. Suck it up."

Then I'm being shoved back and Leo's striding into my room, bottles of beer clanking together as he sets them on the dresser, dropping the box of pizza beside them.

"What are you doing?"

He toes off his shoes, snags a slice and a beer then drops back onto the bed. "You've pissed off Smitty—congratulations on that, by the way. That might have been the first quiet flight we've had since he was traded to the team."

I scowl, but since Leo seems to be settling in for the long haul, let the door slam shut.

Then, because it's there—and because I skipped the team dinner Smitty organized—I walk over to the pizza and beer and help myself.

Leo doesn't speak as I eat a slice. Then two more.

As I drink a beer. Then two more.

Only after I've finished does he ask, "You sufficiently satiated now to not bite my head off?"

I glare at him.

He just grins, helps himself to more food and drink.

I eat another slice, drink another beer.

"Am I turning on *Parking Wars*?" he asks. "Or are you?"

"What the fuck are you talking about?"

"I'm here with your dumb ass instead of bingeing crappy TV in my room so the least you can do is let me watch my favorite hotel show."

"You have a hotel show?"

He snags the last slice of pizza. "What? You don't?"

"I usually just watch shit on my phone," I mutter as he picks up the remote, feeling overly full and a little buzzed and far less edgy as he turns on the TV.

"Lame. Middle of the night cable TV has some serious gems."

"Like *Parking Wars*?" I ask as he pulls up the guide, inputs the channel...and then I'm lying in bed next to my teammate, watching people get parking tickets.

"Why is this entertaining?"

"It's Philly," he says by way of explanation.

And I guess, after having played *against* Philly, it is.

"So," he says several episodes later, "you want to talk about it?"

I go stiff. "Leo," I warn. "I already got this shit from Smitty. I don't need to hear it from you."

"You going to fix it?"

I think of the hurt in Faye's eyes as I walked away and pain slices through me, so intense that when I look down, I expect to see my intestines spilling out onto the bed.

Instead, I appear whole—but that's the biggest lie I've ever told.

Fuck, I miss her with every breath, every heartbeat. I want to call her, beg her for another chance...

But then I think of all the ways I fucked up.

I think of her face when she heard her book was pulled.

I think of those goddamned headlines.

I think—

"I'm thinking maybe it's better I *don't* fix it."

"That mean you won't care if I ask Faye out?"

I move before I realize, clamping my hand around his throat and slamming him back into the headboard. "What the fuck, Leo?"

He just smirks. "I'm guessing that's a no."

"Fuck you," I snap, releasing him with a shove.

"If you don't claim her, someone else will," he rightfully points out.

That doesn't make my rage at the thought of him touching my Faye, talking to her, *touching* her go away, though.

"Relax," he says when I keep scowling at him, "I prefer blondes."

I'm still seeing red. *My* Red. But his words pull me together enough that I remember the caterer, Harper.

Who's blonde.

Right.

"Oh," I mutter.

"Exactly," he says, still smirking, totally nonplussed that I drank most of his beer, ate most of his pizza, then tried to strangle him. "*Oh.*"

I grind my teeth together, focus on the TV.

"Look, man. I don't presume to know what the hell happened between you two or what you need to do to fix it or honestly, even if you *should* fix it, considering the media storm around you, but I'm thinking the way you reacted means that you and Faye aren't done."

I open my mouth.

Close it.

Because what the fuck am I going to say?

He's right?

He is.

And he isn't.

The thought of Faye with someone else is unfathomable. No, it's *infuriating*. It makes me want to rip the TV from the wall, flip the bed, throw the lamp, to do a complete rockstar trashing of this room...and then to get on the ice tomorrow and make every single asshole on the other team pay.

And yet, the thought of being *with* her, of dragging her further into this mess, repeating the same mistakes...hurting her again and again...

"I don't know what the fuck I'm doing," I admit, even as the words burn like acid coming off my tongue.

Leo is quiet for a long moment before he sighs. "Then I guess you have two weeks to get your head together. But man," he adds as he walks to the door, his footsteps on the carpet as heavy as my heart, "think about what kind of decisions *she* can make in two weeks...and whether she'll even want you in her life by then."

Then I'm alone again.

Only it's the last thing I want.

———

"Fuck!" I hiss as the stick comes across my hands, sending pain radiating up my arms and the puck squirting away.

Not for the first time tonight.

If I'm being truthful, I've been fucking useless.

Not a captain.

Not a player the other guys look up to, bringing energy they strive to match.

A fuck up.

Tonight.

No.

For the last week.

Gritting my teeth, I shove everything out of my head except for trying to recover the puck. I skate hard, driving into the fucker who stole it from me, taking it back. I don't try to hold on to it long, instead shoveling it over to Leo, knowing his head isn't fucked up—or at least his head isn't fucked up enough to screw with his game.

He skates it into the zone and I don't join the rush.

Instead, I get my ass off the ice and let someone better take my place.

Which is pretty much anyone else on the bench.

Smitty eyes me as I sink down, his expression screaming disappointment. But it's not stronger than the shame that's been eating me alive.

The headlines on repeat in my head.

Proof of the hurt I caused.

Broken promises...

And history repeating itself.

Smitty sighs but doesn't comment. Just shakes his head and hops over the boards, taking his next shift and doing it a fuck of a lot better than I did out there.

Leo passes the puck over to Aiden, who drops it back to Sawyer at the point.

The crack of his stick hitting the ice is loud and the shot tears through the air, ricocheting off pads and players and eventually, Aiden's stick in front of the net, redirecting it in one final fuck you to the goalie on the other team, who's been struggling to track it through the chaos.

It sails into the net, slipping between pad and glove, and the red light goes on.

And the Grizzlies are up by a goal.

And the hometown crowd boos.

And still...I can't push down the shame.

Or the knowledge that I've ruined the best thing that's ever happened to me.

———

It's not until we're in Boston, my sorry ass in my hotel room trying to sleep on the mattress that feels lumpy (but isn't), attempting to get comfortable on the pillow that feels too thick (but isn't), wanting to watch *Parking Wars* because at least *that'll* distract me (but it's not on TV—or I can't find it, anyway) that I finally turn on my cell.

I've kept it off—not wanting to be tempted…

And it's not like Faye has texted *me*.

Why would she?

I broke up with her.

But now, after my phone boots up, it's her name that pops up on the screen.

Heart twisting, fingers shaking, I tap at the notification.

> FAYE: I've moved my stuff out and left your key on the counter.

Everything in me seizes, pain rippling through my insides.

I mean…what did I expect?

But also—

"Fuck," I hiss, sitting up straight and shoving a hand through my hair, clutching at the locks.

This is what I said I wanted—or if it's not what I *wanted* then it's what I *had* to do. Because it's what's best for Faye.

Sighing, I toss my phone aside.

Don't respond.

Let her move on.

Don't drag her back into the bullshit, that's my fucked-up ability to ruin good things, that's—

Buzz. Buzz.

> FAYE: Thank you for being so kind.

Strands of silken red hair spread on my pillow.

Banana bread crumbs on her cheek.

Her beautiful laugh tinkling through the air.

> FAYE: I've decided to not rebuild. It's...
> nothing's left for me there. I just wanted you to
> know.

My lungs freeze, not working for so long that my vision starts to go hazy, black intruding on the edges.

It was bad enough Smitty was giving me shit and Aiden was looking at me like I was an idiot and Leo was telling me he might ask Faye out because I need to be prepared for some other guy to see how great she is and snap her up.

But...

Not being able to make sure she's okay just next door, not being able to make sure that man is treating her right...

Not being able to be certain she's happy and safe and secure...

"Fuck," I whisper, throat tight, eyes burning, stomach tying itself into knots. The silence of the room is overbearing, stifling... but not as stifling as my thoughts.

I can't allow her to move.

I can't lose her completely.

But...I can't keep her either.

Because if I do—

I close my eyes as pain slices through me, stealing my breath... but not taking the most agonizing thought of all—

That it doesn't matter what I want...

I've already lost her.

FORTY-EIGHT

FAYE

MY PHONE RINGS, AND THOUGH I'VE GOTTEN BETTER about stifling the blip of hope—and subsequent lash of pain—that rises each and every time a call comes through...

It's still there.

"It'll get better soon," I whisper, even though I know that's a lie. Then I take a breath, and seeing Luna's name on the screen, I swipe to answer the call.

But I barely get my "Hello?" out before she's shouting.

"Turn on your TV. Now!"

"Wh-what?"

"Faye. Turn on any cable network. Right *fucking* now."

I don't ask why, just reach for the remote...which is on Gray's nightstand.

It was unwise to spend another night at his house. I hadn't made it to the guest room. Instead, I pulled on my Grizzlies jersey went to *his* room, and—

Slept with his name between my shoulder blades.

One more night with him.

With his scent all around me, pretending the jersey was his

big, strong body cuddling me close. Convincing myself I tried hard to fight for him, that I did all I could, that I can't keep pushing when I'm not wanted.

All the while, thinking this last week has been the biggest mistake of my life.

Giving up.

Letting him walk away.

Praying for him to come back when I could just get on a plane and *make* him see our love is too important to let go of.

Because, God, I *miss* him.

The way his beard catches on the strands of my hair, how his spice fills my nose and the way his lips move on mine, his hard body and soft voice...

Which is coming from the speakers of the television.

Gasping, I turn up the volume.

"...I got in the habit of not discussing my personal life," Gray says and my heart hurts at how tired he looks, how uncomfortable. "It's because of my reticence to trust the media that Faye refrained from sharing our relationship with the world, and it's because of me that her job is being threatened."

I hold my breath.

"And what do you say to critics who say her job is..."

He sits back and crosses his arms, brows lifting. "I'll wait while you attempt to find a word that properly denigrates the beautiful stories that my Faye brings into the world."

My heart starts pounding.

The interviewer opens her mouth, closes it. Then lifts her chin. "Some would say it's filth."

"And yet, I got no pushback about being naked in the body issue of a famous sports magazine and TV shows that are filled with sex and violence get national awards." He raises his eyebrows. "But a love story where the main characters fall in love and find enjoyment in every part of that is somehow... *filth?*"

"Oh, he's good," Luna says.

I jerk, not having realized that I still have my phone pressed to my ear, that she's still on the line.

But I can't hang up.

Not when I'm soaking in every word.

"And have you *enjoyed* being her inspiration?"

"God, where'd they find this bitch?" Luna mutters.

"If anyone finds similarities between me and the heroes that Faye writes then all I can say is that I'd be honored to have a modicum of what makes them so special to her readers." A self-deprecating chuckle. "Though, before people get too carried away, I'd remind them that imagination is a thing...and that I don't have the secret ability to turn into a wolf." He winks at the camera.

Pride bubbles up in my throat.

"Fuck yeah," Luna whispers.

"Let's transition to the topic of your wife," the interviewer says. "Because I do believe you're still married—something I can't imagine the Grizzlies organization is happy about, considering you're carrying on this blatant affair."

Gray's lips press flat. Then he sighs. "As you know, my soon-to-be-ex-wife and I have a long and complicated past, but in the spirit of honesty, I'll share that the divorce papers are signed and filed, and all that's left before the both of us can officially move on is for a judge to sign off on our agreement." He smiles pointedly. "In fact, she recently shared with me the exciting news of her engagement."

"Oh wow, and that doesn't bring up any hard feelings for you?"

"No," he says. "Because I've fallen in love with a strong, smart, resilient woman who's shown me more of the world than I ever thought possible."

"Like what?"

He looks at the camera, and my breath catches because it's like he's right here in the room with me, staring into my eyes, murmuring. "Like how to make banana bread."

There's a pause, a *long* pause.

Then, "Banana bread?"

"Yup." He stands, tugging off his microphone, setting it carefully in the chair. "Now, if you'll excuse me, I have a flight to catch."

"Luna?" I whisper.

"I think he's got his head on straight," she says, pride in every word.

"I...I'm not sure about that. I mean what if he was just doing that to protect me?"

"He was."

I gasp. Because that didn't come through the phone. It came from—

"Gr-Gray," I stutter, desperately trying to process the fact that he was just on TV and now he's standing in the doorway of his bedroom. "I—"

"But it wasn't *just* to protect you, baby. It's because you deserve a man to fight for you, to take on the world for you, to make it clear to every asshole out there that the love we have is the most important thing in my universe and I will never— fucking *never*—be so much of a coward as to walk away from it again."

He's reached the bed now and gently slips my phone from my hand, ending the call and tossing it on the nightstand.

"I was scared," he whispers. "Of all I feel and all the ways it can go wrong, and...I was a fucking idiot."

My breath catches. "I was scared too," I tell him. "And I didn't fight either. I just kept thinking...you're you and I'm me and maybe that's why we couldn't work out..." The rest of my words die in my throat at the furious look on his face.

He leans over me, his hot green eyes holding mine, and he cups my jaw in his hands. "You're not special because you love me, Red. You're special because you're *you.*"

"I—"

"You're the strongest, smartest, most resilient woman I've ever known"—his mouth kicks up—"and I think you know how big that is because I know a lot of smart, strong women."

Luna.

Kailey.

Harper.

Bri.

Me.

I close my eyes against the rush of emotions, so many, so fast it's like regaining feeling in a limb, painful and tingling and overwhelming as the relief and love and fear and hope all battle to take over.

Before I can give voice to any of them, he rasps, "Please don't leave."

"I—"

It's rough and desperate and steals my breath—or maybe that's his kiss as his mouth drops to mine and he takes advantage of my parted lips to slip his tongue inside.

As I sink into his touch I have a fleeting thought—

Maybe the bright, brilliant love I've given my heroines...is something I can have too.

Then I'm not thinking about how miserable the last week has been or how this is likely a really vivid dream or maybe that I've gone insane and slipped into a fantasy because *how can he possibly be here?* Instead, I'm thinking about how good it feels for his big body to be pressing mine back into the mattress and how the hot, slick darts of his tongue set me aflame.

Need burns through me, lips to between my legs, fires in each and every one of my nerves.

It's desperate, trying to suck every bit of sensation out of me —like Gray is trying to turn me into a ball of feeling, of yearning, of *craving.*

But I was already there even before his mouth hit mine.

And when he levers up, yanks the blankets aside, and freezes, my craving hits a breaking point.

If this is a fantasy, *I* want to be the one in charge.

I shove at his chest and he rolls to the side, sprawling on the mattress as I clamber on top of him. I don't take a moment to enjoy the view, just bend and fuse our mouths together.

His hands grip my hips, holding me tightly against him, and it's natural to rock, to ride the hard ridge of his erection.

But there are too many layers between us.

Groaning, I tear my lips from his, reaching for his shirt, yanking it out of his slacks.

A few buttons rip off, hit the floor with little *plinks*, but I'm too busy working at the button on his pants, struggling with the zipper. I shove at the waistband of his slacks and he helps me, lifting his hips, dragging them down.

Along with his underwear.

"Thank God," I whisper as his cock springs free, wrapping my hand around it and desperate to taste him, I bend, sucking him deep, stroking fast.

Too fast.

Too frantic.

But he's here and he's hard and I'm...so damned needy.

His hands go to my armpits and he yanks me up.

I protest when I lose the hard length of him, but I get something better—Gray angling me so he can drag *my* underwear down. He tosses it to the side, settles me over him again.

"No," he says when I reach for the bottom of the jersey, intending to remove it, his gorgeous green eyes blazing into mine, "leave it."

I shiver.

But I leave it.

Then I'm wrapping my hand around him again, shifting forward.

The head of his cock rubs against my clit and I shudder, my orgasm already shockingly close.

"Inside," he rasps as I rock again, rubbing at him, the reverberations of sensation through my body so damned good I don't want to stop.

Only, I want him inside *more*.

So, I shift, angle him and—

"Fuck," Gray groans, head dropping back, the tendons on his neck standing out in sharp relief, his hands gripping my hips so tightly I may end up with bruises.

And I don't fucking care.

Because he's inside me, deep, filling me up.

I rock again, and it's even better with his cock stretching me, his hardness grinding against all the right places.

"Faster," he grunts, hands encouraging me.

And yeah, faster is good.

It's *great*.

And when he starts rocking against me in turn, matching my rhythm, keeping me flush against him as he reaches between our bodies to tease my clit—

"Gray!" I cry.

"That's it," he says, sweat on his brow, his hands clenching tight, his cock so *damned* hard inside me. "Come for me, Red. I'm close, baby. I need you to—"

I explode, his name on my lips, my rhythm going jerky, my pussy—

Clamping tightly around him.

He groans, bucking against me, drawing out my pleasure, and...

Finding his own, his gorgeous face as he comes apart the most beautiful thing I've ever seen.

Or maybe...

Maybe that's his face when I collapse on top of him and he rolls us both to the side, settling his hand on my jaw.

Settling *me*.

Because I know it's not a fantasy.

I know it's not a dream.

I know it's just *him*.

And I'm so not letting him go.

FORTY-NINE

GRAY

"HOW ARE YOU HERE?" SHE WHISPERS.

My lungs are still working hard and though my cock is extremely happy—*extremely*—that wasn't exactly how I imagined my apology tour to go.

I expected groveling.

A lot of groveling.

Not an orgasm that threatened to tear me in two.

"Fuck, Red," I murmur, smoothing back her hair and settling my forehead against hers. "I'm so damned sorry. I was triggered and didn't stop to think. I promised you—I fucking *promised* I wouldn't hurt you again and then I panicked and did the same shit. I know that you can't possibly believe me, but I'm going to make sure it doesn't happen again. I've already gotten a referral for a therapist. I'm going to figure out this crap in my head so it never affects you again."

Her expression...I hate that I can't read it.

"The interview..." she says long moments later. "Why did you really do it?"

I straighten, cup her jaw. "Baby, I fucked up."

"Yes, you did." That has surprised laughter bubbling up in my chest, but she keeps talking before I can. "But you didn't have to do that. I know you hate—"

"I love you more than any headline."

She sucks in a breath.

"I'm done running scared, baby. You're the most important thing in my world and I don't care who knows it."

"But Courtney—"

"Isn't you." I capture her hand, press it to my chest. "You're my heart, Red. I love you and they can make a million videos about us and I won't care so long as you're here."

Her lips tremble. "I should have—"

"None is this your fault," I say firmly.

"But I didn't fight for us."

"Neither did I," I point out. "We hit a speed bump and I took off."

"Because you have trauma. But I don't have that excuse and I still didn't call or text." She scowls. "I just spent a week being miserable and sad and pathetic."

"I hate that you were sad," I murmur, brushing my lips over her forehead. "But you *did* text, baby. It's what finally made me get my head out of my ass."

She frowns. "Um..."

"And it helped me realize how much of an idiot I was being. The thought of losing you forever, of you not being next door—" I cup her face in both of my hands. "It snapped me out of my shit. I can't lose you, Faye." My voice breaks. "I *won't* lose you."

I won't repeat past mistakes.

Won't allow what happened to Courtney happen to Faye.

I *won't*.

"I'm so glad you feel that way, honey," she says, covering my hands with her own. "But I need you to know that I get I made a mistake too. That I should have—*wait*." She frowns, fingers tightening on mine. "Why wouldn't I be next door?"

"What do you mean? *You* told me that, baby."

The furrow between her brows deepens. "I haven't talked to you since that night last week. Something I've been beating myself up for. I shouldn't have just—"

"Okay, so we didn't talk, but you texted." I shrug. "Yeah, I was an asshole who didn't text back, but that's mostly because I was arranging the interview with the PR team and talking with Coach so I could come back and see you." My mouth hitches up. "Of course, I thought I'd have to track you down at Luna's or Kailey's place and beg them to let me see you. I didn't expect to find you in my bed, in my jersey—"

My cock twitches.

Something she feels, if the way she rocks against me is any indication. "But I *didn't* text you, Gray. I spent the week moping and hating that I wasn't strong enough to reach out."

"First, I think I've made it clear that you're strong, Red, and I don't want to hear you say differently."

She opens her mouth, protest in her eyes.

"I'll argue with you about that later," I say cutting off what is sure to be an objection about my *orders*.

Right now, I need to figure something else out.

"You *didn't* text?"

Guilt drifting across her face as she shakes her head.

"Then"—I scoop my pants off the floor, rifle around the pockets for my phone—"what is this?"

She stares at the screen for a long moment then her eyes come back to mine. "I didn't send these."

"Who—"

"Oh, my God!" She sits up so quickly, the sheet falls to her middle, and since the jersey is rucked up, I'm seriously distracted by that plump pink cunt of hers.

I haven't gotten to spend enough time with it.

I need to make it pinker. Wetter.

Thoughts that admittedly sidetrack me from her next words.

Or *word*, rather.

"Luna!" she exclaims sharply, tossing the sheet back.

I shake myself. Focus. "What about Luna?"

"She had my phone last night, and when she gave it back, I thought she looked weird. Now I realize it's because she looked *guilty!*" She snatches her phone off the nightstand, starts jabbing at the screen.

"Maybe you should wait until you calm down—"

She jabs a finger in my direction, and I don't ever think I've seen that particular expression on her face.

And yeah, I know I haven't known her all that long.

I just...

I thought I'd seen her temper before.

Obviously, I haven't seen anything yet.

"Don't," she snaps then focuses back on her cell, prods the screen until I hear the call ringing on speaker phone.

"All work out?" Luna says without a lick of shame.

"What. The. *Actual.* Fuck. Luns?!"

"What's the matter?"

Faye lurches out of bed, starts pacing. "What do you mean *what's the matter? You* texted Gray and lied to him about me moving!"

"You told me you were considering it—"

"I also said I could never leave Nana's house."

The knot in my stomach that's been there from the moment I read the texts loosens.

"I said I had decisions to make!" Faye throws up a hand. "But you knew I had no intention of leaving when you texted Gray—"

"Luna," I say as I push up out of bed. "She'll call you back."

Faye scowls but I don't miss that below her anger is hurt.

She's come so far from being alone...and now Luna's done more than meddle.

She's tried to rewrite our story—hasn't allowed Faye to be the author of her own life.

I love Luna, appreciate her giving me the mental slap I needed to come back and fix this. But she and I will be having a talk.

Because I won't allow anyone—not me, not our friends, not our family—to hurt Faye, not ever again.

"Bye." I snag the phone from Faye's hand, hit the button to disconnect the call.

It immediately starts to ring again.

I shut it off.

Do the same for my own.

Because Faye and I have a future to build.

Without exes or interfering family or viral videos.

Just love and touch and...

And maybe another batch of banana bread.

FIFTY

FAYE

"HEY, RED?" HE ASKS A LONG WHILE LATER.

After my aborted call to Luna, Gray had distracted me, and yeah...

Turns out makeup sex is pretty great.

As was the warmth in his eyes when he propped up the shadow box with my first book near the window in his kitchen.

"Because this is where the dream began," he told me quietly.

Then because neither of us had slept the night before—Gray because he was in an uncomfortable middle seat on the only flight he could get on such short notice, me because I was reeling from what I thought I'd lost—we'd lazed on the couch, action movies playing in the background as we napped the day away.

Now, our bellies have awakened, so dinner is in the oven and I'm doing what I do best— aside from writing, that is.

Baking.

"Yeah?" I ask, mashing the bananas.

"Thanks for not giving up on me."

My heart pulses and I turn, weaving my free hand into his hair. "Promise to not give up on me back?"

"Never again, Red." He brushes his lips over the sensitive spot behind my ear, murmurs, "You're stuck with me."

I lean more heavily against him, loving the scent of him in my nose, the feel of his body pressed to mine. "Sounds like the perfect place to be."

We stand there in peaceful silence until the timer goes. Then he pulls away, going to the oven to pull out the tray of lasagna. At the same time, my phone, which I only turned back on a few minutes ago, rings.

Since it's Luna, I pick up the call. "How dare you—?"

"Hush," she says.

My formerly spent temper begins to boil up.

"Hush?" I ask. "*Hush?*"

"Yup." Her tone is completely nonplussed. "Both of you were about to throw away the best thing you've ever had, so yes, *hush*. I did what I had to do."

I blink.

Stare at my phone, expecting to hear something else. Like an apology.

Then—when I don't—I blink again.

"Luna," I begin. "You crossed a lot of lines."

"Yup," she says proudly. "I sure did. And I'd do it again. Because I love you, and you're my family, and so is Gray, and I do what I have to do for my family."

I still, fingers tightening around the fork I've been smashing the bananas with, her words rushing through me with all the force of a tsunami.

I'm not alone.

I won't *ever* be alone again.

My throat tightens, eyes beginning to well up.

"Dammit, Luns," I whisper, blinking rapidly.

"You both deserve to be happy," she says, her tone going gentle.

God, I really love this woman.

I sniff.

She sniffs.

"Luna," I begin, temper gone, love for her welling up. "I need you to know I—"

"Nope," she snaps, cutting me off before I can tell her what she means to me. "No sappy stuff or you'll face the wrath of pregnant woman tears."

I'm smiling.

When a second ago, I wanted to cry, and thirty seconds before that, I wanted to throttle her.

Such is the power of Luna.

Shaking my head at the tiny tornado that is my friend—no, my *family*—I remind her, "I'm still mad at you."

"You'll get over it," she says flippantly. "Is Gray flying out in the morning?"

"Yeah." He needs to rejoin the team on the road trip.

"Right. Enjoy him"—her voice turns mischievous—"I'll let you yell at me again later."

Laughter bubbles up in my chest. "Deal." Then before she can hang up, I say, "Luns?"

"Yeah, honey?"

"Thanks."

"Anytime."

I grin, somehow unsurprised at the rapid turn of events, thus just shake my head as I hang up.

Because I know she means exactly that.

———

"Babe," Gray calls not much later.

"Yeah?" I say distractedly as I serve up lasagna.

"Yeah, want me to open this box for you?"

"Box?" I frown.

"The big one by the door."

Oh, right. The box Bri brought in for me last night—or the one I hadn't gotten around to opening yet, anyway.

"Did you do something else exceptionally sweet that's going to make me cry and curse your name again?"

"No."

But the way he says that sounds very much like...yes.

I grin.

Such a big, tough hockey player...and such a soft, soft heart.

"You can open it for me, honey," I say, thinking he probably wants to give me whatever he bought me in person now that we've made up. "But then food's ready, so let's eat."

"Got it."

I hear cardboard tearing.

Then a strange hiss.

"Gray?" I call as I set down the spatula.

Because that sounds...*not right.*

The hiss grows louder and I hurry into the other room—

Pop!

I blink.

Then do it again.

Hot pink paint has splattered all over Gray and the door and the floor and...

Oh, my God.

There's glitter too.

Clinging to the paint, coating him practically head to toe.

"What the fuck?" he growls, reaching into the box and pulling out a piece of paper.

One that has him going still as he reads it.

"What is it?" I ask quietly.

"Courtney sent this." A beat. "For you."

I bite my lip.

Because...seriously?

Leaking manuscripts and planting stories and trying to break down front doors...and *glitter bombs that don't even hit their intended target?*

He scowls. "Don't you laugh."

"I—"

I try not to.

I really do.

But pretty soon my amusement is bubbling up in my chest, my throat, escaping off the tip of my tongue. "I-I'll just g-get some p-paper t-towels," I force out through my giggles. It's not funny—except it is. A big, sexy hockey player covered in neon pink paint and gold glitter and...

After everything she's done, is this really all Courtney can dish out?

I turn for the kitchen.

"Faye," he growls.

"Be right back," I chirp, still laughing.

A hand lands on my arm.

A *paint-covered* hand.

"Gray!" I screech as he yanks me into his arms.

But then he's kissing me.

And *then* I'm not laughing.

Because he's pulling off my clothes and he's using his mouth for things that have absolutely nothing to do with laughter and all to do with pleasure.

And love.

And the understanding that it's time for us to move forward.

Together.

Later—*much* later—the rug in the entryway a complete and total loss, our naked—and paint-covered—bodies still intertwined, I call his name.

He trails his fingers through a splotch of paint on my side, making even more of a mess—though I know he's looking forward to washing it off in the shower just as much as I am—and asks, "What is it, Red?"

I snuggle closer. "I just think this begs the question...what the hell are we going to do about Courtney?"

His eyes come to mine.

And instead of the anger I expect, there's plotting.

And humor.

And suddenly I understand that in finding myself amongst the ashes and glitter, burned loaves of banana bread and heart-break, I've also found a world that's messy and imperfect and...so much more beautiful than I ever could have imagined.

And better yet?

I have a man who proves *exactly* that with his next words.

"We're going to sic Luna on her."

I freeze.

Then smile wide.

Because that's the most perfect idea I've ever heard.

Epilogue

Gray, One Month Later

I slip out into the garage and do what I've been doing every single night I've been home since construction began in earnest on Faye's house.

Go through the boxes of debris they've cleared out.

Hoping to find more of her belongings.

Most of the boxes yield nothing aside from ashes, but tonight I get lucky.

Really lucky.

Carefully, I brush off the splinters and ash, extracting a binder from the box.

The cover is charred, almost unreadable.

Except for four letters that have my heart in my throat.

I.P.E. And S.

The spine makes an ominous creaking sound as I carefully open it.

Inside, the handwriting is old and looping, made in the cursive my generation never managed to fully master.

To my Faye.

From my heart to your stomach.
Love,
Nana

I close my eyes for a long moment, trying to find calm, to steady my shaking hands.

Then, when I've got my shit together, I carefully turn the pages.

Mom's Buttermilk Biscuits

Verna's Sugar Cookies with Salted Caramel Filling

Easy Chicken Pot Pie

Homemade Fudge Cake with Double Chocolate Frosting

Dad's Beef Stew

Faye's Stupendous Chocolate Soufflé

And...

Nana's World-Famous (at least to her) Banana Bread

"Fuck," I whisper again, carefully closing the binder. It must have once been blue, but the outside and edges of the papers within are charred and coated in black ash. Combined with the texture of that scorched fabric, it was easy to assume it was just another block of melted plastic.

But it's not.

It's probably the most valuable thing in Faye's house.

I start to stand.

But I don't get the chance.

"You found it," Faye whispers, kneeling at my side, tears streaming down her cheeks as she carefully opens the cover, thumbs through the pages, taking her time, not protesting when I draw her into my lap, when I wrap my arms around her middle.

She reaches the end of the book then just as carefully closes it, holding it gently to her chest before she spins to face me.

Her eyes blaze with emotion as she whispers, "Thank you."

I touch her cheek. "You don't need to thank me, Red."

A nod to the mess of boxes I've slowly been making my way through. "I kind of think I do."

God, I love her. "Then thank me by kissing me."

Her smile is warm and sweet and her kiss is equally so, but as is often the case with Faye, I find my control eroding, my need taking over.

Unfortunately, just as I start to pull her more firmly into my arms in preparation of standing, I hear a familiar pounding on the front door.

Faye looks at me.

I look at her.

Then I sigh and stand, extending a hand to help her to her feet.

My divorce was finalized today—the judge signing off on the agreement—so it's no surprise Courtney isn't happy.

She's shown up a half-dozen times over the last month—despite Luna having been activated to work her magic.

I never thought I'd find someone to match Luna's tenacity.

But Courtney is proving to be just as stubborn.

I just...well, it's not that I don't care. I still feel a sliver of guilt as I walk across my new rug in the entryway, pull open the front door Faye and I repainted a deep brown after I returned from the second leg of the team's road trip last month.

It's just...the doorbell no longer has me fighting the urge to run.

To fix.

To hide.

No shame. No pretending I was completely innocent. And no taking it all on my shoulders.

Faye's doing.

And mine.

And therapy.

Working through acknowledging and being a grownup and trying to build healthy habits.

I hate it—feeling raw and vulnerable and still not completely free of the past and its guilt, of my memories and all my regrets...

But it's also like I'm finally taking full breaths again.

Progress, not perfection.

And lots of banana bread.

Plus it helps that the headlines have become more like—

From Scandal to Sweethearts: Grizzlies Captain and Local Author Prove True Love's No Fiction

Grizzlies' Captain Credits 'The Woman Who Made Me Brave' for Midseason Comeback

The Love Story That Changed the Conversation: How One Romance Novel Sparked a Genre Reckoning

And best of all...

#BananaBreadGoals Trends Again After Faye Sullivan's Cookbook Reveal

"We have bananas, right?" I ask as I see Courtney glaring at us through the side pane of the front door.

"Always," Faye says.

"Up for some baking after this shit is done?"

It's nearly midnight and Faye has spent the last few weeks dealing with her own heavy pile of the past—permits and insurance, managing the rebuilding, her own therapy appointments, dealing with her publisher and own requests for interviews, and working on her revisions, their deadline rapidly approaching now that her book is back on the publication schedule.

She's exhausted—I know she has to be.

But she just takes my hand, lifts on tiptoe, and presses her lips to my jaw. "Of course." Her mouth curves. "We have to try out Nana's recipe."

"I love you," I murmur.

"Damn right you do," she tosses back with a wink.

Which means that when I open the door to confront Courtney, I'm laughing.

"You're a real bastard, you know that, right?" she snaps.

I lean against the doorframe, lift my eyebrows in question, chuckles still emerging from my throat as I ask, "Why am I an asshole this time?"

"You know exactly why!" she snaps. "Winston is angry at me and he may not go through with the wedding."

I smirk. "I think you mean your aging fiancée is finally aware of your crap."

"I *mean* that Winston said if I don't smooth things over with you and get you to recall those bulldogs who are fucking with his businesses then he's going to leave me."

I keep my face neutral.

But inside I'm putting the pieces together.

A year ago, Luna inherited a huge chunk of her family's company...and used that leverage to get into business with a pair of powerful businessmen, Jean-Michel Dubois and Jace Henderson.

Apparently she's been using her leverage with them on my behalf.

I guess that's what she meant about stepping things up.

I fight to keep the satisfied smirk off my face. "Why should I care about *Winston's* business?"

"Because if I don't have Winston then I'll have to come back here." She pauses and I wait for her to say more, to expand on the threat.

She doesn't.

So, I shrug, say, "It's not like that stopped you before."

"*Gray*," she snaps.

I just stare at her and wait.

"Ugh!" She stomps her foot. "You want me to promise to go away and never come back? Fine. I promise. Now call off your dogs."

More staring. More waiting.

Just to give her a bit of the torture she gave me.

"You keep that promise—*and* stop talking about Faye and me to the media—"

She winces, which is all the confirmation I needed.

She planted the stories.

Fucking hell.

But instinct tells me to ask, "The chapter too?"

"I don't know what you're talking about," she says haughtily.

"Faye?" I call.

"Yeah, honey?"

"Will you ask Luna to ask Jean-Michel if lying to the press about us and your book is defamation?"

"I heard you two talking about it!" Courtney snaps. "It wasn't a lie to say you inspired her."

I lift my brows.

She scowls. "Okay, fine," she snaps. "I may have...spent some time in your back yard and..." Her eyes drift away and she coughs. "...taken pictures of a chapter or two—"

Faye gasps.

"You left your laptop on the table," Courtney says in a rush. "And I needed something to read."

My *fucking* ex.

I resist the urge to throttle her and turn to Faye, the only one who matters in this conversation. "What do you want to do, Red?"

Her temper is flashing in those gorgeous brown eyes.

But she only shakes her head, says, "I just want to be done with this."

"Your lucky day," I tell Courtney. "No social media about us, no interviews, no pointed comments or anonymous sources."

She nods.

"You follow through on that, and I'll ask Dubois and Henderson to steer clear. "But," I add as she starts to turn away, "if you renege, know they'll be eager to hop back in and make an example of you." A beat. "And Winston."

Courtney glares as our eyes hold, each of us staring the other down.

But I don't cave.

Because I didn't make her into this nightmare.

And see how healthy I'm getting?

Gold star for my therapy.

"Fine," she growls and whirls around.

"Hey, Court?" I call as she storms down the steps.

She turns back, snaps. "What?"

"You forgot this." I snag the box I ordered a while back from the table just inside the door, having bought it for exactly this moment.

"What is it?" she asks when I hold it up.

"Consider it a going away present." I toss it her way, half-expecting her to let it fall to the ground. Instead, she catches it, glares at me, then continues flouncing away.

Shaking my head—greedy greedy—I move back into the house, start to close the door.

Faye frowns. "What was—?"

Pop!

Courtney shrieks.

Faye's eyes go wide.

I allow myself one peek (and maybe also a pic) of Courtney covered in pink glitter then slam and lock the door, grinning at the shocked expression on Faye's face.

Sometimes happy endings arrive softly, slowly lifted from the ashes to reveal the beauty beneath, and others...burst into life with an explosion of glitter.

But each are beautiful in their own way.

"Gray?" she presses.

Unable to resist, I lean down and kiss the woman who owns my heart. "Seemed fitting," is all I say as I pull back.

Wide eyes again. Another shocked shake of her head.

Then she laughs—and it's the best sound on the planet, tinkling through the air, feeding my heart and soul...and then my stomach as she takes my hand and draws me down the hall and into the kitchen.

"Grab the bananas," she orders.

"On it."

Then—together—we make Nana's banana bread.

It has two eggs, not one.

And it tastes better than any of the other recipes we've tried.

Probably because it was straight from Nana's heart to our stomachs.

———

HARPER

I exhale and roll my shoulders.

Because he's out there.

Leo Richardson.

My sexy as sin one-night stand and talented forward for the San Jose Grizzlies is back in my shop after giving me the best orgasms—yup, that's orgasms *plural*—of my life...and then disappearing into the night.

With nary a call.

Or a text.

Until he showed back up the next afternoon and laid out an entire checklist's worth of reasons why we couldn't work.

Ever.

I rub my temples and take a deep breath.

Unfortunately, that doesn't calm me like it normally does.

Mostly because it makes me feel queasy.

Something that's been happening a lot lately.

Something that had me hurrying to the drug store down the street earlier today and buying a pregnancy test.

Then going back and buying four more.

Four because when the first one showed those two lines, I panicked.

And now I have five tests. Five positives. Five ways to say...

I'm pregnant.

This is a nightmare.

Because the only person I've slept with in the last two months...is standing out front wanting to hire me for an event.

For him and his *girlfriend.*

I'm going to puke.

Again.

But hiding in the kitchen, pretending to pull out some food from the oven is only delaying the inevitable.

I need to go back out there.

And I'm going to accept the job.

Because in this economy and with this much overhead, I can't afford not to.

I suck in another breath, which draws in the scents of my kitchen again...and I'm right back to queasy.

No.

More than queasy.

"Dammit," I whisper, clamping a hand over my nose and mouth, trying desperately to block out the smell.

But the garlic and onion odor is even stronger on my fingers and I fling my hand away, slamming it into the metal table.

A cutting board clatters to the floor, scattering chopped hard-boiled egg in all directions.

I gag, search for any bit of relief.

Spotting the basket of oranges, I sprint over to them, banging my hip on the sharp edge of the table and sending more items dropping to the floor.

Fuck.

"Harper?" Leo calls, concern evident in his voice.

"Just a second," I call back, stifling a gag as I reach for a knife, as I hurriedly cut an orange in half and all but shove it up my nose.

Fresh citrus.

Thank God.

But that relief lasts for only a moment.

Because then I can smell the onion again, the garlic, the *eggs*.

Bile burns the back of my throat, and I slam the orange down, sprint for the staff bathroom...and barely make it in time to lose my cookies.

"Shit," I hear mid-puke, a hand settling lightly on my back for a moment before it lifts away and Leo murmurs, "Let me get you a cool paper..."

He trails off but I'm too busy losing my breakfast—and maybe last night's dinner to immediately understand why.

Then I hear him say, "What the fuck?"

And I know, without a doubt, that I'm an idiot.

Because every single—*positive*—pregnancy test is sitting on the counter next to the sink.

———

Thank you for reading! I hope you love Faye and Gray's story as much as I do! The next book in the Grizzlies Hockey series is KNOCKED UP BY NUMBER NINETY. **He told me it was over...then the pregnancy test turned up positive.**

CLICK HERE TO READ KNOCKED UP BY NUMBER NINETY>

———

And are you curious about Jean-Michel, grumpy billionaire and team owner with a protective streak a mile wide? Check out a sneak peek of his happy ending below in BOTTLES & BLADES. **I fell for a billionaire...I just didn't know it.**
CLICK HERE TO READ BOTTLES & BLADES NOW>

Tiff

"Your total is $23.26," the cashier says, tapping on the register's keyboard, the computer screen above it changing as rapidly as her fingers move.

Clickity-click. Clickity-click. Clickity-click.

She pauses, glances up.

But not at me.

At the man she's currently ringing up, the man just in front of me. The man who reacts after a brief moment, jerking as though jarred from his thoughts and reaching into his pocket.

He's wearing a pair of jeans stained with so much dirt that I pity his washing machine, and his tee isn't much better, filthy and sweat-covered, plastered against a broad, well-muscled chest.

His forearms and hands are stained with something dark.

Clearly coming from some sort of hard, physical work, and on a day like today, summer clinging to the edges of a sunny spring afternoon, I envy him.

Not that I don't love my job—I'm a nanny, and my charge is awesome, and I love that it gives me the freedom to pursue my degree.

But sometimes I wouldn't mind playing hooky and getting out on one of the many trails around us on this side of the Bay, all rolling green hills and old-growth oaks and spring wildflowers.

"Sir?"

I blink, realize that while I've been daydreaming about poppies and blue lupines, the man in front of me has been searching his pockets.

And coming up empty.

"Your total is $23.26," the cashier repeats, a little sharper now.

"Right," the man says, patting his pockets in turn. "Just give me a second. I know my wallet—"

"If you can't pay, I'm going to have to ask you to step aside and let the others behind you have their turn."

Her tone is brusque and cold and—

Filled with disdain.

It slices through me, even though it's not directed at me.

Because I've lived that life.

Because even today, I calculated my own spread on the conveyor belt—sitting behind the plastic divider—to a precise degree. I know that I have exactly the amount in my account to cover my food for the week.

Food and tuition. Medical debts and gas.

All of my expenses carefully worked out.

The man keeps searching. "I know I have—"

Someone sighs behind me—a sharp, irritated sound that zips through the air, stinging as it flies by me.

The man looks up, mid pocket-pat, and I almost gasp at the startling blue of his eyes.

They're as bright as the cloudless sky outside the store and filled with embarrassment that has my heart squeezing.

"If you'll just give me a moment," he murmurs, eyes narrowing as they drift behind me, presumably toward the impatient sigher and the line that's growing by the moment. "I have—"

The cashier starts tapping on her keyboard again, this time angrily. "I'll have to cancel the transaction, sir."

It's the condescension in her tone that unsticks me.

I double tap the side of my cell, take a step toward the man with the dirt marring his strong chin, clinging to the salt and pepper beard on his jaw, his cheeks. I slip between his strong, obviously hardworking body and the payment kiosk, avoiding those bright blue eyes as I say, "I've got it."

That brilliant cerulean gaze comes to mine. "No, that's—"

But I'm already waving my phone at the machine, and it doesn't so much as have to make contact to solve this problem.

Bleep-beep.

And it's done.

"There," I say softly, giving him a small smile. "Enjoy your meal."

His expression...

Well, I'm not sure I can discern the flurry of emotions— annoyance and surprise and embarrassment and...

Gratitude.

"Thank you," he says softly, snagging the sandwich, soda, and bag of chips from the counter.

"No worries," I reply, turning back to the cashier, taking the receipt she passes over.

He waits there for a moment, big body still, eyes on me, so I turn and hold it out to him.

"Did you need this?" I ask, careful to not get lost in his eyes, careful to not notice how handsome he is, all strong muscles and brutal features and those gorgeous blue irises.

"No," he says.

But doesn't move.

Just stares at me like I'm a puzzle to be solved.

And well...no puzzle here.

Just a woman who's barely holding her life together.

"Right, okay." I nibble at the corner of my mouth. "You have a good day."

Another hesitation from the big man next to me.

"You're all paid, sir," the cashier snaps as she starts scanning my items. "You can go now."

I see him stiffen out of the corner of my eye, but he doesn't snap back, and...he doesn't linger.

Just gives a slight nod and walks away.

Some part of me is disappointed.

The rest...is relieved.

Beep. Beep. Beep. Beep—

"Wait," I tell the cashier, as she reaches for the bottle of wine. It's a discount brand, but I'll have to do without it after that $23.26. "I'll pass on the wine," I say softly.

Her eyes come to mine and she rolls hers, silently setting it to the side before reaching for the next item.

A block of cheese.

"And that too," I murmur, doing some mental math. "And the bread," I add when she puts that aside, starts to scan.

More eye rolls, but my math proves to be on point because by the time she finishes scanning—minus the cheese and bread and wine—I have enough left in my account to cover everything else.

I click the button on the side of my phone.

Do another wave of my cell, hear that *bleep-beep.*

And ignore the surly cashier as I bag my items, gather up my receipt, and head out of the store.

I'm putting my bags into my trunk when I feel a presence behind me.

I slam it closed, spin around, and—

See the man from the store standing there, eyes flashing, body big and broad and giving more than a few Daddy vibes.

My heart skips a beat.

Warmth blooms in my belly.

Lower.

He's too old for me.

But my mind is running away with itself anyway.

"Can I help you—?" I begin.

"Come with me," he mutters.

Before I can protest, he wraps his fingers around my arm.

And drags me away from my car.

Grizzlies Hockey

Married to Number Twenty-Two
Divorced from Number Thirty-Eight
Knocked Up by Number Ninety
One Night with Number Nineteen
Friends with Number Ten

Hate missing Elise's new releases? Love contests, exclusive excerpts and giveaways?
Then signup for Elise's newsletter here!

www.elisefaber.com/newsletter

———

And join Elise's fan group, the Fabinators (https://www.facebook.com/groups/fabinators) for insider information, sneak peaks at new releases, and fun freebies! Hope to see you there!

———

If you enjoy my series, considering supporting me on PATREON! Get access to early releases, bonus content, character art, audiobooks, special edition covers, swag, and much more!

CLICK HERE TO SUPPORT ME>

———

I so appreciate your help in spreading the word about my books, including sharing with friends! Please leave a review on your favorite book site!

Also by Elise Faber

***Gold Hockey* (all stand alone)**

Blocked

Backhand

Boarding

Benched

Breakaway

Breakout

Checked

Coasting

Centered

Charging

Caged

Crashed

A Gold Christmas

Cycled

Caught

Cap

Covered

Crushed

Changed

Scored

Breakers Hockey (all stand alone)

Broken

Boldly

Breathless

Ballsy

Bewitched

Blowout

Breathe

Blazed

Sierra Hockey Series

Over the Line

Caught from Behind

The Big Skate

On the Fly

Eagles Hockey Series (all stand alone)

Broken Laces

Lace 'em Up

Knotted Laces

Loaded Laces

Lucky Laces

Oak Ridge Vineyards

Bottles & Blades

Beauty & the Boardroom

The Bachelor & the Break-in

Rush Hockey Trilogy #1

Big Puck Energy

Filthy Puckboy

So Pucking Over It

Rush Hockey Trilogy #2

Love, Pucks, and Other Stories

All's Fair in Pucks and War

No Pucks Lost Between Us

Rush Hockey Novellas

Puck and Make Up

Billionaire's Club (all stand alone)

Bad Night Stand

Bad Breakup

Bad Husband

Bad Hookup

Bad Divorce

Bad Fiancé

Bad Boyfriend

Bad Blind Date

Bad Wedding

Bad Engagement

Bad Bridesmaid

Bad Swipe

Bad Girlfriend

Bad Best Friend

Bad Rebound

Bad Romance

Bad Business

Bad Billionaire's Quickies

Love, Action, Camera (all stand alone)

Dotted Line

Action Shot

Close-Up

End Scene

Meet Cute

Love After Midnight (all stand alone)

Rum And Notes

Virgin Daiquiri

On The Rocks

Sex On The Seats

Life Sucks Series

Train Wreck

Hot Mess

Dumpster Fire

Clusterf*@k

FUBAR

Perfect Storm

Free Fall

Lost Cause

Roosevelt Ranch Series (all stand alone, series complete)

Disaster at Roosevelt Ranch

Heartbreak at Roosevelt Ranch

Collision at Roosevelt Ranch

Regret at Roosevelt Ranch

Desire at Roosevelt Ranch

Phoenix Series (read in order)

Phoenix Rising

Dark Phoenix

Phoenix Freed

Phoenix: LexTal Chronicles (rereleasing soon, stand alone, Phoenix world)

From Ashes

In Flames

To Smoke

KTS Series (all stand alone, series complete)

Riding The Edge

Crossing The Line

Leveling The Field

Scorching The Earth

Cocky Heroes World

Tattooed Troublemaker

ABOUT THE AUTHOR

USA Today bestselling author, Elise Faber, loves chocolate, Star Wars, Harry Potter, and hockey (the order depending on the day and how well her team -- the Sharks! -- are playing). She and her husband also play as much hockey as they can squeeze into their schedules, so much so that their typical date night is spent on the ice. Elise is the mom to two exuberant boys and lives in Northern California. Connect with her in her Facebook group, the Fabinators or find more information about her books at www.elise-faber.com.

[f] facebook.com/elisefaberauthor

[a] amazon.com/author/elisefaber

[BB] bookbub.com/profile/elise-faber

[O] instagram.com/elisefaber

[d] tiktok.com/@elisefaberauthor

[g] goodreads.com/elisefaber